ALY MARTINEZ

Fighting Silence
Copyright © 2015 Aly Martinez

Fighting Silence is a work of fiction. All names, characters, places, and occurrences are the product of the author's imagination. Any resemblance to any persons, living or dead, events, or locations is purely coincidental.

Cover photo by Sara Eirew (http://www.saraeirew.com)
Cover Model: Mat Wolf (http://www.matwolffitness.com)
Cover Design by Ashley Baumann at Ashbee Designs
(https://www.facebook.com/AshbeeBookCovers)
Edited by Mickey Reed at I'm a Book Shark
(http://www.imabookshark.com)
Formatting by Stacey Blake at Champagne Formats
(http://thewineyreader.com/champagneformats/)

ISBN-13:978-1508515036
ISBN-10:1508515034

Other Books by Aly Martinez

The Wrecked and Ruined Series
Changing Course
Stolen Course
Broken Course

Savor Me

Prologue

Till

"GET OUT OF THE CAR." The cool, metal tip of a gun pressed against my temple.

"I don't have any money," I quickly announced, cautiously lifting my hands in the air.

"Get. The. Fuck. Out of the car!" a large, well-dressed man yelled manically before snatching the door to my truck open.

"Take whatever you want, man," I said as I stepped out.

"Oh, I plan to. Where the fuck is my money?" He swung the butt of his gun toward my face, but he was too slow. It breezed past me as I ducked to the side.

The forward momentum sent him stumbling, and I made my move before he could recover his balance. I landed a hard fist to his face, but just as I followed it with a right hook, I heard the gun fire.

"Till!" my dad yelled from somewhere in the distance.

He needed to get the fuck out of there. We both did.

"He's got a gun!" I warned as I scrambled after the man. I had no idea if I'd been shot already, but I knew for certain that I would be if I didn't get the gun away from him.

I was able to knock him off his feet, but I wasn't quick enough to keep him from regaining control of the weapon.

"Move one more goddamn inch and I swear I'll make it your last," he promised, aiming directly at my head from less than a foot away.

I had no choice but to still.

"Fuck!" he shouted, dabbing his mouth with his thumbs. The blood was pouring from his nose, but he simply wiped it on the back of his sleeve then shoved the gun against my chest. "Walk," he ordered with a deep snarl, motioning to the dark warehouse.

"No," I replied firmly. "I'm not going anywhere with you. Take my truck, my wallet, whatever you want."

"You know what I want, motherfucker? My. Fucking. Money."

"I don't have your money!"

"Bullshit!" He grabbed the back of my hair and shoved the gun under my chin. "That bag you stole from Clay Page belonged to me! Just give me the goddamn cash and you walk away without a hole in your fucking head."

Two simple words sent ice through my veins.

Clay Page.

He was the only reason I was there in the first place. About an hour earlier, he'd called me for a ride home. He'd sounded desperate and offered me twenty bucks. I'd figured he was drunk, but with a gun pressing into my neck, it became blindingly obvious that I wasn't just at the wrong place at the wrong time.

I'd been set up.

By my own father.

"I didn't steal anything from him."

"You don't have to lie, Till. Just give Frankie the money," my dad said, limping out of the warehouse. His face was badly beaten, and blood dripped from what appeared to be a gunshot wound to his leg.

My body stiffened at the sight, but so did Frankie's fist in my hair.

"What the fuck are you talking about?" I growled at my dad. "You know I don't have his money!"

He continued toward us until the gun was suddenly removed from under my chin and leveled on him.

"Don't come any closer, Clay. I will drop your ass right fucking there."

Slowly, he stopped and lifted his hands in the air.

With a hard shove, I was pushed forward to join him on the wrong side of the weapon. It was then that I got my first real look at the triggerman.

An unusual dragon tattoo peeked out from under the sleeve of his dress shirt and continued onto the back of his hand. The green monster was breathing flames down each of his shaking fingers, and the gun waved unsteadily. His eyes were wide and glassy, flashing nervously between us. It was a cool night, but he was drenched in sweat. The guy was worse than just pissed off—he was strung out and unpredictable.

"Look, dude. I've got, like, two hundred bucks in my truck. Just take it."

He tilted his head menacingly. "Two hundred bucks? Two. Hundred. Bucks? There was over forty thousand dollars in that fucking bag! And you want to give me two hundred?" He rushed forward, not stopping until his hand was around my throat and the gun planted firmly in the center of my forehead. "That's not even a payment!" Spit flew from his mouth as he lost any sense of composure he had left.

"Just calm down!" I pleaded. "I don't have your money! I never did!"

He swung the gun back to my dad. "That true? I'm putting a fucking bullet in whichever one of you is lying to me."

"No. He has it. I swear!" My father shouted his cowardly lie with such conviction that I almost believed him.

I'd always known that Clay Page was a piece of shit. I'd hated him since I was old enough to realize what a manipulative snake he truly was. But against my better judgment, with only the promise of twenty bucks as incentive, I'd ultimately gotten myself into that situation by not trusting my gut.

Never again.

And right then, my gut was screaming to stay true to what I had been doing since I'd entered the world eighteen years earlier. If I was going to die that night, I was going down *fighting*.

Slamming my head forward, I head-butted Frankie squarely in the nose. The gun fired over my shoulder, but at that moment, I couldn't have cared less about where the bullet lodged—and that included in Clay Page's head.

It had taken only three punches to the face before he fell to the ground, dragging me down with him. I heard the gun skitter across the pavement, and before I landed on top of him, I had planted another fist to his mouth. His head cracked hard against the concrete, but I didn't let it deter me. He eventually stopped fighting back, but the only thing that snapped me out of it was the sound of sirens in the distance.

I stood up, covered in blood, and headed back to my truck. I spared one glance over my shoulder for the man who had brought me there that night. He was holding his stomach and rolling on the ground. He'd made it obvious that he didn't care about me. And as I walked away, I was all too willing to return the favor.

After I'd hoisted myself back into the cab, my truck drove itself down the familiar roads. My father's betrayal filtered through my brain with every turn. I had no idea where I was headed; after that night, I didn't belong anywhere.

I hated my life and all that it was—but especially what it wasn't.

God had already damned me to a future that would gradually fall silent. Teasing me with the present and taunting me with everything I would eventually lose. Even before my own fucking father had been willing to sign my death warrant just to save his own hide, I had already been drowning in the ocean of life. Every gasp of air was a struggle. Just as I would breach the surface, filling my lungs with hope and determination to make it through another day, I was forced back under—harder every time.

There was only one place where the world didn't suck the life out of me. Regardless of how long I was there, seconds or hours, it offered me a reprieve and recharged my will.

I wanted to go *home*.

But home wasn't where I laid my head every night. I didn't actually live there at all, but it was the only place I felt alive. What I needed was the dream that only existed inside those four walls.

I needed *her*.

It had been six months since I'd last crawled out of that window. Six months since I'd watched her naked body take from me more than I'd ever thought I could offer.

Those same six months of living in the real world had destroyed me.

I needed the fantasy only she could provide.

But no matter what I dreamed, I knew she wouldn't be there.

Fuck it. Pride aside. I'd go to her.

With a sharp U-turn over the median, I finally gave in to the pull that threatened to overtake me on a daily basis. I knew where she lived. I knew where she laid her head every night. But above all of that . . . I knew where I belonged.

With Eliza.

1

Eliza

Five years earlier . . .

WHEN I WAS THIRTEEN YEARS old, I met Till Page in a condemned apartment one building over from my own. I immediately recognized him from school. It had been hard not to—he'd been gorgeous even as a boy. It was long before he found the gym or his tattered clothing came back in style. Back then, he was just a scrawny kid with shaggy hair and a wicked grin.

I didn't know what kind of life Till had, but I knew it was probably better than my own. My parents were decent people; they just didn't have time for me. Or, probably more accurately, any desire to make time for me. I was always a burden on them. Most nights, I hid away in my room, listening to them fight over money—or their lack thereof. I loved sneaking away to that run-down apartment. It was my own private fortress of solitude—until Till showed up one afternoon.

He scared me to death when he came crawling in that window. His eyes were red and his cheeks were notably stained with tears.

"Who the hell are you?" he asked, dusting off his already filthy pants.

I jumped to my feet, spilling my sketchpad and the few colored pencils I had managed to smuggle out of art class all over the peeling linoleum floor.

"Crap!" I yelled, rushing to pick them up. When I finished collecting my prize possessions, I glanced up to find him drying his eyes on the backs of his sleeves.

"You tell anyone I was crying and I'll tell everyone you tried to kiss me."

"I didn't try to kiss you!" I shouted, appalled at the very idea—and maybe a little interested too.

"Then keep quiet or the whole school will think you did."

My mouth must have gaped open at his attempted blackmail because he quickly finished with, "You might want to close your mouth before that spider on your shoulder takes it as an invitation."

At the mere mention of a spider, I began screaming and flailing around the dingy room. I tore my shirt over my head, only vaguely aware that his roar of laughter had been silenced.

"Uh . . ." he stuttered when I finally stilled.

It didn't take but a second for me to realize that I was standing in my bra.

"Oh, God!" I squeaked as I turned away, covering my chest with my arms.

"Here." He tossed my shirt, which hit me in the back and sent me into another fit of spider hysteria all over again.

"The spider could still be on there!" I screamed at the wall.

"Or it could be in your hair."

It was then that I decided to give up on covering my barely-there breasts and started ruffling my hair, shaking free any possible unwelcome insect.

He howled with laughter.

"Stop laughing!" I hissed.

He once again picked my shirt up, but this time, he thoroughly inspected it before tossing it back at me. "Spider-free. Till Page guaranteed."

I gave him a side eye but finally replied, "Thanks," as I pulled it back over my head, wishing I could set it on fire instead.

"No problem. At least, now if you decide to run your mouth, I won't have to lie when I tell the whole school you flashed me your bra."

"You wouldn't." I shot him an evil glare that made him smile.

7

"Try me," he said with a staggering confidence I'd never seen in a boy my age. Not that I had any plans of telling anyone anyway, but with one look, he solidified that even further.

"Whatever." I walked back to my small, makeshift storage cabinet and began emptying the contents.

"What are you doing?" he asked curiously while I stacked all of my old sketchbooks and barely there stumps of leftover pencils.

"I'm taking my stuff so you don't steal it."

"I won't steal your crap. I'm not a thief," he responded, and there was something in his voice that made me feel guilty for having suggested otherwise.

"Right. Well. I'm not chancing it. I didn't know anyone else came here." I looked around the room for something to carry the little pile I had accumulated, but as I turned, everything went rolling to the floor. "Ugh," I groaned, immediately diving after them.

"You don't have to take your stuff. I won't mess with it." He squatted down and began helping me collect them. "Besides, I don't have much use for a centimeter-long, pink pencil." He lifted the remnant off the ground and held it out for me. His eyes were warm, completely unlike the ones that had been teasing me only minutes before.

"Thanks," I replied, eyeing him suspiciously. However, without anywhere else to store my drawings, I was forced to take his word for it.

My mother hated that I spent so much time poring over my art. Every chance she got, she threw my supplies away. I thought it had less to do with me drawing and more to do with my father being an out-of-work artist who refused to get a job doing anything else.

"So, do you come here a lot?" Till asked, pulling off a beanie and running a hand through his dark, unkempt hair.

"Well, I did." I rolled my eyes, but he narrowed his and remained silently staring at me from a few feet away. It was the most awkward standoff of my adolescent life, but he didn't budge, and neither did I.

Suddenly, a woman's angry shrill vibrated against the windows, scaring us both.

"Till, get your ass back home right now!"

He quickly grabbed my hand and dragged me flat against the back wall, hiding us from view.

With a finger over his mouth, he urged, "Shhh." He leaned away only long enough to peer out the corner of the window. "Get down," he ordered then pulled me to the floor beside him.

After a few seconds, we heard her voice moving farther away and he let out a relieved sigh.

"Was that your mom? She sounded mad. You should probably get going."

"She always sounds like that, which is exactly why I'm not heading home. She just wants me to watch my brothers so she can follow my dad around and make sure he's not seeing Mrs. Cassidy anymore."

"Mrs. Cassidy? Isn't she married?"

"Yep," he answered nonchalantly.

"As in your girlfriend, Lynn Cassidy? Her mom?"

"Yep," Till repeated, not reacting in the least to my disgusted tone. "Hey. How do you know Lynn's my girlfriend?"

"Because we've been going to school together since kindergarten." I gave him yet another disgusted look and rolled my eyes.

"I knew it! I thought you went to East Side too!"

I knew everything about Till Page, yet he *thought* we went to school together. *How flattering.*

"What's your name?" he asked as I sat down against the wall, pulling my pad and pencils into my lap.

"Cindy Lou," I responded, not looking back up and desperately wishing he would leave.

"No, it's not."

"Daphne?"

"Not it, either."

"Ivy?" I smarted one last time, pretending to be busy by doodling lightning bolts.

"Nope," he responded but didn't inquire any further. "So, you mind if I hang out for a little while?"

"It's a free world, Till. I don't exactly own the place," I said, disinterested—even though, on the inside, I was anything but.

"Okay." He sank down against the opposite wall.

For thirty minutes, he sat there staring at me. It was unnerving, but I tried not to let him see that. I did my absolute best to ignore him, but as my pencil moved over the paper, his eyes began to form within the lines.

Eventually, he got up and headed back to the window.

"See you tomorrow," he called over his shoulder.

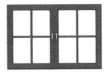

At school the next day, Till didn't acknowledge me at all. It wasn't like I'd expected him to come sit with me at lunch or anything. We weren't friends, but it still stung when he walked right past me, not even bothering to spare a glance in my direction. Maybe it was for the best, though, after the fool I'd made of myself the day before.

That night, as per usual, I made my way to the abandoned apartment as soon as my parents started arguing about the power bill. When I walked in, I saw a small, plastic bag on the ground. On a torn-out piece of notebook paper was a handwritten note.

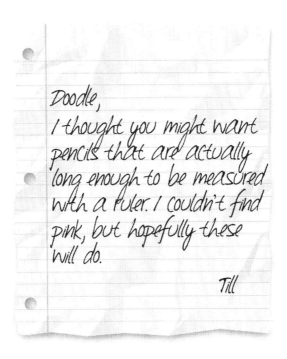

I opened the bag to find a set of tinted charcoals. They weren't top-of-the-line, but they were far better than anything I'd have been able to afford. It boggled my mind how Till had afforded them—or, better yet, why he would have spent his limited money on me. That was if he had paid for them at all. I didn't dwell on those thoughts long as I ripped the box open and began drawing.

"Doodle, you any good at math?" Till asked as he climbed through the window an hour or so later.

"What?" I asked, confused by his sudden appearance and the second use of what I guessed was my new nickname.

"Math. Mr. Sparks is about to fail me. If I fail, I can't play football." He walked over and sat on the floor next to me. "Oh, awesome. You brought food. I'm starving." He shoved a hand in the bag of chips I'd snagged from home as dinner.

"Uh . . . I brought myself food." I snatched the bag away, but not before he stole a handful.

"Hey, you like those pencils?" he asked, crushing the chips into his mouth.

He had given me pencils. *Right.*

I passed him the rest of the chips. "They're amazing. Thank you."

"No prob." He shrugged and tossed me a closed-mouth grin. "So. Math?"

"No, I'm serious, Till. They're really nice. I'm sure they were expensive."

"Nah. It's no big deal." He jumped to his feet and wandered over to the lamp in the corner. "How do you have electricity in here?" He flipped it off and on again.

"I guess the power company never turned it off. It's nice because I bring a little heater in the winter, so I don't freeze."

"No shit? I should move in here," he mumbled to himself. I only understood because it was the same thought I'd had at least a dozen times.

"Can I pay you back for the charcoals?"

"Nope. But you can help me not get kicked off the football team." He shoved another handful of the chips into his mouth.

"Come on. I can pay you a couple bucks a week or something. It'd make me feel better."

"Why? I said it's not a big deal."

"Because neither one of us has the money to be buying stuff like this. I really appreciate it though." I smiled tightly.

"Are you saying I'm poor? 'Cause I'm not!" he yelled, and it quite honestly surprised me.

"No," I said cautiously, not sure what to make of his reaction. "I'm saying *we're* poor. Till, we live in the same apartments. I'm going to guess that your family isn't living here for the luxurious view any more than mine is."

"Just forget it." He jerked the box from my hand and stormed toward the window.

"Hey! You can't take those back. You gave them to me." I darted forward to snatch them back.

Tug-of-war ensued . . . until I pulled the ultimate trump card.

"Ow!" I screamed, cradling my arm as I fell down to the dirty floor.

His eyes flashed wide. "Crap. I'm so sorry. Are you okay?" He kneeled down next to me.

I didn't waste a single second plucking the box from his hand and rolling over to hide it under my body.

"Are you kidding me!" he yelled.

I couldn't help but laugh at my victory.

It was short-lived though because not a second later, he leaned in close to my ear and whispered, "Spider," sending me into full-body convulsions and flying to my feet.

He collapsed on the floor in hysterics. I tried to use *The Force* to shoot lasers from my eyes. Unfortunately, my Jedi mind tricks seemed to be lacking.

"You are such a jerk!"

"Oh my God, Doodle!" He continued to roll around on the floor. "I thought you were having a seizure!"

"I swear I hope you are good at football because you definitely don't have a career in comedy," I deadpanned.

"Oh, but you do?" He began hopping around the room, exaggeratedly yelling, "Ow!"

I crossed my arms over my chest and bit my lips, trying to stifle a laugh. He was making fun of me, but he looked ridiculous while doing it. There was no way I could be mad at that. Some minutes later, he stopped and tossed me a heart-stopping smile. Or at least my heart thought it was.

"I'll help you with math—as long as you promise not to shoplift any more art supplies."

His smile faded as he glanced down at his shoes, embarrassed.

"Thanks for the gift, and don't you dare think about taking it back. But no more, okay?"

"Yeah. Cool," he told the ground.

"All right, Dummy. Where should we start? Please tell me I don't have to go all the way back to two-plus-two," I joked, bumping him with my shoulder as I walked past.

"Soooo funny," he teased but followed me to sit on the blanket.

Two hours later, with three days' worth of math homework completed, he crawled back out of that window. Just before he disappeared, he called out, "See you tomorrow, Doodle."

I didn't know it then, but he had never been more right. After that, there weren't many tomorrows that I didn't see Till Page.

2

Eliza

Three years later . . .

"YOU WANNA MAYBE GO SEE a movie tonight?" he asked.

I chewed on the inside of my cheek to suppress my schoolgirl squeal. "Yeah. That sounds cool," I said nonchalantly before quickly turning to face my locker. He was standing the good kind of too close and I needed an escape. The inside of my dark locker seemed like the most obvious of choices.

I leaned my head inside, pretending to look for a book, and allowed the huge grin to spread across my face. The very idea of telling Crystal about our date gave me almost as much as excitement as the date itself. She was going to have a stroke when I told her that he'd finally asked me out. It had taken long enough—that's for sure. I thought the entire school knew he was interested in me, but I wasn't exactly one of the cool kids. But then again, neither was he. Not many of the jocks were enrolled in every possible art class, including the ones the school offered after hours. He was different, and I liked that. A lot.

"You okay, Eliza?"

I felt his hand on my back, and I literally squeaked. Probably not my subtlest move, but that squeak had suppressed a breathy sigh. I might have only been sixteen, but I knew that "breathy" never helped your case when trying to play it cool.

"Yeah. I'm fine." I twirled to face him, and his hand found my hip. Like the proverbial wheel, I squeaked again.

Suddenly, a pair of unfamiliar, hazel eyes caught my attention. Oh, I knew every single curve on his ridiculously attractive face. I'd drawn each one of them more times than I cared to admit. But inside this building, I didn't know those eyes from the man on the moon.

The smile fell from my face as he approached.

"Bennett, you need to get to the gym. Coach is looking for you," Till said when he stopped in front of us.

I had gotten used to his cold avoidance over the years. He spent hours every night at my side in our condemned apartment, but never once had he acknowledged me at school. It had pissed me off at first. Yeah, okay. It still pissed me off.

"What? Why?" Daniel Bennett removed his hand from my hip.

Instead of another squeak, a growl pointedly aimed at Till rumbled in my throat.

"I wasn't feeling confident about some of the plays. So we're gonna watch last week's videos again." The side of his lip curled into a half smile.

Now *that* I recognized. He was up to no good.

"Seriously? I've got plans tonight," Daniel groaned.

"Sorry, bro. Coach's orders." Till shrugged and tried to wiggle his hands into the pockets of his tattered jeans.

He'd recently found the weights, so his pants were quickly becoming too small to fit his large frame, but he wore them as if that were the sole purpose. Hell, knowing Till, maybe it was.

"All night?" Bennett clarified, tilting his head toward me.

Till sucked in a breath, and I knew he was enjoying it. "So it seems."

I cocked my head to the side, not sure what to make of his sudden appearance, but if he noticed my scrutinizing eyes, he never acknowledged it.

"Shit," Bennett mumbled, turning back to face me. "You think we could do dinner after the game tomorrow instead? Coach loves his videos, so this is gonna take forever."

I let out a disappointed sigh. "I can't. I have to work tomorrow night. The Smokehouse bustles at least twelve customers on a Friday night. How would they ever manage to get them all seated without me?" I replied sarcastically.

He groaned again. "Next weekend then?"

"Yeah. I can do that." I flashed him a sweet smile.

"Okay. Next weekend. Dinner and a movie," he confirmed before backing away.

"Watch out!" I laughed as he plowed over one of the freshmen.

"Sorry," he apologized before tossing me a wink.

Covering my mouth, I tried to hide my smile. I watched until he was out of sight then turned back to my locker, but I paused because Till was still standing next to me.

I wasn't sure why he was lingering. Closing my locker, I opened my mouth to say something, but he beat me to it.

"Doodle," he said in greeting and dismissal.

My jaw dropped open as he sauntered away.

Three years. Three *long* years, and the first time he'd ever spoken to me at school, all I'd gotten was the stupid nickname I fucking loved so much that I couldn't even be mad.

3

Till

Six months later . . .

"HEY, MRS. NOELLE. CAN I borrow your phone?" I asked the crotchety old lady who lived next door.

"Again?" she grumbled, handing me the portable phone through the crack in the door.

"Sorry." I began dialing the number to my mom's friend, Tracie. She had a cell phone, and even though she was a total bitch, I was hoping she would be able to help me out.

"Tracie. Hey, it's Till. Do you know where my mom is?" I asked as soon as she picked up.

"Jesus, Till. Stop callin' and wastin' my minutes. Is your broke ass gonna pay my bill when I go over? I don't think so. I have no clue where the hell your mom is. Stop callin'." She hung up just as quickly as she'd answered.

"Shit." I cursed under my breath, handing the phone back to Mrs. Noelle.

"You're welcome!" she shouted as I headed back to my parents' apartment.

"Yeah, thanks," I responded absently.

I walked back inside and began pacing the den. Eliza was waiting for me. I knew she was. Her boyfriend, Daniel Bennett, had a midnight curfew, so he always dropped her off around eleven thirty. It was bad enough I had to share her with him, but since my mom's trip to buy cigarettes had turned into a six-hour-long excursion, there was a good chance I was going to miss her entire birthday.

I was stuck only two buildings away, babysitting my brothers. Flint was eleven. He probably would have been fine sleeping alone in the apartment, but Quarry was only six. I couldn't just leave.

"Shit!" I shouted, pulling my beanie off and throwing it onto the couch. "Tonight of all fucking nights!" I began to rant to myself.

"Till?"

I heard Quarry as he walked out of his bedroom, fully dressed in dirty clothes. As far as I knew, the kid only owned two pair of jeans. Forget about pajamas.

"It's all good, buddy. Go back to bed."

"Mom's still not back?" he asked, rubbing the sleep from his eyes.

"No, but it's okay. Just go back to sleep." I ruffled his thick, black hair.

"Don't you have a date?"

"Something like that."

It was the biggest understatement of the year. It wasn't something like that. *It's Eliza.* It was bigger than a date. I'd spent fucking weeks saving up to buy her a present. Now, I couldn't even give it to her on her actual birthday.

I rolled my bottom lip with my fingers and debated what to do. Mom would show up eventually, but I was sure it wouldn't be until the morning. God only knew where the hell my dad was. He was even more worthless than she was. I had never missed a night with Eliza, and I sure as hell wasn't about to start on her birthday.

"Hey, Quarry. Put on some shoes. Take a walk with me real quick."

"Okay!" he said excitedly, making me laugh for the first time in hours.

I went to the boys' room and nudged Flint. "Hey, I'm taking Q and going for a walk. You gonna be okay for a few minutes alone?"

"Yeah," he grumbled, rolling over and falling immediately back asleep.

I opened the hall closet and pulled out the vase I'd stashed in the back.

"Ready!" Quarry exclaimed.

I ran my eyes over his dirty shirt and shook my head. "Let's go." I headed out the door with him hot on my heels.

He talked nonstop as we weaved through the buildings. "Hey, where we goin'? Did you make those flowers? Is that for your girlfriend? Do you even have a girlfriend? What's her name? Can I meet her?"

"Jesus! Quarry, shut it!" I growled, but he quieted for only a minute.

"Does she live here?" he whispered, and I gave him a frustrated glare that only made him smile and shrug.

When we got to the apartment, I could see the light peeking out of the window. *She is in there.*

My heart began to race—just like it did every time before I saw her.

"Stay here," I said to Quarry as I started to approach the window, but I heard his footsteps following me. I quickly turned to face him. "What are you doing? I said to stay on the sidewalk."

"It's dark!" he whined as an answer.

"You can't go with me. Just . . . Stay. Here," I continued toward the window, and Quarry once again moved with me. "Stop following me!" I whisper-yelled.

"It's really dark, Till!" he whisper-yelled right back.

I let out a huff. "Then go stand in that breezeway under the light." I pointed to the building next door.

"Fine. Walk me over there."

I gave him an impatient look that sailed right over his head. "Come on." I stomped off, frustrated.

Even at six years old, he actually had the balls to giggle as he followed.

Once I had Quarry planted inches away from a light, I made my way back toward the window. My heart was pounding, and the vase in my hand rattled as I drew near.

It was just Eliza.

Shit. It was *Eliza.* My pulse spiked once again.

"Hey!" she exclaimed as I pried the window open.

My nerves calmed immediately at the sight of her face. *She's still there*. Almost four years later and she was *still* there.

"Hey, birthday girl!" I was careful to keep my hands low so she couldn't see her present.

"Why are you standing out there? Get in here."

"Ugh. I can't. My mom took off . . ." I trailed off, not wanting to dump all of my shit on her tonight. I should have been singing "Happy Birthday" and holding her sketchpad—or, more accurately, staring down her shirt while she leaned over to draw.

"Where'd she go?" she questioned, standing up from a blanket on the floor. I made a mental note to find something more comfortable for her to sit on.

"To get cigarettes . . ."

"Oh, okay."

"Six hours ago," I finished.

"Ah." When she stopped, she was only inches away, but a whole world in the shape of a window divided us.

"I'm sorry, Doodle. I can't leave them alone. I just . . . Well, happy birthday." I lifted the vase filled with paper flowers into her view.

"Till!" she gasped as her hands covered her mouth. Then a loud laugh escaped her throat as familiar tears welled in her eyes.

Eliza was a crier. She pretended that it was only when she was mad. That was bullshit though. She cried every time the wind blew north. Happy, sad, angry—it didn't matter.

I loved it when she happy cried. I laughed when she angry cried. I was gutted when she sad cried. I'd held her through all of them. But her reaction that night was extraordinary. I guessed my present was pretty extraordinary too though.

Eliza had been jabbering about these special paintbrushes she wanted for months. At fifty bucks, they cost a freaking mint for kids like us. But when I realized that her birthday was coming, I knew exactly what I was getting her. I folded a million pieces of notebook paper into these little flower things and taped a few onto the ends of each brush. Then I shoved them into a vase and bam! I had flowers that wouldn't die. I'd thought it was a good idea, but it had actually turned out far better than I'd expected.

"Did you make those?" she asked from behind her hands.

"Yep," I said proudly.

"Are those . . ."

"Yep," I confirmed, and her eyes grew wide. "I bought them," I quickly added when I remembered the first time I'd given her art supplies.

She burst out laughing. God, I loved that sound so much. I knew I'd never be the same when I lost it to the silence. I'd happily give up every noise in the world if I could just keep her laugh. But my life didn't work that way.

"Till!" She scrambled out the window and threw her arms around my neck. "Thank you!"

"You're welcome, Doodle," I whispered into the hair at the top of her head. Holding her impossibly tight, I siphoned the warmth only she could give me.

She leaned away, and her eyes heated as they immediately flashed to my mouth. Eliza always looked at me like that, and as the years had passed, it'd become more and more difficult to stop myself from kissing her, touching her, *claiming her.* But I knew that, if I did, I would eventually lose her. Relationships didn't work in high school. Something would have happened, we would have broken up, and then I would have lost her completely. I needed Eliza too damn bad to ever chance that.

I'd spent years loving her from afar—well, actually only from afar when we were outside of our private little haven. It wasn't safe to notice her outside those walls.

She had always been beautiful. Even at thirteen, her deep, ink-blue eyes had captivated me. Her shoulder-length, brown hair was perfectly straight, but she nervously played with the ends so often that it had formed a permanent curl in the front. Her fair skin had a sprinkle of freckles I could map out from memory alone. And her body . . . Jesus, her body had been made for me. She was naturally thin, but a small curve rounded her hips. Those same curves taunted my hands on a daily basis. I was at least a foot taller than she was and probably had her by almost a hundred pounds, but on the inside, she was the strong one.

See, Eliza Reynolds flew under the radar. Very few people at school knew who she was, and I intended to keep it that way. If she caught the attention of the football team, she'd be flooded with dates. So I ignored her at all costs so as to not draw any attention her way. I couldn't risk that someone would take her away from me.

Sure, she was dating Daniel Bennett, but he was a tool. I wanted to kill him on a daily basis when I saw them together at school. But what was I supposed to do? She wasn't mine—at least, not that anyone knew.

"What did Bennett give you?" I asked just to size up the competition. He wasn't loaded, but he had a car and took her out on dates every weekend. I was curious, but it made her smile fall.

She mumbled something, but I couldn't quite hear her.

"Huh?"

She looked up and repeated, "Ladybug earrings."

I blinked at her for a minute before doubling over in laughter.

"Shut up!" she said sternly. Then she laughed right along with me.

"Doodle, just let me make sure I have this straight. He bought a girl who has never had her ears pierced and is terrified of insects, ladybug earrings?" I went back to laughing.

"Oh, it gets worse. I wasn't sure what to say when I opened them, so I told him I loved them. Now I'm gonna have to get my ears pierced so he doesn't feel bad."

"What? That's ridiculous." I stopped laughing. "You're scared of needles. You know that's how they do that, right?"

"Well, holy crap. Till Page. You actually listen to me when I talk!" She smiled and wrapped her arms around my waist, hugging me again. "Thank you."

"I hear everything you say. Even the boring stuff."

She giggled, and I kissed the top of her head.

"The light turned off," Quarry said, suddenly appearing, scaring us both.

Eliza must have jumped ten feet in the air.

"Jesus, Q! Don't sneak up on people like that!" I barked as I tried to slow my own racing heart.

"Sorry," he said, embarrassed, and I immediately felt guilty for yelling at him.

"Hey, it's all right, buddy."

"Is this Quarry?" Eliza all but squealed.

"We should get going," I grumbled, not wanting her to cross over into the real world.

"Yep. I'm Quarry." He bounced on his toes.

"Wow. You're a cutie." Eliza squatted down in front of him, and all I could think about was that she would notice his dirty shirt.

"Come on, Q." I started to walk away, but they both ignored me.

"Thanks!" Quarry grinned. "Hey, when I'm older, maybe we can go on a date or something?" My head snapped to his as I popped a questioning eyebrow.

"I'd really like that," Eliza managed to say through a muffled laugh. "I should probably tell you my name first though. You know, so you can find me in a few years."

"Oh yeah. I'll need that. Can I have your phone number too?" he asked.

My jaw fell open. Fantastic. My six-year-old brother was even trying to take her from me.

"You are definitely related to Till." She laughed loudly. "Well, Quarry Page, my name is Eliza Reynolds. I'll get your brother to give you my number later. I'm really looking forward to our date." She lifted her hand for a high five, which Quarry enthusiastically returned.

Shaking my head, I broke up Quarry's love connection. "All right, we've got to go. Flint's at home sleeping. Happy birthday, Doodle." I leaned forward and kissed her on the forehead.

She picked the vase up off the windowsill and hugged it to her chest. "Thanks again. I'll see you tomorrow?"

"Of course." I smiled and winked. "Here. I'll help." I scooped her off her feet and eased her back through the window. I'd have used any excuse to touch her.

"Goodnight, Quarry!" She blew a kiss that made a slow smile creep across his lips.

As soon as we got a few steps away, Quarry started talking again. "Are you going to marry her?"

"I don't know. You probably should have checked with me about that before you asked her out on a date. I'm not sure how I feel about you hitting on my girl," I teased, and his smile fell. "I'm kidding." I lightly punched his shoulder.

"Hey, why'd she climb through the window? Does her house not have a door? That would be pretty cool to climb through the windows all the time. Would you have to put a doorknob on the window though?"

"You want to hear something cool?" I interjected just to make him stop talking.

"Yeah!"

"That window she crawled into is *magic*."

"Nu-uh," he said in disbelief, but he stopped walking and turned to look at me.

"I'm serious. It's a magical portal that takes you to a fantasy world. There are no parents or teachers. Everything is nice and clean, and the pantry is always stocked. The best part, though, is that she's always there."

"Is she magic too?" he breathed with wide eyes.

I thought about it for a minute before answering.

Was Eliza magic?

She is to me.

"Absolutely."

4

Eliza

Six months later . . .

"WHY YOU SITTIN' IN THE dark?" Till asked as he crawled through our apartment window. I'd always wondered why he never used the door.

The power to our nightly refuge had long since been shut off. I had told Till no more stealing for me, but when he'd run an old extension cord over to the building next door, I'd made an exception for power. He'd buried it in the dirt so no one could see it, but he'd still had to replace it a few times over the years. He always made sure we had light and a connection for the small space heater I'd bought from a thrift store.

Little by little, Till fixed up that dirty, run-down apartment. His efforts wouldn't have prevented the city from changing its condemned status, but they made it comfortable for us. He brought bits and pieces of discarded furniture as he found them. It was never anything large. I suspected he couldn't carry couches on his own, and I was relatively sure he'd never told anyone about our place. I knew I hadn't.

"What are you doing here?" I asked, quickly turning away to hide my tears.

"Um, I live here," he answered in the smartass tone I had grown to love.

"No, you don't."

"Well, close enough." He eyed me curiously. "Why are you cryin'?" He crossed his arms over his chest, which seemed to be growing thicker every day.

Not that I really noticed or anything. It wasn't like I was checking him out or lusting over his body . . . daily. Nope. Not at all. Till was my best friend, the brother I'd never had . . . and the visual of every orgasm I had ever given myself.

"It's nothing," I said dismissively.

"Why are you cryin,' Doodle?" he repeated, clearly not dismissed.

"It's stupid." I dried my eyes on the backs of my hands. "I thought you were going out with Helen Chapman tonight?" I questioned, trying to distract him.

"What? Who told you that?"

I swear, sometimes, he didn't even remember that we went to the same school. Nothing had changed. Till and I were thick as thieves inside that apartment, but it was our little secret from the outside world—or, more accurately, Till's secret.

"No one had to tell me. The whole school was talking about it." I stood up off the cushions we had made into a makeshift couch on the floor.

A small smirk grew from the corner of his mouth. "You really shouldn't believe everything you hear."

I let out a loud laugh. "Funny, that's not the first time I've been told that tonight."

He quirked an eyebrow and cocked his head, asking for further explanation, but I didn't give it to him.

"You hungry?" I walked to the small filing cabinet he'd converted into a pantry. It was never loaded, but we usually had at least something in case we got hungry.

On average, we spent about two hours a night in our apartment, but on the weekends, we spent almost all day if we weren't working. My parents never even bothered to ask where I disappeared to, and eventually, I stopped sneaking out and started walking out the front door instead.

"Stop avoiding my questions." He grabbed my arm to stop me. "What's got you hiding out, crying in the dark?"

I let out a sigh, knowing there would be no getting out of this. Whether I told him tonight or not, I was sure he'd hear first thing Monday morning when the high school gossip train pulled into the station.

"Daniel hooked up with Crystal," I stated emotionlessly, but my chin started to quiver.

"Bennett? No way," he said in disbelief.

"Totally true." I tugged my arm out of his grip and retrieved a can of ravioli and a fork. "Crystal confessed."

He took the can from my hand but kept questioning me. "Wait. Your girl, Crystal?" Then he peeled back the pull-tab and shoveled a spoonful into his mouth.

"Yep. She called to inform me that they were star-crossed lovers. She rambled about some Romeo and Juliet bullshit then told me they had spent a night under the stars in the back of his car losing their virginity to each other." I summarized her words with my own personal bitchy flare of sarcasm.

Till choked on a laugh, spraying cheap red sauce onto my face. With the night I'd had, I didn't even have a reaction to having been covered with spit and ravioli. It was merely the brown icing on the shit cake.

Placing the can down, he rushed forward. "Shit. Sorry," he chuckled. Lifting the bottom of his shirt, he wiped my face clean—including a few hidden tears that had managed to escape my eyes. "Did you tell her that Romeo was no virgin?"

My eyes snapped to his. "He wasn't?"

"Um . . ." He stalled, nervously rocking to his toes as his eyes flashed around the room.

"Till?"

"It's cool, Doodle. Bennett's got one hell of a mouth."

"What exactly is cool?" I narrowed my eyes, but my cheeks began to heat.

I was closer to Till Page than I was to anyone else in the world, but he was still a guy, and I was a seventeen-year-old girl who was still a virgin. This conversation was awkward.

"Ya know . . . You and Bennett. It's none of my business." Thankfully, he seemed just as uncomfortable. "I mean, you guys were together for, like, a year. Everyone kinda figured you were, anyway."

"They figured we were what?" My embarrassment slipped as my blood began to boil. Unfortunately for me, I cried when I was angry and Till's next words ripped open the floodgates.

"I mean, he . . . uh, told everyone that you guys were doing it." He paused as my eyes grew wide. "Like, on the regular."

"What!" I gasped even though I wasn't really shocked. That was what teenage boys did, right? They lied about sex. The only problem was that this lie was about *me*. Tears dripped down my face as I managed to croak out, "We never . . ."

"Fuck," Till cussed, immediately stepping forward, dragging me into his chest. I could feel his heart pounding and his muscles tense as I unnecessarily ran my hands up his sides. "I'll fix it," he soothed.

"You planning to turn back time? Because I'm pretty sure there is no fixing this."

Right then and there, I vowed to castrate Daniel Bennett. I'd originally intended for it to be a thought, but when I felt Till's chest begin shaking, I realized I had issued my threat out loud.

"You'll lie to the cops for me when I follow through with that, right? I'll need an alibi." I lifted my head to catch his gaze.

He barked out a laugh. "No, I don't want to be the alibi. I'll be happy to hold him down for you though." He smiled, rubbing his hand up and down my back.

Till and I weren't exactly touchy-feely, but we didn't shy away from affection, either. When my mother had shredded the sketchbook she'd found in my backpack during our freshman year, Till had held me for hours as I'd cried. It was the first time I'd realized how much I had come to not only rely on him, but trust him as well. He knew my life and didn't judge me because of it. We were two of a kind. We might not have been the only poor kids with screwed-up parents, but sometimes, it really felt that way.

"Oh, God. I'm going to look like such an idiot at school on Monday. Not only was I supposedly having monkey sex with Daniel, but it wasn't even good enough to keep him from sleeping with my best friend," I whined, stomping my foot for good measure.

"Monkey sex?" Till asked with humor filling his voice.

"Shut up. You know what I mean."

He hadn't yet released me, so I buried my head back into his chest.

If he was offering, I was taking.

"You want me to kick his ass?" He made it sound like a joke, but I knew he was very serious.

"No," I mumbled. My answer had far less to do with worrying about Daniel's safety and everything to do with not wanting Till to get in trouble for doing it.

"Want me to spread some shit about Crystal?" He dropped his arms around my waist and rested his chin on the top of my head.

"No. What I want you to do is find a way to bottle chlamydia so we can give it to both of them."

"Right. I'll begin researching that tomorrow. I know a few girls who could probably supply us with a sample."

"Ew. That's disgusting. Please tell me Helen isn't one of them?" I took a step out of his arms, and his eyes danced with humor.

"Oh, I wouldn't know about Helen."

"Liar," I accused, and his smile grew.

"Hey, you know what I bet would make you feel better?"

"Switching high schools?" I snarked over my shoulder as I walked back to the cushions on the floor.

"Nope. Scratching my head."

"Why does your head itch? You got lice?"

"What? No!" he yelled defensively. "That's like some little kid shit, isn't it?"

"Mostly, but anyone can get it. Besides, how old are Flint and Quarry now anyway? They could have brought it home from school."

"Six and eleven, but we don't share a room or anything anymore." He was blinking a lot and I could tell he was starting to worry.

"Till, just 'cause you sleep on the couch doesn't mean they couldn't have left it there for you. Come on. Sit down and I'll check. Crystal had lice when we were in fifth grade. She was miserable." I paused as an idea hit me. "Hey! If you really have lice, can you give it to Daniel and Crystal before getting rid of it?"

"Sure. I'd be happy to! How do I give it to them?" he asked, so genuinely interested that I couldn't help but smile.

"Just rub your head on them or something. Maybe lend Bennett one of your beanies," I joked, but Till stood there for a minute studying me.

"Sorry," was all he said before diving at me.

He caught me completely off guard, and I toppled over backwards. Before I even had a chance to react, he had my arms pinned and was straddling my hips.

"What the hell!" I yelled as he began rubbing the top of his head against mine. He was thorough too, twisting his head from side to side to touch every inch of mine.

"There," he said before finally moving off me. "Since this whole lice thing was your idea, I figured we should really experience it together." A slow grin slid across his mouth. Obviously, he was proud of his thought process.

"Have you lost your freaking mind? Why would you try to give me lice? It wasn't my idea! You have an itchy head, so I simply asked if you had lice. That's it!"

"Well, shit, Doodle. I didn't realize you would be this ungrateful. I was just trying to be a good friend so we could lean on each other for support during a difficult time." He winked.

Like, actually *winked.* I probably had bugs crawling in my hair, and Till was winking.

That one moment probably summed up our relationship better than anything else. Till always made things hard for me, but in some strange way, he always made them infinitely better as well.

Case in point.

Harder: For twenty minutes, Till lay with his head in my lap as I nervously inspected his hair to see if *we* had lice. We didn't.

Better: For two hours after that, he lay with his head in my lap laughing and holding my sketchpad against his chest as I drew Crystal and Daniel voodoo dolls. I scratched his head with one hand, and he pointed out additional flaws I should add to our Juliet and her Romeo.

Occasionally, Till would go one step further and pull out a *best:* Just as I looked down to ask a question, I met his hazel eyes staring up at me. He didn't look away or become awkward after being caught. Instead, a warm smile lifted the corner of his mouth. His eyes weren't burning with desire the way I'm sure mine were, instead they were deep and content.

Yeah.

The absolute best.

When the intensity of our stare became too much, I cleared my throat and asked, "What time are social services coming tomorrow? You should probably go home."

"Eleven." He glanced at his watch. "You want to stay here with me tonight? I don't feel like going back there. I need to get up early and clean that hell hole before they get there, though. She threatened to take Flint and Quarry last time if things weren't better."

"Crap." I breathed.

"It'll be okay. Flint's done a lot the past week. Mom's leaving to have Tammy do her nails in the morning, so I'm gonna try to make it at least look decent while she's gone. She might not give a damn, but I do. I just can't deal with her shit tonight." He tried so hard to play it off as no big deal, but as he lifted his hand to toy with his bottom lip, I knew he was bothered.

"Okay. I'll stay." I said simply before settling next to him. My parents weren't going to worry if I didn't come home, but I'd worry about Till waking up in time if I left. "You know if you ever need . . ." He interrupted me before I could offer any assistance.

"Night, Doodle." He rolled away, halting all further conversation.

Eventually, I fell asleep. We weren't cuddled up next to each other the way I would have preferred the first time we ever slept together, but after a terrible night, I still fell asleep with cheeks that were sore from smiling.

Even at seventeen I knew I loved Till Page, but I didn't have grand dreams of how perfect our lives would be together. Maybe it was because I didn't want to set myself up for disappointment. But I think it was more because I didn't want to face the fact that there was a future at all—one that may or may not have included him. I just wanted to live with Till in the present where there was no pressure to pretend to be anyone else. A present where I kept his stomach full of canned foods, and he kept me warm and needed. I scratched his head, and he healed my heart.

One day they were going to knock down that building and snatch that life away from us. But with a half boy half man snoring loudly beside me, I was blissfully blinded by the present.

5

Till

THE DAY I FOUND ON The Ropes boxing gym, my life changed forever. I had been going to high school, working two jobs, and spending
almost all of my paychecks to keep a roof over my brothers' heads. I'd
walked past that old vacant building every day on my way to and from
my job at the grocery store. Then, one day, there were about twenty trucks outside and workmen covering the sidewalk. I didn't give it
much thought as I passed, but I swear, by the time I went home that
night, there was a brand-new gym complete with decaled windows.

The next day at school, they passed out fliers advertising a new
after-school program at On The Ropes. It contained my favorite word
in the English language: free. Rumors were flying around that the former professional heavyweight champion Slate "The Silent Storm" Andrews owned the gym and would be personally running the program.
Half the school had plans to enroll just to meet him.

In those days, I liked to keep myself as busy as possible. But when
football season was over, I was left with entirely too much time between school and when Eliza would show up at the apartment. I sure
as shit didn't want to spend that time at the piss pot my parents called
home—the same one I was working two jobs to pay for since they
couldn't get their shit together.

A free boxing program sounded like the perfect fit.

I decided to skip chemistry to scope it out and, hopefully, secure my spot before the after-school rush hit.

"Well, that was fast," Slate *fucking* Andrews said from the front desk as I entered the gym.

The place was amazing. Everything was new and crisp white, red, and black. Two rings stood in the middle of the huge, open room, weights and various types of punching bags filling the rest. Mirrors covered the length of the room on one side, and jump ropes were hanging from hooks in every corner. But my eyes were instantly drawn to the giant words painted in script above the mirrors:

Home of

On The Ropes'
First World Champion

"Your name going in that blank?" he asked when he followed my gaze.

"Uh . . ."

"Okay, maybe we should start with: what's your name?" He pulled a clipboard from behind the tall, wooden counter.

"Um . . ." I continued to stutter, starstruck.

He chuckled and extended a hand. "Slate Andrews."

I wiped my palm on my jeans before lifting it to his. "Sorry. Till Page."

"Well, nice to meet you, Till." He pushed the clipboard in front of me. "Our gym rates are as stated, depending on the membership plan you choose. We have yearly, monthly—"

"Oh, um, sorry. I thought it was free." I looked up, embarrassed.

"Free?" His eyebrow quirked as he crossed his arms over his chest.

"Yeah. I mean the after-school program. Sorry. I must have been confused. I can't afford to join a gym." I stepped away, ready to bolt.

"You're a student?"

"Yeah," I answered.

His eyes narrowed. "It's yes, sir." Then he motioned for me to repeat it.

"Yes, sir."

He nodded approvingly. "Christ you're big for a kid. How old are you?"

"Seventeen."

"Play football?"

"Yes, sir."

"Senior?"

"Junior," I corrected.

He gave me a quick head-to-foot scan and shook his head. "All right, then. Let me switch that out for you." After pulling out a thick, manila envelope from the drawer, he slid it in my direction. "Why aren't you in school right now, Till Page?"

"I don't have class last hour," I lied.

"So, can I expect you here at two every day, then? Ya know, since you don't have class last hour?" He gave me a knowing smirk that read: *busted.*

"Well—," I started but he cut me off.

"You miss school, you don't come here. Got it?"

"Yeah," I answered quickly, but he glared at me. "I mean, yes, sir."

"Better. Look, this program is for kids with integrity. Lying to me will land your ass on the street. So let's try this again. Why aren't you in school right now, Till Page?"

I uncomfortably looked down at my shoes. "I, uh, wanted to enroll in the program. I was worried it would fill up before I got a spot, so I skipped class."

"Okay. You owe me three miles." He walked to a filing cabinet before returning with a neon-yellow piece of paper.

"Three miles of what?"

"Cardio! We have our own punitive system here at On The Ropes. Skipping class is three miles. Just be glad it was only one. Skipping a whole day earns you hand-washing jockstraps." He laughed as I curled my lip in disgust. "It's all outlined right there. As well as the membership fees."

I tilted my head in confusion, "I thought the after-school program was free. I just told you I can't afford gym fees!" My attitude slipped.

His whole friendly demeanor disappeared. He was glowering at me, and even as tough as I pretended to be, it still scared the fuck out of me.

I amended the end of my outburst. "Sorry."

"You don't have to pay me with cash, so technically, it is free. Don't worry. I had a lawyer look over that flier before passing it out. No false advertising here." He winked. "Manual labor is my currency of choice. The back of that"—he nodded down at the paper—"outlines the fees for your time spent here. Everything from sweeping the floors to cleaning the toilets, right down to folding towels, is on there. It also outlines the price of meals in manual labor as well. You need something to eat? I'll feed you. But it's not a handout. You'll work for that too."

"Meals?" I asked, more than just a little interested.

"Yep. You'll probably think they are nasty as hell. Real healthy stuff. Good for your body. I'm training fighters, not slouches."

"Oh, okay," I responded while scanning the "price chart."

Slate had figured out the "cost" for everything from just hanging out at the gym after school to private one-on-one boxing lessons with him. You could "buy" workout clothes or your own gloves with extra jobs as well.

Jesus. He was running a sweatshop, but that was all right with me.

"Max ten hours a week. You do those ten hours then everything opens up to you free of charge: meals, training, summer program, one set of workout clothes a month. And that even comes with my promise to keep my mouth shut when I find you crying about your sore muscles in the locker room." He smiled.

I rolled my eyes.

"I'm not going to bullshit you. I expect hard work in and out of that ring. You go to school and then come here. That's it."

"I work two jobs," I informed him.

"Fine. You go to school, work, then On The Ropes. Nothing else."

That sounded perfect. Well, nothing else except Eliza. Not even professional training with Slate Andrews would stop me from making time to spend with her.

After a few seconds, he cleared his throat. "So, you still interested in joining?"

"Yeah. Absolutely."

"Well, okay, then. Take that packet home and get your parents to sign all the Xs and I'll see you tomorrow after school. Now, go ahead and hit the track out back."

"The track?" I questioned.

"You owe me three miles, remember?"

"I'm wearing jeans," I responded, incredulous.

"Well, maybe you should have thought of that before skipping class." He walked away without another backward glance.

6

Eliza

One year later . . .

A STRICTLY FORBIDDEN BULLHORN BLASTED through the silent auditorium as my name was called to receive my high school diploma. While I never actually saw him, I had not one doubt that it was Till. I burst out laughing as my stomach twisted. It bothered me more than I'd expected that he wasn't walking across that stage with me.

Till's life had been busy. He'd been spending a lot of time at a nearby boxing gym as well as working two jobs: cleaning up after construction crews and stocking shelves at the grocery store. Even with all of that, he still never missed a single night at our apartment. He did, however, miss ninety percent of his math and physics homework, thus having failed both, which left him unable to graduate. He'd acted like it didn't bother him when he'd been told that he didn't have enough credits to walk across the stage with the rest of our class, but I could see the disappointment in his eyes. He'd laughed it off, saying that it wasn't like he had any huge plans to go off to a big-name college or anything.

I, however, had been accepted to the local university on a scholarship. I'd decided to take out every possible student loan I could get and move out of my parents' apartment. Till had laughed when I'd proposed a betting pool to see how long it would take them to notice that I was gone. I bet a decade. He chose a week.

I waited outside the auditorium after graduation was over, looking for Till, but deep inside I knew there was only one place I'd find him.

"Hey," he said, crawling through the window. He froze just as his large body cleared the opening. "Holy hell! Look at you, Doodle. You're in a dress." He smiled a lopsided grin that would have melted other girls. For me, it sizzled.

"See? Just further proof of how messed up the educational system is in this country. I have no idea how they didn't allow you to graduate today with observational skills like those."

"Shut up, smartass. I've just never seen you in a dress before."

"Yeah, I didn't feel like going home to change. My mom was already complaining about having to go to my graduation today."

"Jesus, that woman is a bitch," he mumbled to himself. "Well, you look good. Those college boys aren't going to know what to do with themselves." His mouth twisted into something he expected me to believe was a grin.

I didn't fall for it, but I knew why it was there. "Yeah, I've heard average-looking accounting majors who like to draw and paint are all the rage right now."

His eyes narrowed at my assessment.

"However, on the off chance that I do find someone who appreciates my undeniable awesomeness, I'd still have to explain why some guy is always hanging out at my *new* apartment." I waggled my eyebrows excitedly.

"You got an apartment?" His whole face scrunched up into a painful grimace before he was able to catch it.

"Yep!"

"Which one?"

"Um . . ."

"Which. One?" he repeated slowly, knowing the answer from my reaction alone.

"The one you didn't like." I bit my lip and looked away.

"Doodle, that one was shit. You can't live there. It's dangerous."

"Well, it's kinda my only option at this point. It's all I can afford without selling off my organs. I don't know about you, but I'm pretty attached to my kidneys."

"Come on. Be serious," he chastised in a very unlike-Till way. The crinkle on his forehead was unnatural and looked out of place on his strong face.

Till was no longer a boy in any respect. He stood at six foot four, and every plane of his body was covered with chiseled edges and contoured muscles. His hands were large and callused like a working man well past his eighteen years. Boys didn't look like that. Men did. *Till* did.

It seemed I wasn't the only one who'd noticed the changes in Till either. There was no shortage of women vying for his attention. But if they were lucky enough to catch it, I didn't know. He always brushed my questions about his romantic relationships off. I'd eventually given up and stopped asking. I didn't really want to know the answer anyway.

He cleared his throat to catch my attention, but it only drew my gaze to his throat. I watched as his Adam's apple bobbed when he swallowed. It was a spectacular show I could barely drag my eyes off. And when I did, it was only to move down to the thick muscles at the base of his neck.

"Hello? Earth to Doodle." He waved a hand in front of my face.

I stuttered for a moment before remembering what we were talking about. "Till, my student loans won't take me far. Plus, I have to pay for utilities and crap. Not to mention buying books and supplies. That stuff is expensive. Even if I increased my hours at The Smokehouse, I wouldn't be able to eat half the time if I picked one of the other apartments. It's not that bad, and this way, I can afford the one bedroom." I grinned proudly.

"Oh, fucking fantastic. You're going to be living there alone," he snapped then began to pace a small circle.

"Hey." I stepped in front of him. "If I have my own place, we can ditch this one and start hanging out there." I smiled, excited about the possibility.

Till blankly stared at me.

"Um, hello! This is a good thing. Did you hear me?" I asked.

He barked out a loud, sarcastic laugh. "Yep. Loud and fucking clear." He crossed his arms over his chest and eyed me for a second longer. "You're not living there," he stated definitively, causing *me* to copy his earlier reaction and bark out a loud, sarcastic laugh of my own.

"Oh, I'm not?" I lifted an eyebrow and crossed my arms over my chest, mimicking him. I had a sneaking suspicion my glare wasn't nearly as effective as his, but I held his eyes anyway.

We must have stood there for a full five minutes. I wasn't even sure that I blinked. By the time Till's lip twitched at the ridiculousness of our stare-off, I couldn't contain it anymore and burst out laughing, collapsing to the pillows on the floor.

I used a deep voice to mock his as I rolled around in hysterics, saying, "Doodle, you're not living there."

He wasn't impressed by my uncanny impression.

Finally, I was able to collect myself enough to glance up at him. I fully expected him to be pissed, but he was watching me with a wide smile.

God, he is gorgeous.

"You done?" he asked with a twinkle of something I couldn't quite figure out in his eyes.

"I don't know. Are you done telling me where I'm allowed to live?" I tilted my head questioningly.

He sucked in a breath before releasing it with a hard sigh. "I just worry about you living alone. It's not like your dad's going to get off his sorry ass and be there to make sure nothing happens to you."

"Seriously?"

"Yeah, seriously." He put his hands on his hips, and if it weren't for the fact that I was irritated by his attitude, I would have at least taken a minute to ogle his biceps.

Instead, I focused on the aforementioned attitude. "News flash. I don't need anyone to make sure nothing happens to me. I'm a big girl, Till."

"Right. Of course you are." He let out a frustrated groan and rolled his eyes. "Can we just stop talking about this shit? I got you a graduation present." He headed back toward the window.

"You got me a present!" I squealed. All of my annoyance disappeared.

He had given me a lot of things throughout the years. Most of them were things he found for the apartment when people moved from the building or, more often, got evicted. I loved them nonetheless.

"Well, kinda. I actually made you a present."

"You *made* me a present! That's even better!" I flew to my feet, and he started laughing at my enthusiasm.

"Well, I got to thinking a few days ago. What the hell are you gonna do when I'm not there to hold your sketchpad on my chest while you draw?" he asked with a huge grin, but it deflated mine.

"Why wouldn't you be there to hold my sketchpad?"

I wasn't stupid. I knew what he was trying to say, but it still hurt. I went to great lengths not to think about the prospect of Till not being a part of my future. He had been a constant in the present for way too long.

"Oh, come on, Doodle. You're getting your own apartment halfway across town. You won't have time to chill with me every night in this shithole."

"Are you kidding me? *Yes,* I will."

"Here?" he questioned, and even to my ears, his voice was a little too hopeful.

"Well, I mean . . . Maybe not *here,* but we'll be somewhere together, absolutely."

His eyes lit for a split second before dimming completely. "Yeah. I'm sure. Did you know that that new apartment of yours is five miles from here? That's one hell of a daily hike for two people who don't have a car," he smarted off before turning back toward the window.

"So what? I'm moving closer to my college, *five miles away.* It's not like I'm moving across the country. I'm fully expecting you to help me find a couch and then sit on it every night!" I shouted with a laugh as tears welled in my eyes.

He thought I was leaving. The idea of Till hurting was far worse than the idea of me sitting on a couch without him. And it should be known that that idea hurt pretty damn bad.

"Right." He tossed me a patronizing smile. "When are you leaving?"

"Tonight if you don't stop acting like a dick." I tried to sound stern, but the tears fell from my eyes.

I wanted to blame them on the fact that I was angry, but those tears were so much more. They were five years of codependency, one thousand twenty-six days where I had known someone was waiting for me—and one night when the world felt right as I'd slept at his side.

He swallowed hard. Using the sleeve of his black hoodie pulled over the heel of his palm, he wiped my tears away. Then, after scooping me off my feet, he held me tight and sat us both down on the cushions on the floor.

"Don't cry. It's just gonna be weird not having you around all the time," he murmured into my hair.

I tilted my head back, hoping that, in some way, I could convey my promise through the only simple words I had to offer. "I'm not going anywhere."

"Liar," he whispered, looking down just as I glanced up.

With his lips just a whisper away from mine and closer than ever before, my eyes drifted to his mouth and his head immediately fell back against the wall.

"Don't do that," he groaned. "Not tonight."

"Do what?" I asked innocently as I licked my lips. I lifted my chin so my nose grazed across his cheek. It could have been an innocent brush of skin. It *absolutely* wasn't though.

"Seriously, when do you leave?" He changed the subject and turned his head out of my reach, but his arms still held me tight.

"I don't have to leave." I went back to eyeing his mouth. I wasn't sure what was in the air that night. I'd wanted Till for a long time, but never once had I planned on actually acting on it.

"Yeah, you do. You have college and a way out of here. I'm happy for you, Doodle." His voice was sincere and packed full of lies.

I didn't doubt that he was happy for me; he just wanted to come with me. I wanted that too. So much that the words made their way to the surface before I could stop them.

Deep breath in.

Long exhale out.

Till.

And Doodle.

"I love you. I'm not going anywhere. I swear." His eyes flew to mine.

"Oh, God," he groaned.

"There is no way I could ever leave you, Till. I. Love. You," I breathed, moving even closer. It could have been an innocent and friendly declaration of love.

But, once again, it absolutely wasn't.

That was all it took; his mouth crashed against mine. Finally, those sculpted lips that had haunted my dreams—both day and night—moved against mine. It was needy and frantic.

It was overdue.

I pushed him down flat as I swung a leg over to straddle his lap, forcing my core against his.

"Doodle, please," he pleaded for me to stop even as he lifted his hips to meet mine.

The contact made us both gasp. His hands roamed up my back and down over my ass while his head threatened to divide the pillow in an effort to escape me.

"I can't have you without claiming you for forever."

"Then claim me. I'll claim you too."

"That's exactly what I'm afraid of, *Eliza.*"

I sucked in a surprised breath. If Till had actually known my name before that moment, I couldn't have been sure. But just the sound of it on his lips had ruined it for anyone who would ever utter it after him.

With one quick swoop, he sat up and tore my dress over my head. His mouth latched on to my bra-covered nipple, sending tidal waves of heat crashing through my body.

"Till," I moaned, threading my fingers into his hair.

"Someone touch you like this before, Eliza?"

My breath caught as his hand made its way down to my panties.

"Huh?" he asked, demanding an answer.

"No," I hissed, rising to my knees to allow him more room. Every nerve ending in my body was homed in on the gentle movement of his rough fingers.

"Good," he purred then leaned up to cover my mouth with his own.

His tongue slid against mine, smooth and practiced—at least, on his part. Tilting my head, I greedily took his mouth deeper. I wasn't experienced, but when he groaned down my throat, he made me powerful and brave.

His finger found my swollen clit, working me while his mouth stole the breath from my lungs. My hips glided with his rhythm. I was too lost in his movements to even care how wanton I looked.

I was in *his* arms.

"Say it again. Tell me you won't leave," he tried to order, but it came out as a plea. Then he moved his oral assault to my neck.

"I swear."

"Why not?" he questioned further, and a smile pulled at the corner of my mouth.

"Because I love you."

A deep rumble of approval vibrated in his chest. Suddenly, he removed his hand and rolled so I was on my back, and he settled on his knees between my legs. I was small and Till was huge. He all but manhandled me. Though it wasn't rough, it was definitely rushed.

His chest heaved as his eyes flashed between mine, occasionally glancing down to my bra and more than once to my panties. He swallowed hard.

"I want it all," he whispered, licking his lips before continuing. "Every single first you have to give, I want it." As he spoke, his eyes melted, becoming far younger than his eighteen years and a stark comparison to his physical appearance. They were unsure and dire.

I pressed myself up. While holding his eyes, I reached back and unsnapped my bra, letting it fall down my arms. "Then they're all yours," I promised.

A strangled sigh escaped his throat, and his dark eyes heated in a way I had never seen before. Looping his fingers in the pink cotton, he dragged my panties down my legs, discarding them on the floor beside us.

Completely exposed, I lay in front of Till, awaiting his next move. His eyes traveled over my body, but his hands were frozen at his side.

"Till," I whispered.

"Shhhh." He continued to stare.

Never in my life had I been naked in front of a man. It was terrifying.

"You're making me nervous."

"I've waited a really long time for this," he said with a shaky voice. "I've imagined you like this, every single moment, for years." His eyes flashed to mine. "I never thought I would have you."

"You've always had me. Touch me, Till."

He sucked in a deep breath and then lifted a hesitant hand to my breast. His thumb brushed over my nipple, and I arched off the pillow from the contact.

"Fuck," he hissed.

Starting at my belly button, he slowly trailed kisses up to my breast—sucking it into his mouth before making his way to the other. He was gentle and soft as he explored my body. From my breasts, he moved up to my neck and, finally, my mouth. It was lazy and calculated. But it didn't matter where he touched me—it was exactly the right spot.

I released a moan into his mouth as his hand slid between my legs. His long finger pressed inside my opening, and whatever noise I made was overpowered by his loud growl.

As his finger found its rhythm inside me, I reached out and grabbed the back of his hoodie. "Take this off," I boldly ordered. "I want to feel you too."

His hand froze as he eyed me warily. "Why?" he asked.

At first, it confused me. I assumed "*I want to feel you*" was pretty self-explanatory, but as I looked up into his insecure eyes, I realized it was far more than just a surface-level inquiry.

So I repeated his words back to him. "Because I've been waiting for a long time too. Every. Single. Moment. For years."

The words had barely cleared my lips before Till went wild.

His mouth slammed over mine as he dragged the hoodie off—separating the kiss only long enough for the cotton to clear his head. I followed him as he sat up, and our hands fumbled together over the button of his jeans. He got the denim past his hips before pressing me back down. Using my feet, I hurriedly kicked them off the rest of the way.

Till's naked body covered me completely. His hard-on glided against my stomach as his hips rolled against mine. I allowed my fingers to roam over the rippled muscles on his back, moaning when he flexed as he sat up.

Using both of his hands, he spread my legs wide. I watched as he descended down the cushions, his eyes holding mine until he settled on his elbows. Then his head dipped and he dragged his tongue over my clit.

"Oh, God!" I cried out.

"Have you ever come before?" He licked me again, and instinctually, I lifted my hips.

"Yes," I breathed.

His head snapped up, leaving me utterly lost. "With a guy?" he questioned roughly.

"No."

A one-sided smile tipped his lips. "Good. I want that too."

He quickly sealed his mouth over my sensitive bud, and one of his hands made its way to my opening. He slowly pressed the tip of his finger inside before adding another. I cried out from the surprising and mildly painful intrusion, but as his tongue began a smooth rhythm, the cries morphed into ones of ecstasy.

I writhed under him as he relentlessly drew the impending orgasm to the surface. It wasn't quick, nor was it perfect, but he was dedicated. I came against his tongue and around his fingers while calling out his name.

He continued his torturous strokes even as I came down from my high.

"Till, please," I pleaded when the sensations became more than my tingling body could handle.

I grabbed at his shoulders, trying to pull him up. Releasing a breath as he sat up, he kneeled between my legs. He didn't remove his fingers. Instead, he watched intently as he slowly glided them in and out of me. I wanted to be embarrassed and cover up. It was awkward at best, but the heated look on his face had me brazenly dropping my knees to the sides.

"You're beautiful," he whispered.

"So are you." I dragged my nails over his chest and down over the defined ridges of his abs.

I stilled as I caught my first sight of his straining hard-on. His hand came up and began to stroke it between us. I wanted to look away, but my eyes had other plans as they continuously flashed back to watch.

Till chuckled, and my gaze snapped to his.

"I'd rather it be your hand." He smirked.

I'd rather that too.

I timidly reached out, taking his shaft, and began to mimic his movements. I had absolutely no idea what I was doing, but I knew the gist. It didn't take long before I found a rhythm that caused Till's head to fall back and his eyes to stare at the ceiling.

"Jesus, Eliza." His chest and abs flexed.

I had known that his body would be amazing, but Till naked and reacting to my touch was a sight I could never have prepared for.

I continued my strokes while I climbed to join him on my knees. Starting at his chest, I dragged openmouthed kisses over his pecs and down to his abs. He flinched every time my tongue snaked out for a taste.

Closing his hand over mine, he hissed, "Okay, no more."

Gently pushing me back down, he took my mouth in a hard kiss. I opened my eyes to find him watching me. It was unnerving—and magnetic.

Suddenly, I felt his hand at my entrance as he guided himself inside me. My whole body tensed, and he must have felt it too. Turning his head, Till Page spoke words that solidified his claim on me for all of eternity.

"I love you, Eliza."

I relaxed as he very gradually filled me.

There were fireworks.

Stars.

Every possible cliché I could conjure.

But that wasn't the sex.

No. It was *him.*

We were young and reckless.

There was no condom.

Or discussion.

There were hands, mouths, and tongues.

Fingernails raking his skin and his hand in my hair.

Slow glides followed by deep thrusts.

Desperation.

Comfort.

There was Till.

And Eliza.

7

Till

SEX ISN'T SUPPOSED TO HURT, but with every mind-blowing thrust, a jagged piece was torn from my soul.

This was not supposed to happen. The sex. The pain. Eliza. None of it.

But she *loved* me.

As I watched her naked body tense under me, I knew I had risked it all just to hear her say it again.

She'd said that she wouldn't leave me, but it was a lie. She was finally moving on and starting a life—doing all the things we had dreamed of over the years. But I hadn't even graduated from high school, so she would be doing it all without me. My life was at a complete standstill while hers was sprinting away from me. She'd meet a guy at college who would recognize how amazing she truly was. Then, soon enough, I would be sitting in that apartment alone, haunted by her memories—and reality.

I had to have her, take the pieces I could claim before they were gone forever. I needed her to remember me in her new life, hopefully, even when she was in the arms of someone else. I couldn't make her stay, but I'd sure as hell make it so she couldn't give herself to anyone else.

I'd never had anything I could call my own, but Eliza Reynolds would always be *mine.*

I ran my hands over her small body, memorizing every inch as I went. I made mental notes of the newly exposed freckles, including the one just under her right breast. I burned that one into my memory as I watched her breasts sway each time I pressed inside her.

I'd remember it all.

Because that was all I thought I'd ever have of her.

That one moment.

"Oh, God, Till," she cried and her voice hitched.

"Say it again, Eliza. Tell me," I demanded then roughly filled her. I needed to be gentle. This was her first time, but I was desperate. I had to *hear* her come again.

There was always the possibility that there would be a time in the future where I could find her and convince her to be with me again. Maybe I could get my life together and be deserving of her. Actually have something to offer her.

But even if that farfetched fantasy became reality, there was a very good chance I'd never *hear* her again.

"I love you," she whispered, turning her head to take my mouth.

"You think you can come again for me?" I asked when I pulled away. I forced myself to switch to slow glides.

"I, uh . . . don't know."

"Come. Please." I sat up and found her clit with my thumb.

"Shit." Her whole body arched off the pillows as she dropped her legs open even wider.

"Please come," I chanted, leaning forward to suck her nipple into my mouth.

I wasn't wearing a condom, so I had to pull out. But I had to claim this last *first* before doing it. I wanted to be the last man she ever pulsed around, but I could settle for knowing that I was the first. I poured every resource I had into getting her off. But with every touch, I was forcing myself there as well.

"Damn it," I cursed as I lost the battle with my own release.

Pulling out, I pumped hot cum onto her stomach. Crashing on top of her, I buried my face in her neck and repeated her name as though it would be the last time I ever said it. And it very well could have been.

"I'm sorry." She began to rake her nails up my back.

"For what?" I responded, out of breath and with aftershocks still firing through my cock.

"That I didn't come again."

"Don't apologize for that. I just covered you in cum." I laughed, rolling to retrieve my boxers and using them to clean up her stomach while she giggled and squirmed under me.

With my boxers out of commission, I pulled my jeans on and settled on my side, propping myself up on an elbow to face her. While she had put her panties back on, she remained topless. There was no way I could leave while she was naked. I nabbed my hoodie off the ground and handed it to her. With an eager smile, she tugged it on.

Apparently, she didn't feel nearly as awkward as I did because as soon as she relaxed on the pillows, she curled into my chest. I dropped my arm under her head, and she snuggled in tight. It was absolutely perfect. But I knew it was fleeting.

"You okay?" I asked, slightly concerned that I had been too rough.

"Mmmm, very," she mumbled against my chest, punctuating it with a kiss.

"Eliza?"

"Yeah."

"I meant what I said."

"Me too," she responded lazily, squeezing me.

I held her for several minutes before I *heard* her take a deep breath and release it on a sigh as she fell asleep. It was music to my failing ears. It was also gut wrenching because it signaled the end.

Our goodbye was bound to happen. People like us didn't get handed happiness on a silver platter. We had to work for it. Her working for it meant going away to college, and mine would be hustling and busting my ass just to squeak by.

I didn't want to let her go, but the end was near. She was leaving. I wasn't about to be the one sitting around, watching her go. It might have been considered selfish to some, but to me, it was self-preservation. I'd remember that night. The highest of the highs.

I lay there for a while longer, grieving my loss. I didn't regret having taken the risk for one second though. Even if she forgot me in time, I'd always have one night where, for a brief moment, my fantasy had merged with reality into a world where Eliza was mine in every way possible.

When I was able to slip out of her grasp, I walked to the window and pulled in the easel I had made her as a graduation present. It wasn't anything fancy. Really, it was just the spare scraps of wood I had collected from my job at the construction site. I had one of the guys do me a favor and lend me a sander and some stain so it at least looked nice. It wasn't much, but I knew she'd love it. So I left it there for her to find. I couldn't be there in the morning to see her face when she saw it, but I wanted her to have it anyway.

I considered walking out of the door when I left that night—closing that fantasy world once and for all. Coming in the window might have been a silly superstition I'd started all those years earlier, but it felt real to me. I went so far as to grab the doorknob, but at the last second, I couldn't follow through. So after one last glance over my shoulder at Eliza as she slept in my hoodie, I crawled back out of that magical window for the very last time.

The first few days in the real world were excruciating. My mom was a bitch, and my dad was an idiot who was always up to some bullshit, most of which was illegal. Social services were there once again about Flint and Quarry. It was the same old song and dance, but this time, I had to deal with all of it without the escape that Eliza and our little apartment provided me.

I didn't know how I forced myself to stay away. I started taking a different route to work so I didn't have to pass that abandoned building every day. She could have been there . . . but she probably wasn't. She was moving on, and I was floundering.

Boxing was the only thing that kept me sane. When I missed her, I worked out. When I needed her, I trained. And when the world became too much, I imagined her. Her smile. Her laugh. That one fucking freckle haunted me. Which only made me miss her, so I trained some more. My life was a never-ending cycle that both began and ended with On The Ropes—with Eliza.

However, my body could only take so much abuse. Ten hours was the max a kid could work at the gym, but I was easily putting in at least twenty-five hours a week. Slate started forcing me to leave each night. I would have rather been cleaning the jockstraps than go home though.

Three months after I left Eliza, I was laid off from my job at the construction company. Not only did I become hard up for money, I was suddenly overflowing with free time. It was a nightmare. I couldn't pay the rent and had nothing but time to worry about it. Thankfully, a kid at the gym helped me get a job cleaning up at the auto repair shop where he worked. The money was okay, but I learned a ton from the mechanics. They helped me buy a piece-of-shit truck from a customer who couldn't afford to fix it. It took months to get it running, but as I drove out of the parking lot in a truck that was completely mine, I felt like the biggest success on the planet.

After that, a whole world opened up for me. Being able to travel more than a mile from my house gave me a freedom I had never experienced before. Sure, there was public transportation, but when life went to hell in a handbasket, I didn't have to check the bus schedule now. I could just hop in my truck and drive as far as my usually empty gas tank could take me.

That truck was the reason I ended up with my father the night when everything went wrong. The night when he turned on me and I left him for dead.

The same night Eliza saved me all over again.

8

Eliza

I WAS STARTLED AWAKE BY a loud knock on my window. My heart began to pound from the surprise wake-up call, but as I managed to rouse my lagging mind to consciousness, I automatically knew who was on the other side. I could picture his straight, black hair barely sticking out from under the edges of a beanie and his hazel eyes—the ones that could stir something inside me with only a single glance. I could clearly envision the sexy grin that only tipped one side of his mouth while his thumb nervously toyed with his bottom lip in that way that drew the attention of every woman in a fifty-mile radius.

As I walked to the window, I ran through every possible excuse why I shouldn't open it. Perhaps I should have gone back to bed and sent him away without a backward glance. I wouldn't though. Regardless that he had rejected me, I found myself absolutely unable to return the favor. Unfortunately, I was transparent because Till Page obviously knew that too.

"Doodle, open up," he whispered from the other side of the glass.

"Till, it's late. Go home," I urged, knowing I wouldn't be able to resist opening it for much longer.

"I, um . . ." His words caught with uncharacteristic emotion.

"Till?"

"Please, Doodle." His voice cracked, which shattered whatever imaginary resolve I was holding on to.

I threw back the curtains and pried the window open. Based on the way he sounded, I was fearful of what I would find on the other side. My suspicions were confirmed when I caught sight of his blood-soaked T-shirt.

"Oh my God, Till. Are you all right? Is that your blood?"

"No," was his only response. My eyes raced over his body, looking for any possible injury, but with the exception of split knuckles, there wasn't a mark on him.

"Get in here." I stepped away to allow him room to crawl inside.

"No," he repeated with glazed over eyes. He leaned in only far enough to grab my hips and drag me out the window.

"What the hell are you doing?" I cried out as he carried me to a beat-up pickup truck.

He didn't answer as he placed me on the seat and slammed the door closed behind me. Till might have been there physically, but his mind was lost somewhere else.

Just as he slid behind the wheel, his empty eyes swung to mine.

"What's going on?" I whispered.

"I need you," he said desperately.

"Then I'm here." I reached over to squeeze his arm, but it did nothing to relax his tense, straining body. "Whose blood is that?"

He swallowed hard then shook his head in response.

It wasn't enough though. "Please. You have to give me something here. I haven't seen you in six months, and tonight, you showed up at my window covered in blood. I'm scared," I said quietly, so as not to spook him. This wasn't my rock, Till. This was a virtually unrecognizable, nervous *boy.*

"I'll tell you at the apartment," he muttered, and a pang of guilt stole my breath.

"No. Tell me here," I demanded. "I'm not leaving."

"At the apartment," he repeated.

"There was nothing in that apartment but me and you. So we're already there. Close your eyes." I reached over and folded my hand over his.

He immediately opened his hand and intertwined our fingers. "I just want to go home, Doodle." His voice broke as he leaned over, resting his head in my lap like he had done so many times before.

I went to work running my fingers through his hair, scratching his head in the way I knew would soothe him—but it didn't this time. His huge body crawled even closer, wrapping both arms around me to hug my legs.

"Talk to me," I urged again.

"No. You talk. I want to hear you while I still can."

While I still can.

His words began to ricochet through my ears like a stray bullet fired from an unknown gun. They had been intended to be innocent, but they were deadly to me. They showed me that he wasn't planning to stay this time either. This was but a brief stop for Till. Claiming whatever he needed at the moment before casting me aside yet again. My pulse began to race. I needed to be there for him, but who was going to be there for me when he walked away all over again? Where was he when I needed him?

"You're the one who left, Till. I wouldn't have gone anywhere." I swung the door open and climbed out of his grasp. Then I hurried back to my apartment, wishing this were all just a nightmare and that he had stayed gone.

I heard his footsteps on the sidewalk behind me.

"Doodle! Please!"

I ignored him and kept moving toward my front door—my only refuge from the painful world without Till.

"Please," he continued to beg behind me, and that single syllable destroyed me. "I just need to go home tonight."

Funny, I wanted to go home too. I'd wanted that for a long fucking time though.

My temper slipped and tears sprung to my eyes. I spun around to face him, and he stilled just two steps away.

"There is no apartment, Till. I called the city and told them people were squatting in it. They cleared it out, gutted it, and then boarded it up tight. I sat in the parking lot and watched them do it. It's fucking gone!" I took great pleasure in watching the words hit him like physical blows.

Yeah, kicking him while he was so obviously down shouldn't have felt good, but it eased the pain I had been living with. It was about time that someone else lived with that shit. I was exhausted.

"No. No, no, no, no, no." He stumbled backward before rushing forward. "Why would you do that?" he breathed before repeating it on a roar. "Why would you do that!"

"I needed it to disappear!" I screamed through my tears. "Just like you did." I sobbed, reliving the morning of waking up without him all over again.

"That wasn't yours to take away!" he exploded into the otherwise silent night. His words echoed off the surrounding buildings, each wave slicing me to the quick all over again. "That was *our* place. Not yours." His voice cracked right alongside my heart.

"Yeah, well, there was a lot of stuff that wasn't yours to take either." I held his gaze, desperately trying to be strong, but as his eyes grew wide, I whimpered.

His long legs strode forward, and he stopped only inches away from me. He was crowding me, but he still leaned in closer to my face. "There is nothing in this world that was ever more mine than you," he stated.

Though it was the absolute truth, I wished with all my heart that it were a lie.

"Till," I cried, swiping the tears from my eyes.

"Why!" he shouted, causing his muscles to tense under the force. "Goddammit! I needed that place."

Porch lights flashed on from the surrounding apartments, illuminating not only the dark, but also my rage.

I shoved my hands against his chest. "What about what I needed? You left! I waited in that fucking apartment for weeks."

He didn't budge, but my bare feet slipped, sending me toward the ground. Impossibly fast, Till's hand snaked out and caught my arm. But I didn't let his chivalrous gesture douse my fire. I had six months' worth of words to say to the man I was irrevocably in love with.

"You took what you wanted. Then you left me."

"Doodle," he whispered.

I had been perilously close to the edge of insanity, and with one single word, he'd pushed me over.

I lost it completely.

Pounding my fists against his chest, I screamed at the top of my lungs, "It's Eliza! My name is fucking Eliza! Not Doodle!" I spun to march away, but Till's arms folded around me, lifting me off my feet to restrain me.

I was miniscule compared to him. There was no use in fighting, but I still kicked my legs, irrationally desperate to get away from him—but only because I knew I couldn't keep him for forever.

"Stop it!" he growled into my ear. "I know your goddamned name—probably better than I know my own."

While I was wrapped in Till's strong arms, six months' worth of tears fell from my eyes. He carried me to my apartment and guided me back through the window before following me inside. Then he stripped out of his blood-soaked shirt before dragging the blankets down and climbing into the bed behind me. I cried for a while in his arms, even turning to face him, only to cry against his chest. I had missed him so much.

I knew I'd loved Till years ago, but this was more. I needed him in order to function on a very basic level. Together, the world didn't feel so big and overwhelming. He was my escape—the dream personified.

Till Page was *comfortable.*

His hands trailed up and down my back as he lulled me until the words fought their way out.

"I couldn't stop going back," I announced in a broken whisper. "I didn't know where you had gone. And for the first time since I was thirteen, I was alone inside my own head. God. It was a scary place." I tried to joke, but the tears streaming down my face told the truth.

"I'm sorry," he responded on a sigh. "I couldn't stay."

"Why?" I whined, but I curled in closer against his chest, needing to feel him more than anything else.

"I don't know, Doodle," he lied.

God! It was such a fucking lie. He knew as well as I did. He just didn't want to tell me.

"Where did you go?" I pressed further.

There was no way I ever could have expected his answer, but that wasn't because it was a novel thought. No. His answer was surprising because it was the source of my anguish too.

"The real world." He kissed my forehead.

"Right." I abruptly sat up, drying my eyes. "That's exactly why this hurts. We could have gone together. But you made that choice for both us. I would have given absolutely anything to be in the real world with you."

"You don't understand." He began toying with his bottom lip. "Doodle, you're not real to me."

To date, it was the most hurtful thing anyone had ever said to me. The tears instantly dried, and an unlikely smile crossed my mouth.

Yeah. That stings like the real world.

"Get out," I ordered. For the first time ever, I truly, and rationally, wanted him gone from my life. No one, including my parents, could have hurt me more than he had with those five words.

He squeezed me impossibly tight.

"No. Listen to me."

"Get. Out," I told his chest through gritted teeth, as I lay tense in his arms. I was no longer returning his embrace; I was no longer returning anything.

"You've never once asked me why I was crying that first day when we met," he said randomly, and I tried to wiggle my way out of his arms. He threw a leg over my thighs to lock me in even tighter.

"Let me go!" I began to thrash against him.

He never did follow direction well. Instead, he told me a story.

"The school sent a note home asking my parents to have my hearing tested. Apparently, a few of the teachers had noticed that I didn't always respond when they called my name. It took three weeks for my mom to get off her lazy ass and take me to see someone. I failed the hearing test with flying colors." He laughed, and it enraged me. I didn't want to walk down memory lane.

"Let me go," I demanded once again.

"Nope." He kissed the top of my head. "The doctor did a few tests before telling us that my hearing loss was sensorineural and would cause me to eventually go deaf."

I stilled as my heart dipped in my chest from his matter-of-fact announcement.

"He said it just like that, too. It was quick and to the point, no fluff. I guess you get what you pay for, and unfortunately for me, we were at the free clinic." He laughed again, but my stomach ached.

"Was he right?" I asked with a wince, not wanting to hear the answer.

"Yeah," he confirmed, causing me to gasp. "When I was thirteen, I was hearing at around eighty percent, and they predicted it would go downhill pretty steadily."

"But you're not . . ." I trailed off, unwilling to finish the thought.

"It could take years. It all depends on my rate of degeneration. The clinic sent us to a specialist, but in true Mommy Dearest fashion, she asked what the point of seeing a specialist was if there wasn't any way to prevent me from going deaf. I can still vividly remember her checking her watch as she spoke to the doctor. She must have had somewhere else to be that was more interesting than listening to the diagnosis that would forever change my life."

"Fuck," I whispered.

"As soon as we walked out of that doctor's office, she told me she needed me to keep my brothers because she had plans that day. Plans. Fucking plans!" His voice rose for the very first time during his recount. "It would have hurt if I hadn't already known what a self-centered bitch she was."

My hands found purchase on the muscles on his back, and I pulled him impossibly closer. It was all I had to offer.

"So as soon as we got home, I dashed from the car and took off through the apartments, climbing through the first window I came to. That's when I found *you*. At first, I kept coming back because I thought you were funny and you distracted me from the world that kept spinning under my feet."

"Every girl's dream—a distraction," I snarked against his chest, but if he heard me, I couldn't be sure.

He continued. "But then it became a place where I wasn't bound by my life outside. Inside the four walls of that shitty apartment, I got to be whoever I wanted. I wasn't poor or going deaf. Social services weren't beating down our door, nor were the cops looking for my dad. I was always met with a smile and a sense of belonging. It was *you*. We had an entirely separate life there. Together, we kept it clean. I made sure we always had power and you made sure I didn't starve. That was a hell of a lot more than I got at home. You took care of me, and with what little I had, I took care of you."

I was still mad as hell, but he was speaking the language of longing and acceptance I understood, and that's the only reason I nuzzled my head against him.

"So, Doodle. I fucked up that last night together. I took the risk and merged fantasy into reality."

My body immediately stiffened, but I was unsure which term had hurt more. Who I wanted to be to Till was still a mystery even to me.

With a slide of his hand over my throat, he guided my eyes to find his. "So I decided to walk away from you before you could walk away from me when you realized what a fuckup I was in the real world." His lips lingered close to mine, but it wasn't the good kind. It was the torturous kind.

If I were given the choice with Till, I'd take real life every. Single. Time.

"I am well aware what a fuckup you are," I said, and I felt him flinch. "Did you ever think that maybe I felt the same way about you? My parents couldn't have given two shits about me, but I knew you did. I knew you would always be there. You might be late, you might smell like Rochelle Lane's cheap-ass perfume, you might be in a shitty mood, but you *would be there*. Then, one day, you weren't. I sat in that apartment night after night for two months. Most of the time, I just stared at the window, willing it to suddenly open."

"Jesus. I'm sorry. I just didn't know where else to go tonight. I needed the fantasy back."

"Well, I don't," I said, and he began to roll away. "Stop. Just listen to me. I've put my life back together the last few months. I've moved on in the real world. I don't want to go back to the fantasy. Not even to be with you." I felt his shoulders fall. "But if you want to join me here, I'm okay with that."

"I don't even know where to start being there with you." He sucked in a breath, releasing it on a vibrato.

"Start by telling me whose blood you were wearing tonight. I don't need details, but you have to let me know if I have to testify that you were with me all night. I'm a terrible liar." I raked my nails down his back.

"Some guy named Frankie," he answered weakly.

Our bodies were tangled together. As I stiffened, he became pliable, wrapping around me. Yin and yang. I took the strength he feebly offered. And he held me tight enough to transfer it through mere contact.

"Is he dead?" I finally found the words, but I'd never wanted an answer less.

"No. But my father might be."

"Oh, God." A sob caught in my throat.

"Don't waste one fucking tear on that asshole. I tried to protect him, but he turned on me. He threw me to the fucking wolves!" he exclaimed without ever raising his voice.

His eyes were filled with rage, but it was more than that. He was hurt . . . and disappointed . . . and *abandoned.* I was devastated just watching the myriad of emotions pass over his strong face.

"You really think he's dead?"

"Unfortunately, no. He's probably still breathing. But he's dead to me all the same."

I eyed him warily, unsure how to react to this news. It was obvious he didn't want to talk about it. But there was always one thing that worked for us. Humor.

"Okay. If the cops come calling, you were with me all night. I haven't left this apartment since noon. You came in the window soon after. We ate leftover spaghetti then watched Dancing With the Stars. We had sex—you came, I didn't."

He began to laugh, burying his head in my neck.

"Then you sang me hymns to combat my newfound insomnia."

"Hymns? Really, Doodle? Shit. I'm going to jail for life," he complained before grabbing my ass.

"Hey. Hands!" I halfheartedly slapped his hand.

"Sorry. I needed one last taste of a woman before I'm checking out asses every time soap is dropped in the shower."

I burst into laughter and tears at the same time.

"Shhhh. I'm kidding. I'm not going to jail. Bad guys don't rat out other bad guys to the cops."

"Are you sure?" I asked, staring up through my lashes into his gold-flecked eyes.

"Positive." He smiled and brushed the hair from my face.

"I've really missed you," I boldly confessed.

His eyes warmed as emotion made its way from under his tough exterior. "I've missed you too. I'm sorry I ruined us."

"Hey, you didn't ruin us. In the morning, we just go back to being friends. We're good at that. The past is done. Just friends from here on out. Tomorrow starts real life . . . together. I'm going to help you find an apartment. You need to get out of your parents', and we can meet here every night just like the old place. Only this time, I'll bring the power and you bring the food." I smiled.

"You think we can do friends again?" He looked downright hopeful as he asked.

"Not if you don't get out of my bed and stop grabbing my ass. You can sleep on my couch until you find a place. Okay?"

"Yeah. Thanks."

"Hey, when was the last time you saw a doctor about your hearing?" I asked, causing him to groan.

"About three years ago," he said as he rolled out of bed and headed for the window.

"You need to get that checked out, Till."

"Yeah, I know," he called over his shoulder as he climbed outside.

"I'm serious. That's not something to play around with. Maybe the specialist could do something to prevent it. You never know until you ask."

"I'll make an appointment. I swear," he lied, but I had to let it go.

I couldn't force him into a doctor's office no matter how much this new revelation worried me.

"Where are you going?" I asked.

"To lock up my truck. There was a crazy woman who left the door standing wide open earlier." He flashed me a smile.

"You know I have a door, right?"

He barked out a laugh. "Yeah, I know, Doodle."

"Umm . . . then why don't you use it?"

He stared at me for a few seconds from outside my window before finally answering, "Because I'm afraid it would change everything."

"It's a door, Till. I'm relatively sure the sheer magnitude of you walking through it wouldn't knock the Earth out of orbit."

"Maybe not, but I need you too damn bad to chance it," he said, and it forced the smile to fall from my face. "I decided a long time ago that the window at the old apartment was some kind of portal to a whole other dimension. One where life was easy and people like you existed. I used to think that, if I came in the door, you'd be gone. We might be starting in the real world together, but I'm still not ready to let go of the fantasy."

"Till," I breathed when further words failed me.

"Yeah. Anyway. I'll be right back. Leave this open for me, okay?" He winked before walking away.

Thankfully, I was never kidnapped or robbed, because from that day forward, I never once locked my window. And no matter how ridiculous it was, I smiled daily when Till came climbing through it.

9

Till

I STAYED AT ELIZA'S APARTMENT for a few weeks. It was the best possible feeling, having her around all the time again, but I felt like a worthless dick sleeping on her couch. I spent what little money I had on food to at least make it look like I was helping out, but she still cooked me dinner every night.

Going back to being friends wasn't nearly as hard as I'd worried it would be. Was I still attracted to her? Absolutely. But keeping her in my life meant not acting on it. Our new relationship only vaguely resembled the old one. Gone were the hours spent cuddling or lying in her lap. Before we'd had sex, I'd touched Eliza all the time. There had been nothing to read into from those forehead kisses and innocent moments spent holding each other. But now, I knew her body, so every brush of our skin reminded me what it felt like to have her naked underneath me. Neither of us could deny that the spark was there; we just had to avoid it. I'd only actually had her for one night, but my hands ached to touch her as if it were the norm.

Those first few weeks killed me. Life carried on though. I got word that my father had landed himself in jail after the police had found him bloody and beaten that night. His pockets were apparently filled with meth, so he was slapped with several possession charges, earning himself an extended vacation at the prison. I didn't give a damn if it was a life sentence though. He was dead to me. I told Eliza bits and pieces of the night, but as a whole, I just tried to put it out of my mind.

One day, as I was coming home from work, I saw two guys fumbling a bed down the stairs from above Eliza's apartment.

"Hey, you need a hand?" I jogged over to catch the mattress just before it fell over the railing.

"Shit. Thanks, man," the short guy groaned as we carried it the rest of the way to a truck.

"Damn. That was heavier than it looked." The taller of the two cracked his neck as I pushed it with one hand to wedge it between the two dressers.

I laughed and headed back toward Eliza's apartment, but he stopped me only a few steps away.

"Big man, wait! You wanna make a quick fifty bucks?"

Money.

"Whatcha got in mind?" I asked as I turned to face him.

"I got to get on the road in, like, an hour, and there is no way the two of us are going to be able to get some of that shit down the stairs."

"One hour? Fifty bucks?" I could definitely use the cash, and if I got to combine that with a workout of hauling all his stuff down, I wouldn't complain.

"That's the offer."

"All right. Half now. Half when I finish." I crossed my arms over my chest.

He dug in his pockets, pulling out a wad of bills. "What's your name?" he asked, handing the money over.

"Till."

"I'm Daniel. That's Scott. Follow me, Till. Let's get this knocked out so I can get the hell out of here."

Forty minutes later, I was carrying the last box down to his truck. He didn't have much, so it didn't take me long, but it would have taken those two forever. It turned out Scott was staying in the apartment, but Daniel was moving to Wisconsin to be with some girl he met online. Scott gave him an endless amount of shit about it too. It was hilarious listening to them go back and forth. They both seemed like good guys.

"I am out of here!" Daniel said, bumping fists with Scott. "Hey, please try to find someone to take my room. I can't afford to carry this place more than another month."

My head snapped to Scott. "You looking for a roommate?"

"I am now that this asshole is taking off on me to move in with his mail-order bride. Why? You looking for a place?"

"Yes!" I jumped forward a little too enthusiastically. "I applied here, but they didn't have anything available. They put me on a twelve-mile-long wait list, but I really can't afford anything else I looked at."

Daniel glanced over at Scott, who shrugged.

"You got a job?" Scott asked.

"Two."

"You a partier?"

"Nope. I work, go to the gym, then sleep."

"Rent's five fifty a month. So you'd need to have two twenty-five in cash by the first of every month. If you're late, it's an extra hundred bucks. All the bills get split right down the middle. No exceptions."

"I'm cool with that," I said quickly as I began to get even more excited. That was a hundred bucks cheaper than what I'd thought I was going to have to spend to get my own place.

"Well, okay, then. I know you saw the bedroom, but you want to go up and take a look around the rest of the apartment?"

"Yeah, definitely!" I answered, even though, there wasn't a chance in hell that anything I could see would prevent me from signing a lease. I *needed* a place.

"I'm gonna take off. Let me know if this works out. Thanks again for your help, Till." Daniel pulled out the other half of the money he owed me and passed it with a handshake.

"No problem. Any time." I tucked the cash in my pocket and turned back to Scott. "Let's go check it out."

"Sure. Have a good trip," he called to Daniel over his shoulder as he headed up the stairs.

I followed behind him, hiding the smile that was working its way onto my face regardless how hard I tried to fight it.

"I work nights and sleep during the day, so you won't see me much. I've got a girl who lives across town, so I stay over there sometimes on the weekends."

We walked through the door, and he immediately stilled as we were greeted with loud music blasting through the floorboards.

"Shit. She must be at home. Okay, so maybe this is a good thing." He let out a huff that showed me that what he was about to say was anything but good. "Look, the only catch to this place is that the building is shit. I swear I think the floors are made out of tissue boxes. You can hear everything that goes on in the apartment downstairs. It's a real nice girl who lives there, but her taste in music is almost criminal. She treats us to Justin Timberlake at least once a day. I got pissed when we first moved in. I went down to bitch that her music was too loud, but I swear to you it was louder in our place than it was in hers, so after talking to her, I just let it go. It didn't hurt that she's sexy as fuck." He winked.

My eyebrows popped up in surprise. She was sexy. He at least got that part right.

She was also mine.

He continued. "I'm not home enough for it to bother me, but your room would be right over hers. The bad news is you're able to hear every single sound she makes. However, the good news is that you're able to hear *every single sound* she makes." He finished with another wink, and my self-restraint that day must have been aligned with Mother Teresa because my hand remained fisted at my side and not in his mouth.

"When can I move in?" I gritted through a fake smile.

"You don't want to look around first?"

"Nope. I'll take it. How much do I owe you for this month?" I had two hundred dollars to my name, and that included the fifty bucks in my pocket. There were three weeks left in the month, but I got paid in two days. I could swing the rent as long as I ate at the gym every day.

"Just give me two twenty-five when you move in. Daniel already paid this month's rent, so you can ride out his dollar this month, and I'll use your first payment to cover next month."

I blinked at him and my smile broke free—big time. "Yeah. I can do that," I answered.

"All right. Welcome home, Till. I'll get the sublet form for you to sign." He extended a hand to seal the deal, and I couldn't shake it fast enough.

Eliza chose just that moment to start singing at the top of her lungs. A smile instantly spread across my lips as I listened to her less-than-stellar solo performance.

Yeah. *Welcome home, Till.*

"Can you give me just a second?" I excused myself and hauled ass down the stairs and around to the side of the building.

I shoved her window open and then crawled inside, rushing through her small apartment to find her. She was standing in the kitchen, singing and shaking her ass, but her head was down as her hand was moving over a sketchpad.

I leaned against the wall for a few seconds, watching the show she was unknowingly putting on. I tried not to envision her body naked as she moved with the rhythm of the music. Her breasts swayed with her hips, and just knowing that the fucking freckle was swaying too was more than enough to stir my cock to life.

"Shit!" she screamed when she finally noticed me standing in the hallway. "Damn it, Till," she cursed, trying to catch her breath.

"Come here for a second." I grabbed her hand and dragged her to her bedroom, but not for the horizontal purposes I truly wanted. "Wait right here." I headed for the window, clicking her music off before I climbed out.

"What are you doing?"

"Just wait." I smiled then jogged toward the stairs.

I threw the front door to my new apartment open and then rushed right past Scott. Once I entered my new bedroom, I stared at the stained-carpeted floor.

"Doodle!" I yelled unnecessarily loud.

"Uh, Till? What are you doing?"

I wasn't sure how much she could hear, but her voice hit my weak ears as if she were standing only a few feet away. It was clear that I would, in fact, be able to hear *everything.*

"Oh, nothing much. Just chilling in my new apartment." I played off my excitement, but her squeal let me know she wasn't even trying to hide it.

"I'm coming up!" she yelled.

I rushed to the front door to meet her. Scott watched from the couch as I snatched the door open. It didn't take but a second for her to come plowing through it.

"Are you serious?" She laughed as happy tears glistened in her eyes.

"Completely," I confirmed, which caused her to launch herself into my arms.

God, it felt good as she wrapped her legs around my waist. She laughed loudly into my ear, and I couldn't help but join her.

I glanced over at Scott, who had the good sense to look surprised, and even a little embarrassed, as he watched me hold her tight. I gave him a pointed look when I remembered his comments about Eliza from earlier. The last thing I needed to do was get into an argument with him before I even signed the lease. But thankfully, he immediately lifted his hands in surrender and mouthed, "Sorry."

I lifted my chin in his direction then went back to holding her.

"You're going to live upstairs!" she exclaimed, sliding her feet to the ground and stepping away all too soon. "I want to see your room."

I led her down the hall to the small, empty room that would just fit the bed and a dresser I didn't have.

"It's only two twenty-five a month. I shouldn't have any trouble affording it." I leaned against the doorframe as she looked around.

"What if he's a weirdo?" she whispered.

"Who?"

"Your roommate. I met him once, but I can't swear he's not a serial killer."

"I think I'll be okay. His name's Scott and he seems nice enough. I've been over here for an hour or so. Daniel gave me fifty bucks to help him move out."

"So that's what it was! I heard something going on up here."

Just then, something started beeping. We both looked around the room, trying to find the source, but came up empty. When we left the room, the sound grew louder as we got closer to the kitchen.

"What is that?" Eliza asked.

Luckily, Scott was there to answer. "Your oven timer."

"My oven timer? No way. It's barely that loud in my apartment."

"Way. We can hear pretty much everything through the floor."

Eliza's eyes grew wide.

"Wait. You can hear us too, right?" Scott asked.

"Well, I mean, yeah. I guess. I just assumed you were really loud."

"Nope. Just cheap floors." He shrugged. "So . . . whatcha cooking?" he asked with a smile.

"Oh shit! My pizza." Eliza bolted to the door, and I followed because . . . well, pizza sounded good.

She ran inside through her front door, and I went around to her window.

"So, what do you think?" I asked, pushing myself up to sit next to the oven.

"I think you need to get your ass off my counter and we're both lucky that I didn't burn dinner, but mostly, I think it's really exciting that you're going to be living upstairs." She blew her hair out of her eyes and set the pizza on top of the stove.

I smiled and swiped a pepperoni off the top, burning the shit out of my mouth as I popped it in. "Damn, that's hot," I mumbled, blowing around it.

"Genius. You just watched me pull it out of the oven. Were you expecting it to be cold?"

"No, I was just hungry. Oh, that reminds me." I jumped off the counter and pulled a twenty from my pocket. "Use this for food."

She looked at my hand then began slicing the pizza. "No, just keep it. You're going to need a bunch of stuff for the new apartment. Do you have enough for the first month? I get my student loan check next week. I can help you a little and you can just pay me back—"

I swiftly interrupted her. "Stop. I'm good, I swear. I appreciate it, but I get paid on Friday—"

Then she interrupted me. "But what about your mom's rent? I know you and your dad . . . Well, I just mean . . . Are you, um . . . going to help her this month?" She shyly looked up at me through her lashes. My dad was a sensitive subject, and even mentioning him usually put me in a shit mood.

I sucked in a deep breath. "I don't know. I've been paying their rent for years. But now, I've got my own bills to worry about. I couldn't care less about her getting tossed to the streets, but Flint and Quarry can't be homeless. I don't want to give her the money, though, if she doesn't really need it, because, let's be honest here—I do. But at the same time, she's already a month behind, so if she doesn't pay before the first, they can evict her."

"Okay, well, what if you go in right before the office closes the day it's due? If she's paid it, awesome. If not, you can pay it so she doesn't get evicted, but then make sure she *really* understands that you won't be paying it again. And if you do have to pay it, let me help you at least for this month." She looked up from the pizza and pleaded with her eyes way before she did with her mouth. "Please."

A warm feeling passed over me. I'd never take Eliza's money. She lived counting her pennies the same way I did. But the fact that she was willing to give me the little she had . . . There were no words. It hit me deep.

"All right, moneybags. If it comes down to the wire, I'll let you help out. Let's start with you taking this twenty bucks and then feeding me some pizza."

Her lips twitched. She knew I was lying, but she didn't bother calling me on it. Instead, she took the money and passed me a plate loaded with over half of a pizza.

One day, I was going to buy that woman everything she wanted. I didn't know when or how. I just knew that, one way or another, it would be done.

10

Till

Three years later . . .

"YO, TILL!" DERRICK BAILEY YELLED as I walked into the gym.

"What's up?" I called out, rolling my eyes.

I fucking hated that kid with a passion. He was such a fucking suck-up. He wasn't one of the poor kids. No, his daddy had plenty of money, and he paid a shit-ton each month for his son to be a part of the gym. So while I was mopping floors to earn my keep, he would sit and talk to me. It was obnoxious. Besides being loaded, something about him just rubbed me the wrong way.

"Flint called a minute ago while I was covering the phones. Said you need to go home as soon as possible. Some sort of cop showed up at your mom's place."

"Nothing new," I mumbled to myself. "Yeah, okay. I'll call and see what's going on after I start the load of towels."

"Okay. He was pretty messed up though. He said they were there about your little bro."

"Quarry?" I spun to face him, confused.

"That's what he said, man." He shrugged.

"Shit." My pulse spiked as I dropped all of my bags and sprinted from the gym.

My feet pounded the pavement as I ran the few blocks to my

mom's apartment. Quarry was ten and by no means a golden child. He had a serious attitude. Where Flint was book smart, Quarry was slick and cunning. I had been keeping a close eye on him recently. But the older he got, the sneakier he became.

He was also still a kid though.

I didn't slow down until I'd shoved my mom's front door open. She was sitting on the couch next to some greasy asshole in a silk shirt and across from a uniformed officer. I glanced around her run-down apartment for a second to find it surprisingly not too bad. It was still dingy as hell, but everything seemed to be in place. Clearly, Flint had been busy—and expecting this visit.

"What the hell is going on?" I asked the room, and Flint let out a relieved sigh from the corner. "Where's Quarry?"

"Hey, honey." My mom stood up and walked over to hug me, putting on the fakest show I had ever seen.

"Get off me." I stepped away and put my hands on my hips. "Where's Quarry?" I repeated.

"He locked himself in his room," Flint answered.

My mom glared at him.

"Are you the boy's father?" the officer asked.

I knew my size made me look older than twenty-one, but really? His father?

"No. I'm his brother. Till Page." I extended a hand to the officer.

"You live here?" he asked, eying me but not taking my hand.

"No, sir. I have my own place across town." My use of "sir" seemed to convince him that I wasn't a total juvenile delinquent.

"Well, your brother hasn't been to school in ten days. I was asked by the school to make a trip out here and see what was going on."

My head quickly turned to my mother. "Ten days?" I asked, incredulous.

"Till, honey. I'm just as shocked as you are," she cooed, and it enraged me.

"Ten days?" I repeated on a roar that made her flinch.

The slime ball on the couch jumped to her defense. "Hey! Don't talk to her like that!"

"Who the hell are you?" I growled.

"Till, this is my boyfriend, Ray Mabie."

"Your boyfriend?" I barked out a laugh. "Wow. Congratulations, Ray. You made third-string!"

"Till!" my mom hissed.

"Maybe it's fourth-string? I can't keep up. Let's see . . . Every Thursday, she visits Dad in jail. Then there's the mechanic, Pete, she sleeps with because he pays her rent and keeps this *luxurious* roof over her head. The best part about that is that I actually pay the rent every month because she blows it on penny slots and keeping her nails done. Then there's the manager of the grocery store I work at who insists on personally delivering groceries once a week. Don't even get me started on how she pays for those." I gave him a disgusted look.

My mother's jaw dropped open and she stuttered for several seconds before finding the lies. "You are such a liar!" She turned to Ray. "It's not true, baby. He's just a mean and ungrateful kid."

I could have laughed at her gentle tone, but I had other stuff to worry about. "I'm sorry, officer. I'll personally make sure Quarry gets back to school."

"I'm not sure that will be enough. Quarry was skipping school for ten days and no one at home even noticed. I'm sorry, son. I'm going to have to write up a report and send it over to social services."

"Sir, please. I'll do whatever I have to in order to keep this off the record. Wait! How about this? I'm close with Slate Andrews at On The Ropes. I bet I could get Quarry accepted into the before and after-school programs. It would guarantee that he got to school in the mornings. He's only ten years old, but I'm sure I can get Slate to make an exception."

"I'm not doing slave labor at that gym!" Quarry yelled from his bedroom.

"Oh yes, you are!" I yelled back, never dragging my pleading eyes from the officer.

He looked over at Flint then back to me, ignoring my mother completely. Then he pulled a cell phone from his pocket and handed it to me. "I want proof. Get Andrews on the phone and make the arrangements, but let me talk to him before you hang up."

"Yeah, of course," I rushed out as I dialed the gym number.

"While you're doing that, can you drag Quarry out here and let me talk to him for a minute? Perhaps I can give him a scare."

"Sure. Quarry!" I yelled. "Get out here. And before you say no, I should warn you. If you make me take that door off the hinges, I swear to you that I will *never* put it back on. Goodbye privacy!"

Flint laughed from the corner.

Quarry loved his privacy. About a year earlier, he'd drafted a schedule that allotted specific times so he and Flint both got alone time in the room they shared. I hadn't wanted to know what the hell he was doing in there, so I'd just pretended he liked to read in peace and quiet.

I lifted a finger to the officer and looked down the hall to find the door cracked open. I smiled and went back to dialing. I decided to by-pass the gym number and call Slate's office number instead. We all had it, but it was only to be used in the case of an emergency.

Just as Slate's secretary answered the phone, Quarry timidly made his way into the room.

"Hey, Claire. It's Till. Is Slate around?"

"Hey, bud. He's in the ring. Can he call you back?"

"I *really* need to talk to him." My eyes flashed back to the officer chatting with Quarry. "Can you just take him the phone? Please. It won't take long."

"No prob. Everything all right?" she asked warmly. She was at least sixty and treated all of us as her own kids—even the assholes like Derrick Bailey.

"Yeah. I just need to talk to Slate."

"Okay, sweetheart." Her term of endearment was genuine—unlike my biological mom, who was cuddled into Ray's chest, *playing* the role of a distraught and concerned mother.

A second later, Slate came on the line. "What's going on, Till?"

"Listen, I need a huge favor. I wouldn't ask if I weren't desperate. But . . ." I began to nervously toy with my bottom lip. "Look, my little brother Quarry's been skipping school, and the police are here, and . . . Is there any way you could make an exception and allow him into the program at ten instead of twelve? Please. I'll do anything. I'll work his hours if I have to. I'm just not sure what else to do to keep this from getting reported to social services. We just got off their radar. I can't have—"

Slate cut me off as I started to ramble. "Slow down and just take a breath. I'll take him. It's no big deal."

I let out a loud sigh of relief. "Thank you so much. I'll do whatever you need."

"Is he big like you and Flint?"

I smiled and shook my head. Slate was always thinking about boxing. He trained everyone regardless of his size, but since he was a heavyweight himself, we were his favorites.

"He will be."

"That's what I like to hear. Okay, bring him in and I'll get him set up this afternoon. He can start in the morning."

"Thank you so much, Slate. Hey, I think the officer wants to talk to you for a minute? Is that okay?"

"Yep. Put him on. I'll see you in a few."

I passed the phone over and turned my attention to my mom. "I'm gonna let the boys sleep at my place tonight. I'll take Q to the gym in the morning."

"Okay, this is a great plan, Till. Are you going to need me to sign the release forms like I did with Flint?"

I blatantly rolled my eyes.

She didn't sign those fucking forms when Flint turned twelve and entered the program a few months after I did. They'd sat on the counter for a week before I had forged Dad's name and taken them back myself.

"I wouldn't dream of asking you to do something so strenuous. I'll do it." My voice was dripping with sarcasm.

"Don't be silly. You're not his parent." She smiled and moved even closer to Ray.

I lifted my eyebrows and crossed my arms over my chest "Well, that makes two of us then, because *neither are you*. Just because you gave birth to him does *not* make you his parent. Boys, get your stuff. I'll meet you outside." I headed out the door, and the officer followed me without another word for my mom.

"Okay, Till. You need to keep him out of trouble and in class from here on out. Mr. Andrews speaks highly of you. Don't let this happen again, or the next officer might not be willing to lose the paperwork."

"Thank you. You have no idea how much I appreciate this."

He nodded then headed down the stairs.

The door was barely closed after the boys came out of it, when I heard the deadbolt click from the inside.

"Is the cop gone yet?" Quarry asked, looking out at the parking lot just as the police car pulled away. "Oh, thank God. I thought he was gonna follow us to the gym." He turned back to the front door.

"Where the hell are you going?" I grabbed his book bag, forcing him to stumble backward.

"I'm not cleaning that gym. You and Flint enjoy mopping the floors, great. But I'm not doin' it!" he declared, shrugging out of the straps on his bag.

"Fine. You're right. Everyone deserves to make their own choices." I took a menacing step forward. With my hands planted firmly on my hips, I bent at the waist and leaned down to his level. "Either you walk your ass to On The Ropes or I will *carry* your ass to On The Ropes. But in the next five minutes and then every single day after that, your ass *will* be at On The fucking Ropes." I narrowed my eyes. "So, what's it going to be, Q?"

He didn't drop the attitude, but he did have the good sense not to smart off. Flint was innocently watching our showdown. Quarry's eyes found him as he seemingly weighed his options. I fully expected Flint to chime in in an attempt to keep the peace, but he remained surprisingly silent. Finally, Quarry turned and headed down the stairs.

"I don't think you're supposed to say 'fucking' to kids," he mumbled.

As he passed me, I reached out and smacked him on the back of the head. "Don't fucking cuss."

"Riiiight," he drawled sarcastically, which caused Flint to laugh as he jogged down the stairs behind him.

11

Eliza

"DOODLE?" TILL CALLED FROM MY bedroom window while Justin Timberlake was blaring through the small speakers of my stereo.

"I'm in here!"

"Doodle?" he yelled again.

I rolled my eyes. Wiping my hands on a towel, I walked to my bedroom. "What?"

"Oh good! You're home. You didn't answer through the floor." He grimaced as he rubbed his shoulder.

"I was in the kitchen. Why are you just standing out there?"

"Honestly? Slate killed me today at the gym. My entire body hurts. You'd have to be dying or have that cheese potato stuff for me to come in tonight."

"It's a twice-baked potato, Till. I told you how to make it."

"I tried! I wasted my last five bucks on burnt potatoes. No, thank you! I'll just wait for you to make them again." He leaned in and sniffed the air. "Now, I'm hungry. You're not making them tonight, are you?"

"No," I answered then began to laugh when his shoulders fell with disappointment.

"It's probably for the best. I've got the boys tonight. They'd just eat it all. Hey, can you come up and help Quarry with his homework? It's official—fifth-grade math is over my head. It was a real blow to the ego."

"Oh, God, no! Not your fragile ego!" I slapped my hands to my cheeks and feigned horror, earning me one of Till's one-sided grins.

"I know. I took it hard. I had to flex in front of the mirror for a full five minutes before I was able to come down here."

This probable truth earned him one of my wide grins. "Just five minutes?" I asked suspiciously.

"Okay, fine. You got me. It was ten." He played along and threw his hands up in the air, only to wince from the movement.

"Give me a second. I was making a meatloaf. I'll cook it at your place. Did you guys eat at the gym?"

"Yeah, but I'm always down to eat some more."

"You got any rice? That way we won't all starve splitting one baked potato?"

"I've got noodles!" He waggled his eyebrows, knowing exactly how much I hated his coveted ramen.

"Right. Okay, then. I'll bring the rice."

He laughed and shook his head. "I'll meet you out front."

After packing the food up, I met him outside. Till immediately took the pan from my hands and waited for me to walk up the stairs ahead of him.

"Why do you have the boys on a school night?"

"My mom got a visit from a truancy officer today. Apparently, Q thought collecting cans for recycling was more lucrative than going to school. He skipped ten days straight. Thank fuck the officer was willing to brush it under the rug after I asked Slate to take him into the program early."

"Wow! Ten days?"

"Yep. He wants to drop out. Warning: he's pouting about it too. So he'll most likely be a rude little shit tonight."

"Oh, please. Quarry loves me. He won't be rude to me."

Till shrugged and pushed his front door open.

My eyes immediately landed on Quarry, who was lying facedown on the couch with Flint sitting on top of him. Quarry's arms and legs were flailing and Flint was laughing.

"Hey! Get off him," Till growled.

"He tried to take off when you went downstairs." He turned his attention to me and grinned. "Hey, Eliza."

Flint Page was fifteen-years-old and virtually a carbon copy of his older brother—same black hair and one-sided smile. The only exception being his baby blue eyes. He loved to box and, by all accounts, was amazing at it. But his true love was between the pages of a book. He was a voracious reader that you would never find without a book from the library.

Every other Saturday, the boys would spend the night at Till's. I would take Quarry to the gym to watch Flint and Till fight in the local amateur league Slate hosted in conjunction with a few other local gyms. I had never seen Flint lose, but, to be honest, I had never even seen Till take a decent punch. They were both the top seeds in their divisions.

"Hey, Flint," I responded, and he winked.

He was the quiet type but still a flirt just like both of his brothers.

"Get off me, you dickhead." Quarry struggled to get up as Flint held his position sitting on his back.

Till stomped over and leaned down into Quarry's face. "Did you just say dickhead? What the fuck did I tell you about cussing? You are ten, not twenty. Act like it!"

Quarry stilled under Till's angry gaze. "Then make him get off me," he whined, reminding me how young he really was.

"You gonna try to take off again?"

"No."

"I swear to you, Q, if you leave this apartment, I will hunt you down and then drop you off at the police station myself. Who knows! Maybe Dad could use some company in prison."

The mere mention of their father sucked the energy from the room. Quarry immediately looked ashamed, and Flint's eyes dropped to the floor. I hated seeing those faces. I might have only been in love with one Page man, but I absolutely loved all of the Page boys.

"All right. Flint, get up," I ordered, and he stood without question. "Till, put that meatloaf in the oven, and, Quarry, let's do some homework. I bet you have a ton to catch up on."

At least they followed directions well. Till went to the kitchen and turned on the oven, Quarry grabbed his backpack, and Flint cracked a book open.

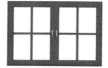

"What do you mean she's gone?" I asked Till three days later as he paced a hole in my bedroom floor.

"I mean the apartment was empty! I went to the front desk and they said she wasn't evicted, but she didn't turn in her keys when she left either."

"What about all of the boys' stuff?"

"It was gone too! I found some clothes in the closet, but all the furniture and their stuff, like Quarry's video games and Flint's books, were gone."

"Maybe she got robbed?" I offered the only reasonable explanation I could think of.

"She took off with that asshole. I can almost guarantee it. She doesn't give a fuck about anyone but herself. My father was a piece of work, but he was the only thing that kept her rooted to the family. I can barely believe she lasted three years without him." Till stopped pacing and ripped the black beanie off his head before throwing it against the wall. "She fucking abandoned them!" Then he shook his head and pinched the bridge of his nose.

I took a deep breath and looked knowingly at the ceiling. "I know this is overwhelming, but they're better off with you anyway."

He lifted his eyes to mine and whispered, "I'm not sure they are."

"Are you kidding me? You love them, and sometimes, that's the hardest thing to get as a kid."

His eyes grew warm with understanding.

"You would never leave them, so that security alone is better than whatever they had with her."

"So, what do I do? I share a two-bedroom apartment. Scott's cool when the boys stay on the weekends, but moving them in is a little different."

"Till, he's never there anymore. He spends every single night with Anna. If you didn't have to help your mom with rent, you could afford to carry the whole apartment by yourself. Maybe bring it up to Scott.

Who knows? He might be happy to get out from under the lease and move in with his girlfriend."

He stared at me, nervously toying with his bottom lip. "Keep going," he urged.

"Let Flint get a job."

"No," he answered firmly.

"Till, he could help out with some of the bills."

"No," he repeated.

"We were both working almost thirty hours a week when we were fifteen."

"Yeah and I also didn't graduate high school because of it. He makes straight A's and actually enjoys it. He's not getting a job. That's the end of it."

Suddenly, Flint's voice came through the ceiling, joining the conversation. "What if I only work a few days a week or on the weekends? I promise I won't let it mess with school."

Till's chin fell to his chest in defeat. "What if you stop eavesdropping and butt out of our conversation? Go watch TV or something."

Then Quarry spoke up, making me bite my lip to restrain my laugh. "Can I just say, I like Eliza's idea too. I'd way rather live with you than go back to Mom's. I can't believe she took my damn Xbox."

"Quarry!" Till and I yelled in unison.

"Sorry. It slipped."

"Go!" Till barked at the ceiling before looking back at me with exaggerated frustration.

"You can do this. I know you can."

"Fuck," he mumbled. "Won't I have to do all kinds of custody stuff? I don't have money for an attorney."

"I wouldn't even bother right now. She took off. Do you really think she's going to show up tomorrow and fight for them? If, by some miracle, she suddenly decided to get her shit together and be a mom, that's when we can worry about it. Just keep the boys in school and out of trouble and no one has to know they live with you. It won't be long before Flint can move out if he wants to, and we'll worry about Quarry if the time comes."

He stared at me blankly and started rolling his bottom lip. "I'm really nervous about basically being a parent at twenty-one."

"Well, would it help if I made twice-baked potatoes for dinner to help ease you into your new role?"

His eyes snapped to mine. "Don't tease me, woman."

"I just bought a whole bag of potatoes," I playfully sing-songed.

"Damn it! Say yes!" Quarry yelled from upstairs.

Which was followed by Flint scolding him. "Really freaking smooth, Q."

"What? I want those potatoes!" Quarry retorted, making me burst out laughing.

Till let out a huff and shook his head, but he stepped forward, pulling me into a hug. "Okay. You get the potatoes, and I'll call Scott."

"Score!" Quarry celebrated upstairs.

I understood, because wrapped in Till's arms, I was celebrating too.

"Ehm." He cleared his throat as I snuggled in even closer.

"Oh, right. Potatoes."

"Just so you know, I'm going to need two. You know . . . fuel for my added duties and all."

"Right. Of course." I played along. "How about I just make all of them?"

"I like the way you think, Doodle. That is one sexy brain you are working with."

My cheeks heated at his compliment. After one last squeeze, Till let me go and headed for the window.

"I'll make burgers. Bring the potatoes up and make them at my place. Quarry would *love* to help," he announced over his shoulder, causing Quarry to groan and stomp from Till's room upstairs.

12

Till

SCOTT WAS THRILLED WHEN I told him that I wanted to take over the apartment. His lease wasn't up for another nine months, but he was planning to propose to Anna, so the timing really worked out for everyone. After hearing why I needed the apartment, he made me a killer deal on his bed and furniture. So by the end of the phone call, I had not only a room but also a bed for the boys and a dresser for them to store the trash bag full of clothes I had been able to recover from my mom's.

Finally, something was going my way.

Two weeks later, everything was going as smoothly as possible. The boys were in school, Quarry seemed to be getting his shit together, and Eliza came over every night when she got off work to help with their homework. We were still counting pennies to pay the bills, but we were together. It had been well worth the sacrifice.

Flint was pissed when I put my foot down about him getting a job. So he decided to take it into his own hands and tattled to Slate, who, thankfully, took my back on the issue—kind of. He agreed that Flint needed to focus on school, but he also thought that it was Flint's right to be able to contribute to our household. So Slate did what he always did for us—he fixed it.

Flint became the first kid hired at On The Ropes to be paid in actual cash. He still had to earn his keep around the gym, but for two hours every afternoon, Slate paid him to tutor the kids who were struggling in school. Flint loved it, and every week, he signed his paycheck over to me. I'd be lying if I said that it didn't help. It did, but we weren't exactly eating steak and lobster every night. Kids were fucking expensive. Especially two growing boys. Jesus, they could eat.

I loved having them around. We felt like an actual family for the first time ever. We still fought over bullshit things, and Quarry wouldn't stop cussing no matter what I did, but they were good, honest, and respectful kids. I couldn't for the life of me figure out how that had happened when they had been raised by two wheeling-and-dealing scumbags like our parents. I had Eliza to thank for the way I'd turned out . . . but they had figured out how to be decent people all on their own.

It was Saturday night and we were headed to a league fight at On The Ropes. I loved fight nights, but this one in particular had us all buzzing—especially Eliza. It was the night Quarry would debut in the ring. He'd only been boxing for a few weeks, but Jesus, he was a natural. I knew I was good, but I'd never seen someone take to a pair of gloves like Quarry "The Stone Fist" Page. (He announced the nickname approximately twelve seconds after Slate agreed to let him fight.)

"Yo, Till!" Derrick Bailey strutted into the locker room in a pair of khaki slacks and a teal button-down. He was such a tool.

"'Sup. You not fighting tonight?" I asked only so I didn't look like a dick when I ignored him.

"Nah, man. Slate didn't tell you? He's taking me pro!"

I tilted my head questioningly. Not only were my ears failing me but they were now making up words just to fuck with me on their way out.

"I'm sorry. What?"

"Yep. I'm going professional. My first fight is next month." He bounced on his toes and put his hands up triumphantly. "I'm gonna get paid to fuck people up in the ring." He threw a slow-motion uppercut under my chin.

I was too stunned to even play along with his little game. "Slate doesn't do pro," I stated, confused.

"Well, he does now. I guess he decided he couldn't just pass up talent like mine." He dusted off his shoulder playfully, but he was wearing at least a hundred-dollar shirt, so he just looked like a douchebag.

"Yeah. That must be it," I bit out as I turned to face the locker.

Derrick was a decent boxer, but he wasn't a champion.

There are two types of boxers: the opponents and the champs. Opponents are often less-than-kindly referred to as bums. Sure, they can be good boxers, but not great. Everyone starts as an opponent, but the ones who fall become bums, and those who rise and separate themselves from the pack are your champs.

Really, it all boiled down to good versus great.

Derrick was good in the amateur ring, but there was no doubt he would be outclassed in the sea of professionals. So it boggled my mind—and, quite honestly, pissed me off—that Slate would even agree to transition him.

"Page!" Slate boomed into the locker room.

"Yes, sir," Flint and Quarry answered at the same time.

"Shit, there are a lot of you now. Sorry. I meant Till."

"I'm here."

"Listen, we're switching up the order of the fights tonight. The bus carrying the lightweights from one of the other gyms got a flat. We're starting heavy and working backwards to give them time to get here. We're pushing back the first bell a half hour to give you guys time to finish warming up. Meet me in the dressing room. I need to get you taped up." Then he turned and walked out, leaving me once again staring at Derrick Bailey's shit-eating smirk.

"Okay. I'm gonna go grab a seat. Give 'em hell. I hear the guy you got tonight is a beast. Keep your left up, and get a few more wins. Maybe Slate will take you pro too."

I suddenly had an overwhelming urge to keep my left up, all right. Preferably up around the level of his fucking mouth.

Just as the door closed behind him, Flint whispered, "What a prick! Did Slate really take him pro? He's going to embarrass the entire gym."

"I don't know. Something's not right though."

"You're the best fighter here. Why would he pick Derrick?"

That was a good fucking question, and I fully intended to find out.

"Just get dressed and worry about your fight," I said, striding out of the locker room.

I found Slate laughing with one of the other trainers in the dressing room.

"You ready for me?" I asked.

"Yeah. Have a seat on the table." He finished up chatting then grabbed a roll of gauze and tape from the cabinet. "How you feeling?" he asked as he started wrapping my hand.

"Um, honestly? I'm a little confused."

"Oh yeah? Why's that?" He looked up but continued methodically moving the gauze around my hands while holding my eyes.

"I heard you're taking Derrick pro. That true?"

"Yep. I got him his first fight scheduled for next month. It's nothing big, but it will get a little money in his pocket and start people talking while we work him up."

"I thought you didn't do pro. You sent Hutchins to a whole new gym when he wanted to transition."

He shrugged. "Things change. I miss it, I guess. I love the amateur stuff, but the true talent makes the leap."

"Exactly. And you choose to start with fucking Bailey?" I snapped.

His eyes shot up to mine. "Excuse me? You got a problem, then spit it out, but don't you dare catch an attitude with me."

"Yeah. I got a problem. How much is he gonna make on that fight next month?" I was still pissed, but I dropped the majority of my attitude.

"Not much. Four or five hundred bucks."

"Right. Not much," I scoffed. "I'm easily your best fighter. If this was just something you were itching to do, why the hell wouldn't you ask me? I need the money. Bailey's a bum and you know it."

"Till, you have more than enough on your plate right now without adding something else on top of it. Derrick's chasing a dream. I'm not stupid. I realize that. Do I think you're more talented than he is? Absolutely. But you have a family and responsibility outside of that ring.

"Do you have any idea how much time goes into fighting professionally? It's not something you do for an hour or two every night after you get off work. At least it won't be for any of my fighters. It's a full-time fucking job. Forty-plus hours a week. In this gym. Working out, sparring, studying, working out some more. You *cannot* afford to do that."

"You managed, didn't you? You've told me at least a dozen times how you had nothing except for your talent when you crossed over.

You were just as broke as I am when you started. How the hell did you manage it?"

He finished wrapping my first hand, and I jumped up from the table, physically unable to sit still any longer.

"You're right. I had *nothing* when I started. But you have *something* . . . in the form of two little brothers who depend on you to eat and keep a roof over their head."

I hated every single word that came from his mouth, but I knew he was right.

I would have given anything to become a professional boxer. I'd shadowboxed that championship fight in the mirror a million times. It wasn't just the money either. I knew that boxers didn't make much in the beginning. But I was already broke, so it wasn't like I'd have to get used to the struggle. No. This was about finally getting to do something that could really better my future. However, like most things, that wasn't my life.

This was reality.

And I couldn't even afford to dream.

"This is bullshit," I mumbled to myself but settled back down on the table.

"Look, how about you increase your hours at the gym and we'll reevaluate in a few months?"

"Increase my hours? I work close to sixty hours a week. Then I spend another twenty at the gym either cleaning shit to pay my dues or training. Where exactly would you like me to pull these extra hours from? I barely even have enough time to sleep as it is."

"I don't know what to tell you. You know I'd do damn near anything for you. But putting you into a professional ring without the proper training and watching you fail is not one of those things."

"Right. I guess I just wasn't aware Bailey was the next Muhammad Ali." I was acting like a petulant child, but I was pissed and frustrated.

"That he is definitely not. But his daddy is funding his grand pursuit at going pro. It won't hurt me one bit to watch him lose."

"Well, maybe it should. He's going to make you look like a fool as a trainer," I bit out just as he finished wrapping my second hand.

I stomped to the door, and just as I pulled it open, I heard him say something else behind me that I couldn't make out.

"What?" I let out an exasperated sigh and turned to face him, but he was already storming in my direction.

When he reached me, Slate used the heel of his hand to slam the door shut. Leaning into my face, he growled, "And that's another thing. You would have to go to the fucking ear doctor for your new physical. I set you up with a doctor and even prepaid for the appointment, but you still couldn't seem to drag your ass in to get your hearing checked."

I blatantly rolled my eyes at his concern.

Stepping up, Slate bumped his chest with mine as he leveled me with a glare. "You know what? I'm done. I've let you throw a fit. You're pissed. I got it. But I am not going to stand here and watch you act like a punk-ass kid. Remember who the fuck you are talking to or march your ass out of my gym for good."

We stood nose to nose staring at each other.

He was wrong. I wasn't just pissed. I was *jealous.* Of him. Of Bailey. Of anyone who got to follow their dreams. Of the people who had money. And most of all, the people who didn't have to crawl through fucking windows just to feel a single minute of contentment in their lives.

But none of that was Slate's fault. He might very well have been the closest thing to a father I'd ever had. But what blew my mind was why he did it. He was good to all the kids at the gym, but he had gone out of his way since day one to help me, then Flint, and now Quarry too.

"I'll go to the doctor next week," I promised.

"That'd be a good start." He took a step away.

"And I'll add a few hours on Sundays in the ring."

"Another good answer."

"Sorry," I finally mumbled.

Slate reached out and squeezed my shoulder. "I get it, Till. I fucking know how you feel. You're hungry for more in life, and that's a good quality for a man to have. Don't ever lose that. Stay hungry. Stay driven. Stay focused. But you need to remember that I'm looking out for what's in your best interest. Always."

"I know. I appreciate it all. I really do."

"I know you do, son. So before you go and get soft on me, let's keep that adrenaline going and get you warmed up. Let's make a deal.

You take him two rounds, then you have my full permission to knock him the fuck out in the third."

My eyes grew wide. "Seriously?"

Slate always encouraged us to take it the full three rounds. He drilled into us all that the local league was there for practice and experience, not for laying your opponent out. It still happened sometimes, but it was never the goal.

"His trainer is talking all kinds of shit today. This guy's apparently the new golden boy over at Three Minutes. I saw a video of him fight a few weeks ago, and I swear he's just a fat kid who can take a punch. But to hear them tell it, he could go ten rounds with Holyfield."

I laughed at his assessment. "You know, most people would end that sentence with your name."

It was Slate's turn to laugh. "Go on. Get out of here. I'll meet you out there."

"Thanks, Slate," I responded, and we both knew it was for more than just taping my hands. It wasn't enough. But it was all I had.

13

Eliza

"HERE WE GO! HE'S UP!" I stood from my metal folding chair to clap.

"So, how long have you known Till?" Derrick asked beside me.

I had been drawing in one of the notebooks I kept stashed in my purse when he'd surprised me by sitting next to me. I'd met him briefly a few times over the years of watching Till fight. There had been a half-hour delay, so we'd had plenty of time to chat while we'd waited for the fights to start.

"Jeez, um . . . eight years. We grew up together," I answered with a smile.

Derrick was a good-looking guy—I couldn't deny that. He was a little preppy for my tastes, but he didn't seem snobby, so I could overlook the slacks. His hair was sandy brown and perfectly styled. He had sparkling, blue eyes. His bright, white smile was blinding, but not in the heart-stopping way Till's was.

"So, you two . . . together?" he bumbled out uncomfortably.

"No. We're just friends."

"Good," he whispered, and my cheeks heated to pink.

About that time, Till "The Kill" Page entered through a side aisle. I freaking loved watching the guys fight. It was such a rush.

I glanced to the other side of the ring, just as Till's hulking opponent stepped inside.

"F.uuuck!" I breathed. "He's huge!"

Till was big, but this guy had him by at least two inches and fifty pounds. Where Till was hard and defined, the man across the ring had a thick layer of fat over muscles I could barely make out.

"They call him the 'The Brick Wall' for a reason," Derrick chimed in.

"Is he any good? Till didn't mention anything about this guy."

"They only added him to the card last week. I'm not sure Till even knew who he was. I've heard this will be his only amateur fight before he goes pro."

"Shit! He's going pro?" I gasped, never dragging my eyes off the ring.

"Yep. Just like me." He tossed me a toothy grin.

"You're going pro? That's awesome! Congrats," I responded as everyone started sitting back down.

"Thanks. I'm pumped about it. Being able to make a career out of something you love . . ."

He continued to ramble, but I lost my focus when, just as I found my chair, Derrick's arm slid around the back. It wasn't touching me, but I was all too aware that it was there. He reclined in his seat and crossed his legs knee to ankle. I took a second to turn away and bite my lip before looking back to the ring.

I was met with a hard glare from hazel eyes.

Till was standing in his corner, shaking out his arms, but his eyes were not homed in on his opponent like they should have been. They were narrowed on me—or, more accurately, the arm Derrick had draped around the back of my chair.

"What?" I mouthed to him, confused. I mean, Till didn't exactly love when I talked to or dated guys, but he usually just ignored it. The same way I did when we ran into other women who obviously *knew* him. We were friends—nothing else. However, the inferno brewing in his eyes said otherwise.

He shook his head and turned to Slate, whispering something in his ear.

"No," Slate said loud enough to be heard over the chatter of the crowd.

Till shrugged and started bouncing on his toes and pounding his gloves together.

Within seconds, the bell rang and I jumped to my feet.

"Let's go, Till!" I screamed, causing the couple in front of me to turn around in disapproval. I didn't care. We were at a boxing match, not the library, and above that, my man—er . . . something like that— was in the ring.

The first round flew by. When the bell rang and the fighters moved to their corners, I glanced down to find Derrick already sitting and scrolling through his phone. His arm was still firmly planted around the back of my chair. I hadn't torn my attention away from the fight, so I couldn't be certain if he had watched at all.

"Wow. That guy can take a hit," I said, flopping down.

"Yeah. Till's gonna have to do way better than that," he snarked, not looking up from his phone.

"Umm, he totally won that round in points." I snapped and his eyes finally rose to meet mine.

A slow smile crept across his face. "Oh, I didn't mean that in a bad way. Of course he won that round. He just needs to be careful not to tire himself out. That's all." His hand moved to my back and he soothingly rubbed my shoulder. "Till's got this, I'm sure." He winked, and my cheeks heated once again.

I physically felt the moment Till's eyes once again found me. It might have been because of his angry gaze, but more likely, it was because Derrick had chosen that exact second to reach up and tuck a stray hair behind my ear. He too was well aware that Till was watching us.

I dragged my attention away from his hypnotizing, blue eyes just as the bell sounded. I barely made it to my feet before the fight was over. With three punches, Till forced "The Brick Wall" to crumble. The ref hadn't even finished counting when Till started using his teeth to remove his gloves. Slate might have been shaking his head in the corner, but he was smiling while doing it.

Till didn't linger to bask in his victory. He quickly disappeared. It took several more minutes for them to get "The Pile of Bricks" off the mat, but eventually, he walked out of the ring to what could only be described as a polite round of applause. The only obvious injury was to his ego.

The next bout was in the second round when Till suddenly climbed from the row behind us and into the chair beside me. Before he had even settled, he shoved Derrick's arm off the back of my chair, replacing it with his own.

Derrick looked around me in absolute disbelief, but Till didn't even acknowledge him.

"'Sup, Doodle," he said casually, as if he hadn't just pissed a semi-circle around me.

Men were ridiculous. So instead of arguing, I reached back, removed his arm, and decided to play it casual too.

"You dropped that guy! Nice job!" I offered a high-five.

He tossed me a side smile and smacked my hand. "It's no big deal. He wasn't as good as people built him up to be." He sniffed, trying to play it off.

"Oh, shut up. He was good and you destroyed him," I said, calling his bullshit and causing his smile to grow.

"I know, right!" He squeezed just above my knee.

"Stop!" I burst out laughing while trying to pry his torturous hand away.

"What's wrong?" he asked, faking concern while continuing to tickle my leg.

"Till! Please!" I folded down in the chair, using both of my hands to unsuccessfully stop only one of his.

"You okay, Doodle? You look like you're having some trouble there?"

I continued to laugh, all the while threatening his life under my breath. I finally resorted to violence by punching his thigh with my knuckle.

"Damn," he cussed, rubbing his leg, but he did release mine.

"I seriously hate you sometimes."

"No, you don't." He dropped his arm around my shoulder and pulled me to his side for a brief hug, but it wouldn't have been Till if he didn't complete the piss circle by kissing my temple.

Derrick cleared his throat, reminding me that he was, indeed, watching our little tussle. We might have been twenty-one, but we pretty much always acted like we were thirteen again. Some things never change.

"Sorry," I said to Derrick, embarrassed for having acted like a giggling fool.

He smiled warmly and opened his mouth to speak, but Till got there first.

"Hey, Q's in the dressing room getting wrapped. You want to come with me to wish him good luck?"

"Yeah!" I all but jumped out of my seat.

I could watch Flint and Till fight all day long, but I still thought of Quarry as such a little boy, so I was a bag of nerves. And Till knew it because he'd spent half of the morning laughing at me as I'd tried, unsuccessfully, to convince Quarry to give it a few more months.

I stood up without another thought of the sexy, blue eyes on my other side.

Till guided me through the crowded gym with a hand planted securely on my lower back. I'd long since stopped reading into his every touch. That had become way too time consuming over the years. But just because I didn't dwell on his advances didn't mean I'd stopped throwing my own. Just as he pressed his hand to urge me forward, I seductively arched my back. I honestly couldn't help myself. He let out a loud grumble, but I couldn't tell if it was because he didn't like it or if, even worse, because he did.

A few people stopped to congratulate Till on his big win, but eventually, we made it back to the dressing room. My nerves calmed as soon as I saw Quarry sitting on a table in only a pair of boxing trunks. Slate was standing in front of him, taping up his hands.

"That's just gross. You have muscles!" I cried out teasingly.

"You like what you see?" Quarry flexed his arm, showing off a tiny, yet totally defined, bicep.

"Are you smuggling grapes, Q?" I joked, and his smile grew.

"I could ask the same question to your bra," he responded, and my mouth gaped open.

"Hey!" Till and Slate scolded at the same time.

"What?" he yelled innocently. "I was kidding. We were just joking around. Tell 'em, Eliza."

I was afraid that, if I spoke, the laughter I was desperately trying to suppress would leak out. "Yeah. Joking. Totally."

I bit my lip and turned to Till, who had his hands planted on his hips. Because I'd been fully expecting him to be pissed at Quarry, I was surprised to see that his shitty attitude was aimed at me.

"What's that look for?"

His shoulders flexed as he cracked his neck. "I don't want you talking to him anymore."

"And here we go," Slate mumbled from across the room.

"Uhh . . . who? Quarry?" I asked in shock.

"Derrick. I don't like him, and I sure as shit don't want you anywhere near him." He narrowed his eyes at me, taking me aback by this sudden attitude.

It was unusual for Till to be an ass to me, but it wasn't exactly an anomaly. I knew exactly how to handle him.

I very calmly pasted on a patronizing smile. "Well, I didn't know that, *Till*. Perhaps it would be easier if you made me a list of who I'm allowed to talk to," I said condescendingly as I dug into my purse and pulled out a sketchpad. Dramatically, I licked the end of the pencil before poising it over the paper. "Or wait. A leash might be better for full control over who I'm *near*. I'm sure we could temporarily rig one up with a jump rope or something. Please just let me know what works best for you." I popped an eyebrow and crossed my arms over my chest.

"Well, that could have gone better," Quarry told Slate as they started laughing behind me.

"Don't give me that shit, Doodle. I don't like him. He's a self-centered, arrogant prick. "

"Oh, well, you should have just said that, then. I already have one of those. I don't need another," I smarted off.

"Burn!" Quarry whispered, but neither Till nor I shifted our focus.

"Seriously?" He crossed his arms to match mine.

"I don't know. You tell me. Are *you* serious with this crap?"

He sucked in a breath through his nose. It was angry going in, but he held it until he released it on a resigned sigh. "Look. I have never once asked you not to hang out with someone. Never. You make your own decisions about guys, and no matter how big of a douchebag they are, I keep my mouth shut. But I can't bite my tongue here. I do not like that guy. It makes my skin crawl that you are even on his radar. We're family, right? Well, family watches out for each other. So, Doodle, I'm *asking* you. Please. Stay. Away. From Derrick."

I held my attitude for a few seconds longer, but it wasn't because I was still mad. Rather, if I spoke, I knew I'd start crying.

We're family.

There was no way he could truly understand the depths of what those words meant to me. I swallowed hard, trying to force the emotions back, and for once, I actually succeeded.

"Okay."

His head snapped back as if I had slapped him. "Um . . . okay?"

"Yeah. Okay. If you had started with that explanation instead of being all bossy, this conversation could have been a whole lot shorter. I get it. You don't like him. I'll steer clear."

Till smiled, and it reflected on my own lips.

"Besides I'm in a very committed relationship with Justin Timberlake right now."

"Good. Keep it that way." He cupped the back of my neck and pulled me up against his chest.

I wrapped my arms around his waist and held him as his hand slid up and down my back.

Till and I both knew we had a strange relationship. It was more than a friendship, but there wasn't romance or sex. There was definitely love though. Immeasurable amounts of it. I knew that Till had this grand fantasy about me. But what he didn't realize was all that he gave me in return. He was the only thing I'd ever had that I honestly thought I couldn't live without. Till Page was my soulmate on every level. I'd accepted that it didn't have to be sexual between us. Truth be told, I'd have been happy to sit in an empty room for the rest of my life as long as he was sitting beside me.

But it was moments like those, when his arms were protectively folded around me, and his heart beat a strong rhythm in my ear, that made me want *more.*

14

Eliza

"I NEED TILL TO SIGN this paper for school," Quarry said as I opened the door.

"Uh, okay? He's not here."

"Really? His truck is here."

I glanced out into the parking lot, and sure enough, Till's truck was parked front and center. "I haven't seen him at all today, actually."

"Well, he wasn't at the gym this afternoon either. Slate drove us home."

"And you checked his room?"

"No. But I didn't hear him come in. He must have snuck past."

I headed back to my room. "Till?" I yelled at the ceiling. But I didn't get a response. "Till!" I yelled again.

"Yeah."

I heard his voice, but it wasn't coming from the ceiling. "Where are you?" I looked around my room.

"Purgatory," he slurred then began to laugh.

I traced his voice to the window, but when I lifted it, I didn't see him anywhere. "Till?" I called again, getting frustrated.

"Jesus. Stop calling my name."

I leaned outside and found him sitting on the ground with his back against the brick exterior of the building. His long legs were stretched out in front of him, and a bottle wrapped in a brown paper bag was at his side.

"What are you doing?"

"I told you. I'm sitting in purgatory. And they say I'm the one going deaf."

"Oh, well, that clears things up," I said sarcastically. "Quarry was looking for you."

"Fuck." His voice broke as he began frantically scrubbing his face with his hands.

His reaction instantly worried me.

"Give me a second. I'm coming out." I shut the window and ran back to the door, where Quarry was still waiting. "I found him. He'll be up later."

"Can you ask him to sign this? I'm about to go to bed."

"Um . . ." I responded, remembering the way Till had slurred his words and the bottle at his side. "Here." I snatched the pen and paper from his hand. "Does your mom spell her name with 'ie' or 'y'?"

"'Ie.'"

I scribbled "Debbie Page" across the paper and handed it back.

"Hey, thanks!" He smiled and dashed away.

I made a mental note to discuss the big, red F on the test I'd just signed later, but for now, I needed to see what the hell was going on with his brother. I snagged one of my many sketchpads off the coffee table and walked around the side of my building.

"Doodle!" Till yelled in greeting as soon as he saw me.

I kicked the sole of his boot. "Scoot over, drunky."

"You want some?" He lifted the brown bag.

"Um. Hell yeah!"

"That's what I'm talking about." He smiled and passed me what I discovered was beer.

I immediately poured its warm contents into the grass before handing it back empty.

"Not cool, Doodle. Not. Cool."

"Oh, whatever. You don't even drink!"

"I know, because that shit is expensive, and you just wasted it!"

I shrugged. "I can live with that. Now, scoot."

"Okay, but you don't belong in purgatory, so you can only stay for a few minutes."

"Why exactly is the flowerbed under my window purgatory?" I asked as he lazily moved over a few inches.

Using a finger, he pointed over his head to my window. "Heaven." Then he motioned to everything in front of us. "Hell." And finally, he pointed to the dirt where he was sitting. "Purgatory."

I gave him a confused look that made him fall over in laughter. I wasn't sure if he was laughing at me or at his own joke. I'd never seen Till drunk before, but I knew right then I preferred him sober.

I sat next to him and patted my lap and handed him the sketchpad. "Here. Hold this and lie down."

His eyebrows shot up. "Look at you going all old school on me. You must be really worried," he teased, but he didn't waste any time getting situated so his head rested in my lap.

It wasn't the most ideal position, with his legs wedged crooked-ly between two of the overgrown bushes, but he didn't complain. He opened the sketchpad and handed me the pencil.

I began scratching his head with one hand and drawing his eyes with my other. I didn't say anything for several minutes, and eventual-ly, I felt his shoulders relax as he let out a content sigh.

"I'm going to assume it didn't go well at the doctor today," I said quietly.

His eyes snapped to mine. "What?"

"I said, 'I'm going to assume it didn't go well at the doctor today'."

He slightly shook his head. "I'm still hearing at about seventy per-cent."

I stopped drawing and looked down at him. "That's good, right? It's only gone down, like, ten percent in six years. It's fading slowly. That means you have years before you have any real issues, right?"

"He couldn't predict that. He said everyone's different. Some-times, it's slow. Sometimes, it's rapid." He didn't seem too thrilled, but I felt an overwhelming sense of relief.

Later. We could deal with this *later*. Many, many years later.

I went back to drawing in an attempt to downplay my enthusi-asm. This should have been good news, but with his lips sealed tight, I couldn't figure out what exactly was going on with him.

"So, why were you drinking, then? I thought Slate had a strict no-drinking policy."

"That's only for the kids. I'm twenty-one. He can't stop me from having a drink if I want one. Besides, are you planning to rat me out?" He reached up and tugged on a piece of hair that had fallen free of my ponytail.

"Maybe." I shrugged, filling in his long, black eyelashes on the paper. "Now, tell me what's really going on."

Till avoided my question by glancing down at the paper. "You always make me look like a chick when you draw my eyes."

"No, I don't. And who said those were your eyes?"

"Okay, then whose eyes are they?"

"My ugly, old accounting teacher."

"Well, he has some seriously sexy eyes, then."

"She really does, doesn't she?" I smirked, and Till burst out laughing.

He suddenly sat up, causing my sketchpad to fall to the ground. His laughs were silenced as he dragged me onto his lap and buried his head in my neck.

"Oh, God, Doodle." The agony in his voice shredded me.

"Talk to me," I said louder than necessary since he wasn't looking at me.

"The doctor I saw today thinks it's genetic," he confessed against my neck. "He wants to test Flint and Quarry."

My stomach twisted.

"What am I supposed to tell them? If they have this too . . . I . . . Fuck! I can't do this."

"Okay. Let's stop for a second." I crawled off his lap so I could see him. "What exactly did the doctor say? He *thinks* it's genetic, so he doesn't know for sure?"

"He's pretty positive. He said he couldn't be sure, but I didn't fit into any one category of sensorineural hearing loss, so he's assuming it was some combination that was passed down."

"All right. What did he say were the chances of Flint and Q having it? They haven't shown any symptoms, have they? I mean, you were already at eighty percent by the time you were thirteen, right? Surely, we would have noticed something, at least in Flint. What type of test would he want to run on them? And when does he want to do it? The sooner the better, right?" If I just kept talking, I felt like I could sort it out. But the more questions I asked, the more it seemed to piss Till off.

"I don't know!" He jumped to his feet and drunkenly stumbled.

"Well, let's figure it out."

"Goddammit, I don't know how to figure this out!" he shouted, startling me.

"Hey! Don't yell at me! I'm just trying to help." I pushed to my feet and brushed the dirt off the back of my pants.

"Well, you're not. You're making me feel stupid for not asking all that shit." He shoved a hand through his hair.

"I'm trying to figure out a way to fix this!"

"You can't fix this! No one can. They are either going deaf or they aren't!"

"Calm down and let's—"

"No. This is a fucking nightmare. I'm going to bed. I can't do this." He stormed off, tripping over the edge of the flowerbed.

"Not a bad idea. Sleep that shit off," I barked as he staggered away.

"You ruined purgatory!" he yelled over his shoulder, and I rolled my eyes at his dramatics.

Drunk Till was an ass.

I walked back to my apartment, and I heard his feet clomping up the steps. I knew he wouldn't want the boys to see him drunk, and as much as I wanted to stay pissed and not care, I still did. I went straight to my bedroom and dragged off my shoes. And after crawling into bed, I listened for Till to make his way to his room.

Several minutes later, when I still hadn't heard his door shut, I began to worry.

"Till?" I called to the ceiling.

"Yeah," he replied, lifting my window open.

"Shit!" I cried. "What is wrong with you? Why are you never where you are supposed to be tonight?" I shouted at him as I tried to slow my pulse.

He folded his bulky body inside. As much I wanted to hold on to my anger, with his next words, Till Page robbed me of my God-given right as a woman to be mad at a stupid man.

"Maybe I'm exactly where I'm supposed to be."

"Maybe you're drunk," I snarked in order to hide the way my heart skipped.

Throwing back the covers, I issued an unspoken invitation for him to join me. It wasn't unusual for Till to hang out in bed with me. We would lie there late at night and talk about random shit. We didn't exactly cuddle anymore, but he always found ways to touch me.

"I'm sorry." He kicked his shoes off the end of the bed, making it quite obvious that he was planning to stay for a while. "It's just . . . I'm in over my head, Doodle." He paused to cross his arms behind his head. "I want to give those boys so much more than we had growing up, but I just don't have it to give." He turned to look at me, and his eyes sparkled with desperation. "I want to be there for them, but in order to pay the rent and buy the shit they need for school, I have to work damn near twenty-four-seven. Then there's the commitment at the gym. I love the way I feel inside that ring, but I guess I could give it up. We eat two meals a day there though. If we quit doing that, I'd have to pull more grocery money from the already negative bank account.

"Then Quarry's just starting to fit in at the gym, and he's really showing talent. I'm not sure what would happen if I stopped showing up to train him every night. He's still not sold on the work ethic Slate instills. Although, it's been a month since he tried to skip school, so I guess that's progress. And Flint . . ." He went silent. I had almost convinced myself that he had fallen asleep when he boomed, "Christ, that kid is smart! I can't pay for it, Doodle. All the after-school stuff he wants to do. And I mean the good stuff that parents pray their kids will be interested in. He's a beast in the ring but equally as talented out of it. They've never had it easy, and now, they have to be tested to see if they are ultimately going to struggle for the rest of their lives. It's just not fucking fair."

"Okay. First off, they already have more than we did by you caring enough to be freaking out about this right now."

"I'm not freaking out," he mumbled to himself.

"Yes, you are. And that's a good thing. We didn't get that from our parents. I had you and you had me. That's the way it's always been. Well, now, Flint and Quarry have you, but guess what, they have *me* too. I can't do much to help in the financial department, but I can pitch in with getting them to and from the gym to allow you some more time in the mornings or afternoons. Maybe you could pick up a few extra hours at the shop to help loosen things up."

He stared at me as I spoke, and I could see the weight lifting from his shoulders with every word. Yeah, I loved Till, and I had grown to love Flint and Quarry too, but my offer to help was completely selfish. He wasn't alone in this. Because if he were, that would mean that I was alone too. I needed the Page boys far more than they needed me.

Till did things a little differently that night. He started with the *best.*

"I don't deserve you." He rolled over and pulled me into a hug. "You and those boys are all I have," he whispered into my hair, and I melted against him.

Then he pulled a *better.*

"You know I love you, right? I don't say it enough, but I do."

My response was muffled against his chest. "Yeah, I know."

"Good. Just checking." He laughed and tickled my sides.

I squirmed back to my side of the bed.

"So, what do I do if they test positive? What if my worthless parents passed this shit down to all of us?"

"We do what we always do. We go to battle against the world." He grinned with both sides of his mouth, and it was a truly amazing sight. "You're a fighter, Till. This is no different."

He barked out a laugh. "I can't fight the inevitable."

"Maybe not. But *we* can." I returned his smile, but his fell instantly. He blinked at me in what I could only describe as awe for several beats.

Just as I began to question his reaction, Till made everything *harder.*

With both hands, he cupped my face and pressed his lips to mine. He took a deep breath as he held my mouth hostage. My eyes were wide with shock, but Till reverently closed his own as he opened his mouth and slid his tongue against mine. I didn't know why my mouth opened with his or why my tongue stroked against his, and I had no clue why a moan escaped my throat as he rolled on top of me. Why wasn't even part of my vocabulary at that moment. I knew but one word.

"Till."

15

Eliza

I GASPED AS HE SLID his heated mouth over to my neck. His tongue left a wake of chills as it made its way down to my chest.

"Take this off." His callused hands glided under my shirt.

Lifting my arms, I gave him permission to pull it off. He watched as I licked my lips. Then his eyes heated before he roughly took my mouth again.

It was then that I tasted it.

Beer.

I slammed my arms back down to the bed. "Till, wait. We can't do this." I turned my head to disconnect the kiss, but it only caused him to latch on to my neck again.

"Yes, we can," he growled, raking his teeth across my skin.

Yes, we could.

"No. We can't. Remember last time? It almost ruined everything." I groaned as he ever so slightly rolled his hips against my core. "Seriously, we have to stop. You're drunk and not thinking straight. You'll thank me in the morning." I shifted to the side, trying to squeeze out from under his large body, but he had me pinned.

His hand found my breast, sending a rush of heat between my legs, bypassing my brain completely. "I'm not drunk. Yeah, I was drinking, but I've wanted to have you again since the second I pulled out of you the first time. I need you."

But I needed him too—in a totally different way.

"No. Last time, you disappeared for six months. I can't go through that again." I shimmied myself up the bed to escape the mounting pressure his hard-on was coaxing as he continuously slid it against me.

"I won't leave ever again. I swear. It's me and you forever, Eliza."

Eliza.

Forever.

With Till.

His hazel eyes studied me as I weighed my options. I knew that it was going to rock our world, but with his promise of forever still ringing in my ears, I didn't care if the entire world flipped upside down. I could have sat there all day and tried to rationalize everything out, but the fact was that my body had made its decision the moment he'd said my name.

I licked my lips again then leaned forward and licked his. "Take it off."

He let out a loud growl then tore the shirt over my head. His mouth covered mine as I began fumbling with the button on his jeans. I barely even had them unzipped before I wedged a hand inside and wrapped it around his cock.

"Fuck," he gasped, dropping his forehead to my chest and rolling his hips, gliding his shaft through my hand.

Supporting himself on an elbow, he popped a breast from my bra and sucked it into his mouth. My hand froze as I arched off the bed. I remembered the first time Till's tongue circled my nipple, and this was nothing like that. This was rough and raw. His teeth nipped and his tongue soothed. His hand kneaded the soft flesh as he held my breast to his mouth.

Suddenly, his mouth disappeared, but it reappeared in the form of a gentle bite at my side. He dragged his tongue up the curve of my breast and plucked my nipple between his fingers before sensually rolling it.

"Oh, God!" I gasped and grabbed the back of his head, trying to aim his mouth somewhere, although I wasn't particularly sure where I wanted him to start.

My hand fell away as Till rose to his knees. He watched as I undulated under his skilled touch. He wasn't the only man I had ever been with, but he was the only one my body recognized.

"Fucking hell, Eliza. Do you have any idea how hard you make me?" He glided his other hand up my stomach until it reached my breast. "I fucking love when I get here and you're already in bed. Your nipples get hard for me the second I crawl through that window. I can't tell you how many times I've left here with blue balls from these fucking nipples alone."

That was definitely news to me. Fan-fucking-tastic news to me.

He firmly squeezed my breasts before leaning forward and swiping his tongue across one. Then he switched to the other and came back again.

"Goddamn, I love your tits," he said through breathy kisses then sucked as much of my breast into his mouth as he possibly could.

His hand massaged and his tongue swirled. I wished I could have come from that alone, but I needed more. My legs opened and I inched myself down the bed as I sought out some form of pressure against my clit.

"Please. Till." My hips circled off the bed but came up empty.

He noticed my need and shifted up the bed, pressing his thigh against my covered core. Sparks ignited me the moment I found friction. Just as I reached down to once again find his cock, his hands disappeared, causing a strangled objection to escape my throat.

"I need to see it," his jagged voice demanded, but it wasn't like I was trying to stop him. I'd have shown him damn near anything he wanted at that point. I just didn't know what he was referring to.

He guided my back off the bed, and then, with one hand, he unclasped my bra and slid it off my arms. No sooner than I was exposed, he groaned deeply and brushed his nose across my nipple, laving his tongue under the curve of my right breast.

"I haven't been able to come without envisioning this freckle. It fucking ruined me."

"It's just a freckle. It can't ruin you," I said breathily, continuing to grind myself against his thigh.

"Bullshit. It's *your* freckle. It could destroy me."

My chest seized at his words, and my hips stilled.

It had always been Till for me, but with that sentiment, I felt like maybe it was always me for Till. The sense of overwhelming belonging set me ablaze. The burning heat made its way to my hands as I threaded my fingers in his hair and fisted it to tilt his head back.

"I want you. Now," I said brazenly.

He drew in a hiss through his teeth, leaning away from my grasp to increase the tension. The muscles of his neck flexed as his eyes narrowed, and a one-sided smile tipped his lips. It was the wrong side though. This smile was dangerous, but under his touch, I was fearless.

"Take whatever you want. It's all yours anyway." He finished with a nip.

I tugged his shirt off then went to work on his pants. They were already unzipped, but I wanted them gone. I roughly pushed Till down to his back and slid off the bed, taking his pants with me. After that, mine gave his company on the floor.

His cock sprung free, and without a second of hesitation, I kneeled on the bed and took him in my mouth.

"Fuck," he groaned through clenched teeth as his hands made their way into my hair. He brushed it to the side and watched me intently. His abs rippled as I worked him, but as much as I loved his every involuntary reaction, his eyes were what really commanded my attention. They owned me, and we both knew it.

Till gently guided my head into a rhythm. It was unapologetic yet permissive. Possessive yet desperate. Dominant yet seeking validation. It was the ever-present dichotomy of Till Page. The boy and the man.

I wished that I'd had more time to really enjoy watching Till lost in the sensations I provided him. But there would be plenty of time for that later. *Forever.*

With a groan, he dragged me up his body. "Goddammit, Eliza. I could fuck your mouth for days, but I'm not finishing until I've had you completely."

After he rolled us so he covered me, his mouth crashed into mine in a needy meeting.

There was nothing gentle as his hand dived between my legs. I had barely adjusted to the intrusion of his fingers before they were gone and his length pressed to my opening.

"God, Till," I breathed, lifting my hips to urge him forward. Knowing I was only seconds away from having him again—and getting to keep him—made me impatient.

He dragged the head of his cock through my folds. "You get wet like this for everyone?" he asked with a painful groan. He was torturing me almost as much as he was himself.

"Just you," I whispered, and his head popped up, signaling that he hadn't heard me. "Just you," I repeated.

"*Just* me."

It wasn't confirmation of my answer—it was an order. A menacing smirk formed on his lips. I didn't recognize it from Till's repertoire of smiles. But then again, I'd never lay naked in front of Till the man.

My mouth fell open as he pressed inside. My muscles clenched around him, relishing every inch he gave me.

He stilled once he'd filled me. "Tonight, you come on my cock. It's the one thing I've been missing." He glided out agonizingly slowly and then drove back in. A sharp cry escaped my throat. "Oh, fuck you feel good, Eliza."

"Ahhh!" I breathed as he once again eased out.

My eyes closed and my head fell back against the pillow as I anxiously anticipated another deep thrust. But he froze with only the head of his cock nestled inside me.

"You need me to take it easy, baby?"

"No. Please don't. Fuck me hard, Till."

His eyes grew wide, and his cock twitched inside me. "Jesus Christ. I should fuck your mouth more often."

The small smile that tilted the corner of his mouth gave me a flash of the boy I'd originally fallen in love with. I loved this sexy and dirty version of Till, but that one twitch of his lips turned me on more than any words he could ever utter.

And when it was replaced by a core-clenching smirk, I knew that, no matter what happened after that moment, I'd never be able to go back to being friends. One glance and I was addicted.

Till

I buried myself to the hilt inside her.

My mind was foggy from the alcohol, but I knew exactly what I was doing. I was a thief, but I had convinced myself that it wasn't wrong. I was only stealing what was rightfully mine. The way her eyes had lit when I'd said, "Forever," told me that she thought this was more. I would have corrected her if I hadn't meant it from the bottom of my soul. I'd just known I couldn't follow through.

"Till!" she gasped.

"I need to feel you come." I drove into her in the way I fucking loved, and judging by the sound of her moans, so did she. But despite how hard I took her, she didn't come.

She cried my name and her body writhed, but she wouldn't step off the edge.

"Goddammit, tell me what you like?" I growled, taking her mouth in a frustrated kiss.

"Here." She pushed a hand between us to find her clit.

I knew how to make her come with my hands. Based on the last time we had been together, that was easy. But I had three years of dreams fueling me with an overwhelming desire to make her come with my cock.

"No hands." I grabbed her arms and pushed them above her head, securing both of her wrists in one of my hands. "I want you to come because of this." I pointedly pumped inside her, driving myself toward the brink of orgasm with every thrust.

"I can't," she whined, struggling to free her arms.

"Yes, you can."

I continued a hard rhythm that was slowly driving me mad. Her moans and cries were encouraging, so I waged war against my own release.

She could do it. I would give it to her. I would *take* it from her.

"Use *your* hands then," she bargained.

"No. Damn it. It's the only thing I don't have from you, Eliza. If I have to fuck you until I go soft, then I'll lick you until I get hard again. You will come without using your fucking hands."

Her eyes flashed to mine in shock . . . *and arousal.*

"Christ, Till."

"I've got all night. Tell me how to get you off."

"I don't know! Damn it, please just touch me," she panted, raking her nails down my back.

I was so focused on trying to figure out how to take the last piece I needed to finish my Eliza Reynolds collection that I missed the fact that I was ruining it for her.

"Okay, okay." I continued a rhythm but finally dropped my hand between her legs.

The minute my thumb brushed her swollen nub, her whole body spasmed. She didn't come, but I knew she was on the way.

"So, my dick gets you close, but this is what you need?" I circled her clit, and she tensed around me. *So fucking close.*

"Yes. I'm sorry." She rolled her hips to ride me from the bottom.

"Apologize by milking my cock. Come on, Eliza." Sliding an arm under her ass, I lifted her lower half off the bed to allow for a better angle. With my thumb moving furiously, I drilled inside her.

Fucking finally, her whole body quaked and her muscles pulsated. *There it is.*

"God. Till."

Oh, I had missed the sweet sound of her ecstasy.

"Fuck," I grit out as my cock shot off inside her. I fell forward, catching myself with my arms beside her head as I filled her. "Goddamn, Eliza." I tried to catch my breath, but the aftershocks continued to course through my balls.

"I love you so much." She took my mouth until I began to soften inside her.

"I love you too. Always," I promised between kisses.

For the next half hour, we lay in bed kissing and getting to know each other's naked bodies in a much less sexual nature. It was casual but needy. The sex was amazing, but those moments were what my fantasies were really made of.

Fantasy, but not reality.

Eliza

We didn't talk as we fell asleep even though I was well aware we had a lot to discuss. I wasn't stupid. I knew Till, and he was probably muddling things up in his head even as I drifted off in his arms. I was much too sated to talk him down from whatever ledge I was sure he had climbed onto the minute he'd come and was no longer driven by his dick. But we could figure it all out later. He had never once lied to me, so I slept easily knowing that forever truly meant forever.

But getting there would be a totally separate issue.

16

Eliza

"HEY." MY CHEEKS HEATED AS I walked into Till's apartment.

Memories of his mouth against my breast flooded my mind and ensured that my nipples immediately hardened. I would have used that to my advantage, but the boys were present, so I quickly crossed my arms.

Quarry rushed me as soon as my feet hit the carpet. "Eliza, guess what? I won my fight at the gym tonight! So next week, I get to fight Chris. He's, like, really, really good, but I can take him. He does this thing where he drops his hands. I'm gonna . . ."

He continued to ramble about boxing, but my attention was on Till, who was standing in the kitchen with a spoonful of peanut butter frozen in midair. His free hand jumped to his bottom lip as soon as we made eye contact.

"Hey, *Doodle.*"

His greeting immediately put me on guard. The way he'd said, "Doodle" might as well have been the Great Wall of China for as much as it divided us. The night before, I was *Eliza.*

I tilted my head to the side. "Why'd you call me that?"

"I always call you Doodle," he responded, but even that sounded distant.

Oh, yeah. There had definitely been muddling going on in his head since he'd crawled out of my bed the night before.

"Not always." I narrowed my eyes, and he narrowed his right back at me.

Quarry continued to talk about his day, and Flint read on the couch. As usual, they were both oblivious to the stare-off that Till and I were engaged in.

Finally, a small smile played on his lips as he flipped the spoon over and shoved it in his mouth. I might have moaned as he slowly dragged it out. It wasn't meant to be sexy, but the memories from the night before made it damn near electric. However, it did manage to soothe my exposed nerves—and drench my panties.

"You hungry?" he asked, breaking the awkwardness that was partially because of our first after-sex encounter and partially because I was openly gawking at him as he ate freaking peanut butter.

"If you are making anything except mac and cheese ramen, yes."

"Soooo, you're not hungry, then?" He lifted a bag of shredded cheese off the counter and tossed a fistful into the pot on the stove.

I laughed and continued trying to gauge what direction his mind had taken him over the last twenty-four hours. The nickname had spoken wonders, but his eyes drifted down my body, saying something else altogether.

"No. I'm definitely not hungry, then. Look, I can't stay tonight. I have a big test tomorrow in accounting, but I just wanted to see if anybody needed help with homework before I disappeared."

"I'm good," Flint answered, not taking his eyes off his book.

"I finished all mine at the gym," Quarry called out, spooning his own peanut butter into his mouth.

"Okay. Good deal." I turned my attention back to Till. "You still coming over tonight?"

He hesitated for a second. "Um . . . do you . . . still want me to?"

"I just figured since, ya know, you come over every night."

"Right. So then why would you ask?" He arched an eyebrow.

Then it was my turn to feel awkward. "I . . ." I trailed off.

Quarry's eyes were bouncing between us questioningly, and even Flint took notice of our uncomfortable conversation.

"All right, you guys get something to eat," Till instructed as he walked in my direction. Then he guided me to his front door.

"So, I'll see you tonight?" I asked as he stepped outside with me.

He shoved his hands into the pockets of his jeans and looked over my head as he asked, "Are we good?" His eyes nervously flashed to mine.

It might have been wrong, but his nerves made me smile. "I'm *really* good," I purred. Deciding to put his fears to rest, I wrapped my arms around his waist and snuggled my head against his chest. "Are *you* good?"

He released a loud breath and then chuckled as he looped his arms around me. "I'm good."

"So, I'll see you tonight?" I repeated then glanced up to find him staring down at me. It was a brief second, but whatever worry I had that Till had jumped ship on his promise to me vanished.

Forever blazed from his eyes.

"Leave the window open."

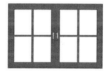

Both times I had been with Till in the past had been spontaneous, but later that night, I actually had the opportunity to prepare first. I showered, blew my hair dry, shaved—everything. Instead of washing my face like I usually did, I applied makeup before crawling into bed. I donned a sexy, see-through bra that usually hid in the back of my drawer and a matching thong, which was equally as sheer.

"Hi." I stood up off the bed as he started climbing through the window.

His eyes went wide when he saw me, causing him to momentarily lose his balance on the windowsill and go crashing to the floor. "God. Damn," he cursed as he rose to his feet while taking in my new wardrobe. "You . . . I . . . um . . ." His hand went to his lip.

He was rooted in place only a few steps away, but his eyes traveled over every inch of my body and back again.

Till was speechless. I had never felt so empowered in my life.

"Are you okay?" I feigned concern as I slowly approached.

"Not even close," he told my breasts, making me giggle.

After sliding a hand under the edge of his T-shirt, I raked a fingernail over each of his abs before dipping it into the waistband of his jeans.

"I'm sore today," I announced, closing the distance between us. My breasts were pressed against him, but he still hadn't even attempted to touch me yet. I had plans to remedy that. I smirked then stood up on my tiptoes, kissing the base of his neck. "Make me sore for tomorrow too." At the last second, I darted my tongue out to the hollow dip at the base of his neck. It was meant to tease him, but as the taste of his skin hit my tongue, I was flooded with memories of taking more of him in my mouth. The moan escaped before I'd even felt it coming.

A loud rumble shook his chest, but that was the only warning I received. Suddenly, I was off my feet and sailing through the air. Just as I landed on the bed, Till crashed on top of me. His mouth roughly landed on mine.

"Tell me we can't do this again," he demanded as his hands found my breasts.

"We're definitely doing this again." I arched into him.

"It's gonna get so messy, Eliza. Please." He groaned as I reached into the front of his jeans.

"I'm okay with messy," I breathed, guiding his hand from my breast and into my panties.

"Fuuuuuck" he cursed when he discovered exactly how thorough I'd been with the razor earlier. His finger pressed inside me as his body traveled down the bed and settled between my legs, stripping my panties off during his descent.

He added another finger in a less than gentle but overwhelmingly intoxicating rhythm.

"Tell me to stop, Eliza. We can't do this again." He grazed his teeth on the inside of my thigh.

"We're already doing it."

"Tell me to stop."

"No."

"It's going to ruin us."

"If you don't stop talking, you're going to ruin this."

"I'm serious." He kissed the inside of my other thigh, his fingers never faltering in their steady pace.

"So am I. Stop trying to talk yourself out of this while your fingers are buried inside me." I threaded a hand into his hair and gave it a gentle tug.

"Goddammit. Tell me to stop!" he demanded one last time, but his fingers sped before twisting in the most delicious way.

I decided to give him what he wanted, but only because I knew he wouldn't follow through.

"Stop." I rolled my hips, forcing him even deeper.

"Well, it's too fucking late now."

I would have laughed, but his mouth sealed over my clit and stole my breath, words, thoughts, and orgasm. My body shook as he pushed me higher even while I was falling. It shouldn't have worked like that, but whatever voodoo magic Till Page was working with that night was all right with me. He didn't stop swirling his tongue until I used his hair to pry his mouth away.

"Too much!" I cried.

He looked up with a wickedly proud grin. His hand disappeared, and seconds later, his cock replaced it.

The sex wasn't drawn out the way it had been before. He wasn't desperate to make me come, but he still did. Till coaxed me to the brink of orgasm and then used one hand between us to send me flying off. Then he quickly followed.

With my legs wrapped around his hips, he breathed my name as he came. "*Eliza.*" He rained languid kisses over my mouth and neck as he rocked inside me until he softened. Several minutes passed before he settled next to me and tucked me under his arm. Trailing his fingers gently over my breasts, he whispered, "You're beautiful."

There were no declarations of love, but they were as present as ever.

"You worried me earlier when you called me Doodle," I confessed against his chest, punctuating it with a kiss.

"We're good, okay? Always."

"Yeah. Always." I squeezed him tight. "Hey, Till?"

"I'm right here." He returned my squeeze.

"Please tell me you're better at using condoms than you have been with me."

"Shit. I'm so fucking sorry. I swear . . . I always use one. I just don't think straight when things start happening with you."

"Yeah, I get it. I don't exactly think straight with you either. I'm not on the pill or anything, but I think we're safe as far as timing goes."

"Okay, good." He sighed and kissed the top of my head.

"But next time, we have to use one. No more chances."

"Next time?" he questioned, and I could hear the smile in his voice.

I looked up to find him grinning. "Yep. There are going to be a lot of next times. You should probably invest in the economy box."

His smile grew. "Well, in that case, I don't get paid until Friday, so you're gonna have to keep it in your pants until then."

"See, that's exactly the problem. We *have* been keeping it in my pants. Maybe we should try keeping it in *your* pants for a while."

We both laughed until Till dropped his head back against the pillow.

"How the hell is this going to work?" He rolled to his side.

I shifted up to share the pillow, and then tucked a stray hair behind my ear as I settled.

"The same way it's always worked," I said. "Only now, you get to see me naked."

"So, like, friends with benefits?"

"Uh. No," I stated firmly. "Like two people who love each other and have decided to take it to another level and actually be together."

It wasn't storming outside, so I couldn't be completely certain, but judging by how quickly Till scrambled off the bed, I decided that he must have been struck by lightning.

I only felt it through a searing pain in my heart when Till yelled, "We can't do that!"

I blinked at him. I'd expected this to some degree. I had known that Till would overthink us taking this step, but I was nowhere near ready for the wild eyes that stared back at me.

I did my very best to remain calm as I asked, "And why not, exactly?"

"Because it won't work and then you'll be gone." He stated his assumption as if it were a definitive fact I could look up in an encyclopedia.

"That's not true. Forever, remember?" I tried to ease his mind, but he was already dragging on his clothes, ready to bolt. "Just chill out.

Please. Sit down and let's talk." I pulled my robe on and watched as he started pacing the length of my bed.

"I can't be with you, Doodle. Not in the way you want."

"Um, why the hell not?"

He opened his mouth, but I quickly cut him off.

"And I swear to God, if you say the words 'fantasy' or 'reality,' I will lose my fucking mind."

"Because I can't lose you. I need—"

"Or that! Don't say that! You can't be with me because you can't lose me? What the actual fuck does that even mean?" I yelled.

"It means what if we don't work out as more!" He matched my intensity. "We are good at friends. Let's stick with that."

"Well, what if I decide to move to Zimbabwe to become a missionary?"

He arched his eyebrow. "What the hell are you talking about?"

"Oh, I'm sorry. I thought we were playing the 'what-if' game," I replied sarcastically. "Because my what-if is just as plausible as yours. Hell, maybe even more likely."

"Stop fucking around and be serious here."

"I've never been more serious in my life." I sucked in a deep breath, grasping for some semblance of calm that had obviously escaped me. "Till, you cuddle with me during scary movies and take out my trash if you notice it's full," I stated, and he stopped pacing long enough to tilt his head in confusion. "I cook for you almost five days a week and do well over half of your laundry after the 'black sweater with the white towels' fiasco. You are the first person I run to when I've had a bad day because you wrap me in your arms so it doesn't seem so bad anymore. You've never, in eight years, missed my birthday or, miraculously, a single night when I've made twice-baked potatoes. We lean on each other in virtually every facet of life. When you've had a bad day, I'm not sure if I'm the first person you run to, but I know for a fact that I'm the only person you fully trust to unload on. You would protect me with your life, and I would do the same for you. If you have a problem, I solve it—"

"That's actually Vanilla Ice."

"*And* I laugh at your jokes even when you tell them at completely the wrong times."

"Sorry," he said with an unapologetic shrug.

"We love each other ferociously—and if the last few days are any indication, we are undeniably attracted to each other sexually too. Till, we've been basically married for a long time. Facing the facts won't change anything."

"I can't risk that it will, Eliza."

"Well, it's too late. We took the risk last night, and not five minutes ago, we were risking it all over again. I love you. That's not ever going to change."

"Bullshit! It *will* change. You're right. We do lean on each other for almost everything, and if you weren't here, I'd end up flat on my ass. Those six months when we were apart damn near destroyed me. I love you and would go to the ends of the Earth to keep you. But I am *not* fucking this up by trying to make it into something it may or may not be."

"Oh, but you were okay with fucking *me* up last night?"

He grimaced. "Don't act like that. That's not fair. I wasn't trying to—"

"Not fair? Oh, so now, we're talking about fair? Well, let me tell you how fucking *not fair* this is to me. I fell in love with a man whose fantasy is crawling through my window to escape reality. All the while, *my* fantasy is walking out that door to navigate reality by his side. I'm pretty sure *that* is the definition of not fair."

"Eliza." He shook his head.

"No. Shut up. I'm so sick of living in your goddamn fantasy. You know what, fuck it!" I grabbed his hand and dragged him out of my room.

He didn't put up a fight as we headed toward the front door, but he threw on the brakes the moment I snatched it open.

"Stop," he said quietly.

"Come on, Till. We've been doing it your way for eight fucking years. It's my turn." I was beyond the point of rationality. I was madder than I could remember ever being, but not one single tear fell from my eyes. I really was done.

His feet didn't budge.

"Let's go!" I yelled again, pulling on his arms.

I'm not sure what I was trying to prove. I just wanted my fucking way for once. It wasn't an issue of if Till wanted me or not, loved me or not, or could have me or not. It was all about his silly little need to keep me squirreled away because he was scared I'd eventually leave. He couldn't understand that leaving him would have killed me too. I couldn't have done it even if the world suddenly caught fire. I would have died at his side before my legs would have carried me away.

He silently stared at me as the tears finally made it to my eyes. I walked past him, and he turned, snagging my arm and dragging me into a hug.

"I love you. I swear I do. Please let that be enough," he pleaded, stroking my hair and holding me tight.

We were it for each other, and there was nothing but a little boy's dream world standing in our way.

"Okay. We'll be fine." I sniffled and stepped out of his grasp.

His whole body sagged as his chin dropped to his chest and his eyes closed in relief.

And then I ended it.

I rushed forward, and with both hands, I shoved Till as hard as I possibly could. Catching him off guard, I sent him stumbling out the door.

He stood dazed and in shock. His mouth hung open as his eyes blinked rapidly. It was physically painful for me to witness, but it had to be done.

"The fantasy's over. Let me know when you're ready to use the door." With one swift push, I slammed the door on my relationship with Till Page.

I didn't lock it. I actually stood there willing him to rush back through. He could be as mad as he wanted if he would just open that door and walk inside. I didn't budge until I heard his footsteps head toward my bedroom. I sprinted back to my room, and just as he approached, I slammed the window too.

His gentle eyes turned murderous. "Open the fucking window," he demanded through the glass.

"No."

"Open the window!" he shouted.

"No more, Till. I love you, but I'm sick of living in your fantasy. My door will always be open for you." Tears fell from my eyes as I watched each word land on his gorgeous face. "No more windows. No more pretending."

"Eliza, don't do this. We'll start over. Go back to friends."

"I can't go back to that. Not after experiencing what we can be together."

"Doodle! Open the window." He pounded the heel of his hand against the brick building.

"Goodbye, Till."

His eyes went wide as I slowly lowered the blinds. "Stop. Eliza!" he yelled until I drew the curtains.

Half of me expected him to shatter the glass to get back inside, but I guessed that would have ruined his magical window forever.

After several minutes, I heard him make his way back upstairs, which was immediately followed by several minutes of him yelling and breaking things. I couldn't listen to any of it. I pulled my headphones on, curled into a ball on the bed, and allowed myself to lose it too.

I couldn't lie to myself. There was always something romantic about Till's crawling in my window and the way it made me feel to be so special that he was afraid to use the door. He wasn't delusional—he knew the truth. But, sometimes, in the world we lived in, where everything was a struggle, it was easy to become dependent on the things that numbed the chaos. Some people turned to drugs or alcohol as an escape. But I had Till . . . and he had the fantasy.

17

Till

IT EXPLODED. ONE MINUTE, I was holding her in my arms as she came calling my name. And minutes later, she was gone. I nearly tore down the building that night. I sure as hell destroyed my room. In all seriousness, I considered prying up the floorboards and dropping into her bedroom through the ceiling. It was crazy, but that was exactly how my life felt too. Flint came to check on me, but he didn't ask a single question about why I was suddenly on a rampage against my furniture. It was safe to assume he and Quarry had heard the whole thing and knew what a delusional fool their brother was. *Outstanding.*

For a full twenty-four hours, I wallowed. I had no choice but to go to work. I went through the movements, but my mind was consumed with all things Eliza. I was a zombie. My mind scattered through scenarios that would get her back, but I knew there was only one solution—the impossible.

The first night without her, I snuck down to purgatory and left a new sketchpad against her window.

The second night, I stared a hole in my floor.

The third, I lay in my bed and talked to her—at least I hoped she could hear me.

I confessed to every time I had copped a feel and disguised it as something innocent over the years. I was completely unaware of how long that list really was until I hit the two-hour mark.

I missed her.

It had been three days, and I craved her on every level. She would come around though. We'd talk it out and go back to how we used to be. But what honestly pained me was that, even though I knew the way it had to be, I didn't want to go back to being friends. I wanted to crawl through the floor and bury myself inside her.

I threw myself into the only thing that seemed to distract me—On The Ropes.

"What's up, Leo?" I shook his hand, but he pulled it in for a back pat.

"Not much, man. How the hell are you guys doing?"

Leo James was the head of Slate and, his wife, Erica's security team. He was up at the gym a good bit and often brought his family with him. I couldn't quite figure out the dynamic with that group, but I thought maybe Leo and Erica were related somehow. They were super close, but for as protective as Slate was over Erica, he never seemed fazed in the slightest by how tight they were.

"We're good. Jesus. You running a day care in here?" I stepped away as I was almost plowed over by an angry heard of toddlers.

Slate and Erica had two kids; Adam was three, and Riley was still a baby. I'd have been hard-pressed to take a guess at her age though. Then Leo and his wife, Sarah, had Tyler, who was two, and an nine-year-old daughter named . . .

"Hey, Liv," Quarry greeted from behind me.

"Hey, Q," she responded shyly before going back to playing with Adam.

"It sure as hell feels like it sometimes," Leo responded with a laugh. "We're headed out to dinner, and Slate said you'd watch the kids."

"What?" I asked as my eyes flew to Slate, who was chatting with Erica on the other side of the room.

"Yeah. It's an overnight thing. I packed extra diapers, so you should be good. Just keep an eye on the boy. I snuck him a few Pixy Stix on the way over. He's gonna be wired."

Erica must have read the fear in my eyes from across the room, because she shouted, "Leave him alone! Ignore him, Till. We're meeting a friend here then heading out. *With* the kids."

"Oh thank God," I breathed, causing Leo and Slate to burst into laughter.

"Speaking of . . ." Slate nodded to the gym door.

A big, tattooed dude and a smoking-hot blonde came walking in arm in arm.

"Where are the kids?" Sarah yelled with disappointment.

"Wow. It's great to see you too, sis," the blonde said sarcastically. "We left them with Brett and Jesse. There is no way we are finally going out of town, getting a nice hotel room, *and* bringing the kids with us."

"I told you I had a nanny!" Erica whined, obviously sharing Sarah's disappointment.

"Look, we haven't been alone since the twins were born." She waggled her eyebrows suggestively, and the man at her side smirked.

"Well, okay, then." Slate changed the subject as the women started giggling. "Caleb, this is Till Page. Till, Caleb Jones."

"What's up, man? I've heard good things about you." He extended a hand.

"Really?"

"Yeah. Slate's been telling me for years that you're the next big—"

Slate cut him off. "All right. Let's get out of here. Till, I need you in the ring with Derrick tonight. You both need a good workout, so make it happen." He pulled a key chain out of his pocket. "You think you can lock up tonight?"

I looked down at a silver boxing glove.

"Those are yours. Don't lose them."

I blinked rapidly. It was just a key on a pretty sweet key chain, but it was so much more to me. As far as I knew, no one had keys to On The Ropes except for Slate. And the fact that he was giving me a set meant more than I would ever be able to explain.

I cleared my throat so I didn't sound like a bitch getting all emotional. "Um . . . I get to keep them?"

"Yep. Go with Leo, and have him set up your code for the alarm."

I get my own code for the alarm too? Shit. I really was an emotional bitch.

A half hour later, the whole crew left. The gym quieted down, and

I was finally allowed a few minutes to obsess about Eliza again. *Fuck.* She would have understood what those keys meant to me. She probably would have gotten all excited and jumped up and down, giving me an opportunity to watch her tits bounce. *Double fuck.*

"Till!" Flint called from the ring, snapping me out of my thoughts. "You coming?"

"Shit. Sorry. Yeah, I'm coming." I grabbed a set of pads and jogged over.

Distraction. That was just what I needed.

Flint was killing it as Derrick Bailey came strutting into the gym. Why the hell he came to the gym in slacks and a pink button-down, I would never understand.

"Where's Slate?" he asked from the corner.

"He took off. He had some friends come into town," I answered absently as Flint's gloves continued to pound out a rhythm. "He wants us to spar tonight. Go get warmed up."

The bell rang, and I finally gave him my attention.

"Nah. I'll work out on my own while I wait on him to get back. He'll be back later, right?" he asked with his eyes glued to two of the rich girls who used the gym like a country club.

"Nope. I'm locking up tonight."

His head snapped to mine. I fucking loved that feeling. He didn't have keys—that much was certain.

"You?"

"Yep. Slate gave me a set of keys." It was an obvious statement that had been implied with the whole "I'm locking up" thing, but I really just threw it out there to rub salt in the wound.

He slowly nodded as he stared at me. God, it felt good to be one up on that asshole.

"Get changed and warmed up. I'll meet you in the ring in an hour. I've got to finish this up then switch over the towels."

"You ever get sick of being the maid, Till?" He laughed as he said it. That was Bailey's way—an insult laced by a laugh to mask it. His mouth painted the picture, but the words told the story.

"Sorry. I don't have a rich daddy that I can leech off," I shot back. No laugh. Just an evil glare. That was *my* way.

"Right. Well, how is your dad? He doing well in lockup?" He

smiled.

My nostrils flared. I didn't have a clue if Bailey knew anything about my father. It wasn't like I ever spoke about him. But with that shit-eating grin chiseled on his asshole face, I knew that he had done some homework on me.

"Let's finish." Flint stepped in front of me, blocking my view. I tried to look around him, but Flint mirrored my every move. "Forget about it," he urged quietly.

Yeah. I'd forget about it—until I stepped into the ring with that motherfucker. Sparring with Bailey suddenly sounded like a whole lot more fun.

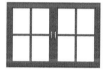

An hour later, with my temper no less quelled, I headed for the ring.

"Go tell Bailey I'm ready for him!" I yelled to Flint, who was oddly not showered or changed yet.

"Nah. I'll let you get him." He smiled awkwardly.

"He's doing it with that girl in the locker room," Quarry announced as he took a bite from an apple.

"What?"

"You know, *doing it.* Like, having sex," Quarry clarified as if that were the part I couldn't understand.

Flint smacked him on the back of his head then nodded, letting me know that Quarry wasn't wrong.

"Dumbass," I cursed as I stormed into the locker room.

The door to the massage room was shut, but even I could hear the moans echoing around. I slammed my fist against the door and heard a woman squeak in surprise.

"Let's go, Bailey." I was fucking pissed. Not because I really cared that he was fucking some sorority girl. But rather that he was doing it at the gym with several kids still milling around. Slate would destroy him if he found out.

"Give me a minute . . . Maybe five," he called out, causing his girl to giggle. Within seconds, the moans started up again.

I was going to fucking kill him. Plain and simple. I stomped out of the locker room but only long enough to dig the keys out of my bag. With the flip of my wrist, I swung the door open to their not-so-private refuge.

"Son of a bitch!" Derrick cussed as the chick grabbed her shirt to cover her breasts.

"Get out!" I growled.

He didn't budge, but the chick shimmied up her shorts as she scrambled past me. "Really?" he huffed, dragging his own pants up.

"There are fucking kids here. What the hell is wrong with you?"

"Well, currently, blue balls. Thanks for that, dickhead. You think I can convince the other one to suck me off?" His eyes, tone, and face were stone-wall serious. So much so that I decided he had problems way bigger than me or even Slate.

Then he smirked.

"Are you fucking kidding me?" I barked.

Reaching into his pants, he snapped a condom off. He made a less-than-half-assed effort to look for a trash can before dropping it on the floor. "Have housekeeping clean that up for me." He laughed. "Oh wait . . . That's you."

I was honestly too stunned to react as he walked past me. Bailey was a fucking prick, but he didn't have balls. And if he suddenly thought he was going to grow a pair, I was going to rip those fuckers off.

I spun around and grabbed his shirt, slingshotting him hard against the wall.

"Who the fuck do you think you are?" I roared into his face.

"Wow. That got your hackles raised." He stood there grinning at me as if he didn't have a fucking care in the world.

I couldn't breathe without worrying about the myriad of some-things ever brewing in my head. Yet, even with my forearm across his throat, he grinned. It enraged me.

"You sorry sack of shit." I shoved him harder, but the brick wall behind him failed to yield to my will.

I wanted to release the week's worth of the hell I was living with onto his face. Hands, fists, hopes, dreams, fantasy, and—most of all—reality. I wanted to shatter it all—preferably over his skull. Just as I convinced myself that Slate would understand if I committed murder in his locker room, Flint came flying in between us.

"Stop." He shoved me backwards.

I stumbled, but Bailey straightened his pansy shirt with a grin.

Like the fool he was, Bailey prodded, "What the fuck is your problem? Don't act like you haven't dipped in the On The Ropes waters. Oh that's right. You're too pussy-whipped by that poor artist chick. Eliza, right?"

The sound of her name rolling off his tongue was more than enough to secure my spot on death row. However, the bastard wasn't done yet.

"Maybe I should see what she's up to right now. I bet that tight little ass of hers could more than cure my blue balls."

My brain exploded, shooting adrenaline directly into my veins.

"No!" Flint yelled as I dived past him, landing a hard fist to Bailey's chin.

Finally, that fucking smile was wiped from his face.

Flint pushed and shoved between us, trying desperately to separate us. He was barely able to keep us far enough apart to where we couldn't land anything else.

"Stop! Calm down!" he barked into my face. "You're both going to get booted from the gym."

I couldn't have given a damn about On The Ropes in that second though, but I did care about Eliza.

"Goddammit, Till. Stop. It's not worth it."

My body fought, but my judgment finally caught up. I stared savagely at Bailey as I allowed Flint to push me away.

"You stupid fuck," Bailey cursed, rubbing his chin.

"Chill!" Flint pleaded, holding my eyes. "This is not the time or the place. Just let it go."

I took a deep breath and tried to reel it in. The desperation in my brother's eyes was the only thing that grounded me.

I begrudgingly started toward the door, but then I heard Bailey mumble words I couldn't quite make out. Flint's entire body went stiff beside me, physically revealing their severity. But before I could even ask what was said, Flint spun and, with one unexpected right, dropped Derrick Bailey to the ground.

Out. Cold.

"Holy fuck!" I grabbed Flint as he dived back in for seconds.

"Yeah. Say it again now, bitch!" Flint yelled over my shoulder as I shoved him out of the locker room.

A few of the guys lingered around the door, obviously listening.

"Jacob. Sam. Go check on Bailey," I ordered as I dragged Flint up to the office.

He wasn't fighting against me, but he was obviously fuming.

"What the fuck did he say?" I asked as soon as the door closed behind us.

"Nothing." Flint flopped down into the chair. His legs and arms were noticeably shaking as the rush of adrenaline left him.

"Oh it was something if it set you off like that."

"He's just a dick. That's all." He looked up nervously. "Am I gonna get kicked out of the program?" Flint had recently turned sixteen. He was huge and would easily be bigger than I was in a few years, but he was still just a kid in a man's body, who was worried about getting in trouble.

"Nah. I'll talk to Slate. It'll be fine."

"Okay."

It seemed to be enough to ease him.

"So you're really not gonna tell me what he said?" I asked him.

"Nope. You'd end up in jail. Just let it go."

We both turned to look out the glass windows as Bailey made his walk of shame out of the gym. He didn't say a word as he left, but his tail was firmly tucked between his legs. I found it especially gratifying when I saw his girl from earlier watching from the treadmill.

"Hey, we should celebrate. It's not every day you get to knock out a big-time, professional boxer." I looked over at Flint, who erupted in laughter.

18

Eliza

IT HAD BEEN ALMOST TWO weeks since I'd shoved Till out of my front door. I hurt. I missed him. I missed the boys. I missed the everyday, routine life we had. It sucked. When I'd made the decision to slam that door, I'd had no idea that it would shatter *my* fantasy as well.

I'd tried to stay gone as much as possible during those weeks. I'd taken up studying at the college library and picked up every possible shift I could get at work. I just hadn't been able to stay in that apartment. Life had gone on for my family upstairs. And every time I had been forced to listen to them talking or laughing, it'd shredded me.

Late one night, I heard a loud commotion upstairs. I assumed that it was Flint and Quarry arguing or Till wrestling with them. Any other day, I would have been up there before the first shout. But at that point, I had lost them all.

"Quarry, stop!" Till yelled before the door slammed.

Feet pounded down the stairs, and the wall shook with the sound of glass shattering.

I glanced out my window for long enough to see Quarry sprinting away. He stopped at the end of the sidewalk as if it were the edge of the Earth. He looked to the left, then the right, and then crumbled to the ground.

I raced outside after him, completely unsure what the hell was going on but still positive I needed to help.

"Quarry!" I called, rushing toward him. "What's going on? Are you okay?" I squatted down and scanned his body for any possible injury. But only his tear-stained cheeks seemed to be worse for wear.

He didn't say a word as he turned and threw his arms around my neck. He was nearly the same size I was, and I struggled to remain upright. It was pure force of will that I didn't topple over.

"What's wrong?" I turned to gain better traction, but if the shake of my knees the moment I met Till's devastated eyes were any indication, the ground had fallen away completely.

He stood on the upstairs breezeway staring down at us, his hand furiously rolling his bottom lip.

"What?" I mouthed up at him while holding Quarry tight in my arms.

It was such a simple gesture that it should have confused me, but my heart dropped to my stomach the second he lifted a finger and tapped his ear.

Oh, God. Quarry was going deaf too.

Till

I helplessly watched her holding him. I wasn't sure if Quarry was crying, but I knew with absolute certainty that salty tears were flowing from Eliza's eyes. Right then, as they were wrapped comfortingly in each other's arms, I wasn't sure which of them I was more jealous of. I made my way down the stairs, stopping just before I reached them. What the hell would I even say? So, like a coward, I backed against the wall out of sight.

"Hey. You want to go somewhere with me?" Eliza asked Quarry.

"Where?" he replied brokenly.

"Just come on."

I wanted the best vantage point to see how she was going to handle this. I had failed earlier as I'd tried to work the results of the genetic testing into a casual conversation. I hadn't known what else to do though. Eliza usually would have helped me with something like that. She would have known exactly how to tell Quarry that he going to go deaf and warmly assure Flint that he wasn't.

I quickly jogged back up the stairs, fully expecting her to take him back to her apartment, but Eliza surprised me as she guided him around the side of the building.

I leaned over the railing and watched her stop at the edge of the flowerbed.

"Welcome to purgatory."

"Um. Purga-what?"

"Purgatory. You know . . . the suffering point halfway between heaven"—she pointed to her window then out into the space in front of them—"and hell."

"Till made this up, didn't he?"

Eliza laughed. "What gave it away?"

"No one else is weird enough to consider your window heaven."

"This is true," she softly giggled.

I bit my lip and shook my head to keep from joining her.

"Come on. Sit down," she told him. "In purgatory, you can cuss as much as you want."

I lost them as they sat, and their voices became muffled from my position in the breezeway. I quietly snuck down the stairs and settled on the cold concrete beside Eliza's front door—only a corner divided me from joining them.

"I don't want to know that I'm not going to be able to hear one day. It's not fucking fair! Why did he have to tell me? He's such a dick!" Quarry shouted.

"So, you're pissed at Till for telling you?"

"Damn right!"

"Q, he didn't have a choice. You're going to have doctor appointments and treatments and all that stuff. Was he supposed to lie you? This is kinda need-to-know information."

"No! I don't know. Maybe."

"He's not going to lie to you. And I know for a fact you wouldn't want that."

"You don't fucking know what I want!" he yelled, but then they fell silent. A few seconds later, his voice returned on a whine. "Eliza, I don't want to go deaf."

It broke me. I didn't want that either. I should have been the only one. I'd gladly bear that burden alone.

"I know. It *fucking* blows!" She exaggerated the curse for his benefit.

I was sure his eyes lit and hers watered.

"But it's not Till's fault. He loves you, Q. I know the old 'misery loves company' saying, but I can guarantee that he would way rather face this on his own."

Fucking mind reader.

God, I *missed* her.

God, I *loved* her.

"A couple of weeks ago, I sat right here in purgatory with Till. He was a mess, freaking out when he found out that it might be genetic."

"I wasn't freaking out," I mumbled to myself.

"You *were* freaking out," she replied, making my eyes go wide.

"What?" Quarry questioned.

"I mean, um, earlier," she said, covering up our conversation. "You were freaking out . . . just like your brother. You know, you and Till have a lot in common. Maybe, instead of being pissed at him, you should talk to him. There's no magical solution for this, but it can't hurt to have your big brother beside you on this journey." She spoke the truth. She always did. Even when I was too stupid to recognize it.

Since I had been busted, there was no use hiding anymore. I walked around the corner of the building to find Quarry facing away from me. His head was resting in her lap, his hands awkwardly holding the sketchpad I had left on her window. It was a position I had perfected years earlier.

She was drawing long, fast strokes I immediately recognized as eyelashes. She didn't look up as she lifted the hand that was buried in his hair and waved me away. I stood still for a second, reliving the moment when I first found out about my diagnosis. Eliza was the only thing that had held me together then too—and honestly, every day after that. It was only the promise of Eliza that kept the world from falling apart when, every single day, I was faced with overwhelming adversity.

I can't lose that.

I knew what she wanted, because it was the exact same thing I'd have killed to have with her. But there are few things in life that trump the fear of losing your soul mate. I wouldn't allow the desire to consume her to be one of them.

We were good at friends. We could leave it at that.

We *had* to.

I sulked back around the corner and listened to the two of them talk some more. As the intensity of the conversation decreased, so did the volume of their voices until I eventually lost purchase on their words.

I was content with the knowledge that she was still with him though. If there were one person in the world who could mend Quarry's wounds, it was *her.*

Always her.

It must have been at least an hour later when they rounded that corner. I immediately found my feet. Quarry was startled to see me, and while Eliza sucked in a deep breath, it wasn't from surprise.

"Hey." I dusted off my jeans.

"What are you doing?" he asked, drying his red eyes.

"I was waiting for you." My mouth told Quarry, but my words were for Eliza.

She rolled her eyes and looked away, but not before I saw the moisture glisten from behind her lashes.

"Sorry. For you know . . ." Quarry trailed off weakly, snapping my attention back to him.

"Don't worry about that. We're good." I grabbed the back of his neck and pulled him against my chest. He was far too much of a man to hug me back, but he didn't fight me either. "I swear to God I'll make this okay for you. I can't fix it, Q. But I *will* make it okay." I felt his shoulders softly quake, and it was all I could do to keep mine from joining him.

"I'm going to bed," he announced, quickly walking away.

I stared at Eliza while we listened to his footsteps as he made his way upstairs.

Just before the door to my apartment shut, he called out, "Thanks, Eliza."

"Anytime, Q," she replied, holding my gaze.

"Can we talk?" I asked her.

"I don't know. Can we?" She smacked the sketchpad against my chest.

"I miss you. I really need you right now, Doodle." I took a step toward her, but she stepped out of reach.

"Well, you know where I'm at, Till." She shoved her door open and backed into her apartment. "You want to come inside?" She tilted her head.

We both knew what it would mean if I crossed that threshold. Even above my ridiculous superstitions, it would mean forever.

"Doodle, please."

"That's what I thought." With the flip of her wrist, she swung the door shut—once again.

"Shit." I fisted my hair.

I dragged myself back to my room. As soon as I crashed into bed, I opened the sketchpad. I knew what I would find, but I would have given anything for it to be her softly curved eyes inside instead of my own.

But I was wrong on both accounts.

Quarry's were the first to meet me, followed by Flint's a few inches below. It was pages upon pages of the boys' eyes with a few of my own scattered throughout.

It sucked for me to not have her, but I'd completely forgotten that she was all alone.

"You can see them any time you want, you know. Even if you don't want to see me. You don't have to ask," I said out loud, knowing she could hear me. "How about tomorrow? You can pick them up from the gym and I'll make an excuse why I have to stay later so you can just hang out for a few hours."

She didn't reply.

"Not me. Just them."

Her emotion-filled voice broke the silence. "Okay."

It was a single word, but it cut me to the bone. I was losing her faster than I could figure out how to make it right, and it was terrifying.

"I love you," I choked out, but she remained agonizingly quiet.

Eliza

"I love you too," I whispered inaudibly to the ceiling with tears streaming from my eyes. "I love you too."

19

Till

"YOU STUPID SON OF A bitch!" Flint yelled as he charged through the front door.

My eyes swung to Quarry as I tried to figure out what he could have possibly done to warrant this kind of explosive reaction, but when I turned back to Flint, his rage had homed in on me.

"Are you talking to me like that?" I asked, dumbfounded.

I'd seen Flint lose his cool before, but never like this. That just wasn't who he was. Me or Quarry, sure. But with the exception of when he'd lost it at the gym on Derrick Bailey, Flint was pretty chill.

"You're an idiot. You fucked us all!" he screamed, stopping only inches from my face.

I wasn't sure what the hell kind of *Freaky Friday* bullshit had happened that had transported Quarry into Flint's body, but clearly, something unnatural had taken place. I was so confused that I couldn't even formulate a stern response.

"Me?" I asked one more time just for clarification, causing Quarry to laugh beside me.

"What the hell is wrong with you? You couldn't get your shit together, so now, she's dating Derrick."

"Who?" I questioned even though I knew the answer. But my throat had suddenly closed, and it was the only word I could force out.

"Eliza!" he roared, shoving my chest with both hands.

I stumbled a few steps, but it had less to do with his physical push and everything to do with her.

"No." I shook my head, rejecting his statement.

"Oh yeah. I just passed them strolling arm in arm to his Mercedes." He stepped back into my face. "Why? Why? Why!" he screamed.

"Why what?"

"Why can't you get your shit together? Goddammit, she's going to leave us! He's a fucking piece of shit who hates you. You might as well have wrapped her in a pretty, red bow and handed her to him." He stepped away and started to pace a familiar pattern. "Till, he's rich. He's gonna take her to nice places and give her nice things. She'll get a taste of that life and won't want to come back to us. She'll be gone. "

He was irrational, yet I hung on his every word.

"He's gonna charm her into believing that he's something he's not and then take her away."

"She's not stupid. She won't fall for his bullshit." I stated matter-of-factly, but in my head, each sentence was punctuated with a giant blinking question mark.

"Why would she go out with that douchebag?" Quarry asked, but I couldn't focus.

"You have to fix this." Flint stilled. "Start using the fucking door."

I sighed and grabbed the back of my neck. "It's not that easy."

"Oh yeah?" He turned and stormed out of the front door only to immediately walk back in. He made a show of turning the knob and swinging the door. "I'm pretty sure it is that easy, brainiac."

"You have no idea what you're talking about," I shot back.

"Oh, I don't? Maybe you've forgotten that these floors work both ways. I've heard all your fantasy bullshit arguments with her." He gave me a pointed look.

"Truth," Quarry chimed in.

"Then you should understand that I can't give her what she wants!"

"Pull your fucking head out of your ass and stop being such a pussy. You living in this ridiculous-ass fantasy world is fucking up reality for the rest of us. Including her." He strode to his room, slamming the door behind him.

"Christ." I dropped my head into my hands, feeling more lost than ever.

"For the record, are you not going to yell at him for cussing?"

"Get out of here, Q."

"I'm just saying that—"

"Go!" I barked, and he wandered down the hall, joining Flint in their bedroom.

"What the fuck am I doing?" I whispered to myself, but Eliza wasn't there to answer for me. She'd know exactly how to fix this.

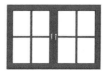

I sat on those stairs for well over three hours. I repeatedly flipped through the pages of her sketchbook, tracing my fingers over the lines just because I knew her hands were the ones that had drawn them. It mildly calmed the chaos in my mind.

Finally, around ten, she came strolling up the sidewalk—surprisingly alone.

"Hey," I said, taking in her sexy, red heels and hating Bailey that much more because he'd gotten to enjoy them.

"Hey," she replied, nervously twirling her ponytail.

I sighed. "Really, Doodle? Derrick?" I shook my head in disappointment—at myself.

"He's not a bad guy, Till. He's actually pretty nice."

"Sure." I nodded. "But why him? Is this to get back at me? Some sort of punishment for not giving you what you want? Because you should know, it's working. Really fucking well." I laughed without humor.

"I'm not trying to punish you." She stopped and tilted her head from side to side. "Well, maybe not completely." She smiled, and it hurt so damn much.

That smile was an oasis for me. I knew it would vanish, but it would tease and taunt me while it lasted.

"Right." I took a deep breath. "I don't have the right to ask this, but I'm doing it anyway. Please don't go on a second date with him. Doodle, that guy is no good. This is not coming from a jealous place.

I just don't want to see someone as amazing as you getting mixed up with a scumbag like that."

She gave me a knowing look. "Not a jealous place?"

"Well, maybe not completely." I chuckled, and tears sprung to her eyes. "Come here."

She didn't move, so I closed the distance between us and folded her into my arms.

"I'm so sorry I fucked this up. Just tell me how to fix it."

She sniffled and backed away. "Open your eyes, Till. I'm sick of letting the Earth spin under my feet while you circle around me. We belong together, but if that isn't going to happen, I have to start moving on." She paused to wipe away the tears that were steadily dripping off her chin. "I don't want to live in a world where the windows are locked and the Page boys don't eat me out of house and home. So I am begging you, Till. Wake. Up."

I didn't have a chance to find the words to reply before she walked away.

I made my way back to my apartment and crashed into bed. I was exhausted, but I never found sleep that night. I also couldn't figure out how to wake up either.

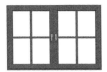

"Whoa! Take it easy. I just bought that bag." Slate laughed as I pounded my aggression out. "I'm closing up in five. Go get changed and get out of here."

I stopped and shook out my arms. "You mind if I stay for a little while longer? I'll lock up when I leave."

"What's going on with you? You spent the better part of the night terrorizing my equipment, then you left with the boys, and less than an hour later, you're back alone. Don't get me wrong. I like the dedication. But there has to be more to this."

I let out a huff and stared down at the ground. "Derrick's car was parked at my apartment when I got home. I just can't go back there right now."

"What's he doing at your place?"

"He's not. He's at Eliza's."

Slate's eyebrows shot up as understanding crossed his face. "Did you two break up?"

"Who? Me and Eliza? We were never together."

Slate barked out a laugh. "Sorry, buddy, but I think you were the only one who believed that."

"No. Seriously. We're *just* friends."

"Well, of all the times I've seen you two together, she wasn't *just* anything to you."

"Whatever." I blew him off, but only because I knew he was right.

"So, what's your hang-up with Derrick being there, then?"

Now *that* I could answer. "I fucking hate that guy. I don't want him anywhere near her."

"Yeah, I heard you two went at it a few weeks ago."

My head snapped to his.

Before then, he hadn't mentioned a single word to me or Flint about that night at the gym. Slate had a strict "no fighting outside of the ring" policy, so I'd figured we would have for sure heard about it if he'd caught wind.

"Yeah. About that—" I started, but I was quickly interrupted.

"So, you'd be okay if it were any other guy at her place?"

"You got eyes for my girl, Slate?" I smarted back, and he laughed. "Nah. But it's definitely worse because it's him."

"I get that." He squeezed my shoulder. "Okay, stay as long as you want. Take it easy on my bag though." He shot me a smile as he turned to walk away.

"She wants more," I blurted. I needed someone to talk to, and the speed bag just wasn't cutting it.

He turned back to face me, crossing his arms over his chest and signaling for me to explain.

"What if we took it to that next level and it didn't work out? I'd lose her for good. But I can't get her to understand, so I'm afraid it's gonna happen anyway." I tucked a glove under my arm and tugged it off.

"You want advice or you just want me to listen?"

"Advice. Please. Anything."

"You're going to lose her no matter what you do."

"Wow. You are terrible at this," I snarked.

"Till, she's not the girl you hung out with in high school anymore. One of two things is gonna happen. Either you take the next step and make her your woman or you sit back and watch someone else do it. It's gonna happen regardless of how much you try to fight it though. If it's not Derrick, it *will* be someone else."

"No. She's dated in the past, but she's never gotten serious with anyone."

"She's not a kid anymore though. She's twenty-one years old and starting to make plans for the future. People don't stay the same forever, especially women. But you have to face the facts that you *can't* lose that girl you're so desperate to hang on to . . . She's already gone."

"She's not gone!" I shouted as the panic began to set in.

"Yeah, she is, son. You need to let go of whatever you two had before and make something new. I'm not saying you have to marry Eliza, but I think you need to figure out what you want before you find yourself sitting in a church, watching her marry someone else." Slate walked forward, swinging his keys around his finger. "And you better figure it out fast, because women like her don't stay single long."

I didn't have a response as he backed away. The fact that someone hadn't already swooped Eliza off her feet was a miracle in and of itself. But she'd always made it clear that she loved me. It was stupid and naïve, but I hadn't worried that she would end up with anyone else. The scenario of watching her get married seemed so farfetched that I couldn't even conjure the image.

So, instead of focusing on Eliza's imaginary wedding, I closed my eyes and pictured *my life* with someone else.

20

Eliza

I WAS ECSTATIC WHEN I heard the unexpected knock on my apartment door. But when I opened it, I felt a deep sense of disappointment when I found Derrick standing on my welcome mat. He'd brought Chinese food to apologize for having to dash after our date the night before. Little did he know, but that had been my favorite part of the entire date. My manners won out and I invited him in.

We'd hung out and talked for a couple hours. It had been a fine evening. Not great. Just fine. When I made the excuse that I was getting tired, he took the hint. I offered him a chaste hug at the door, but he had other ideas. His lips softly brushed mine, and instead of feeling the spark of excitement that should precede a first kiss, I cringed. He didn't seem to notice, so with promises of a date the next night, I hurried him out.

Derrick was a nice enough guy. He was charming and all that crap, but there was no chance in hell we would ever turn into more. He was no Till. I was afraid no one ever would be though.

I was lying on my couch, fighting my hands as eyes flowed from the charcoal, when yet another unexpected knock at the door startled me.

"Um . . . who is it?"

"It's me." Till's voice shook on two simple syllables.

I snatched the door open, praying that it would be the moment I'd been waiting for, but his feet never even shuffled forward.

"I'm ready to let us go," he announced abruptly.

Never in my life had I felt a pain so deeply.

My heart seized.

My bones ached.

My soul withered.

"What?" I squeaked.

"We're not the same anymore. I get it. It's my fault. I'll own it." His eyes were as hollow as my chest felt. "Eliza, I can't do this any-more."

Eliza. Oh, God.

Every nightmare I'd ever had was playing out in front of me.

"Stop." I choked out around the lump in my throat.

"I'm sorry."

"Is this because of Derrick? Nothing happened, Till," I rushed out.

"No. It's not that. I should have done this a long time ago."

"Why are you doing this?" I cried, barely holding myself together.

Then it happened.

The most unlikely one-sided smile grew on his mouth, breathing new life into his empty expression.

"Because I'm ready for a new reality . . . with you."

With one sentence and two steps, forever began. Till Page walked through my door for the very first time.

My mouth gaped open as I blinked rapidly, expecting the visual in front of me to vanish. I should have been elated, but I was so fucking confused.

"I don't know how to react right now. Are you coming or going?"

"Both." He folded me into his chest.

I went willingly, needing the comfort and strength I knew his arms could provide.

"I've been fighting for years to keep us inside the safety of my comfort zone, but during that time, *everything* changed. You changed, the world changed, our situations changed, our desires changed. But I wasn't willing to change with them. I'm sorry. I'm an idiot."

"You really are." I sucked in a shaky breath.

"So I'm giving up on that part of us. I quit. I want to start over with a new relationship, preferably one where I get to touch you. Naked. A lot."

I laughed through the tears.

"I love you, Eliza Reynolds, and if I had my way, I'd lock you up in a room and keep you all for myself. But if you insist on doing that whole 'living a real life' thing, I want to go with you."

"Kidnapping and imprisonment. So romantic." I sniffled, and it was Till's turn to laugh. I took a deep breath, filling my lungs with the promises that infused his words. Then I leaned away and looked into his eyes. "Are you really serious about this?"

"Absolutely."

"Are you freaking out about this?"

"Absolutely," he exhaled, causing us both to laugh.

"What if I said I don't want you anymore?"

His smile fell and his eyes narrowed causing my eyes to narrow in return. A classic stare-off ensued.

Unblinking, he slid a hand down and squeezed my ass. "Then you'd be lying to us both."

I held his hazel eyes, unwilling to look away, but I was scared that, one day, I wouldn't have a choice. His grand entry through the door had been amazing, but it hadn't cured my anxiety.

"I need you to swear to me that this isn't one of your impulsive, half-assed decisions, because I can't handle that, Till. I need this to be real."

Leaning forward, he lost the staring match as he captured my mouth. It was a *really* good kiss, but it wasn't an answer. I tried to move out of his grasp, but his arms tightened around me.

"She was terrible," he whispered.

"Who?"

"My wife."

My head snapped back. "Excuse me?"

"Her name was Natasha. She talked all the time and was addicted to shoes. Flint and Quarry hated her, but that was okay because she hated them more. She bit her nails, so it didn't feel very good when she scratched my head. Her boobs were a decent size, but there wasn't a single freckle on them." He sucked in a dramatic breath before playful-ly choking out, "She didn't even know how to make those cheesy potatoes. It was torture." He smiled then grazed his teeth across my neck.

"What the hell are you talking about?" I snapped, not even remotely amused by his little story.

"I spent the last hour envisioning the nightmare I would eventually find myself in if I didn't get my shit together and actually wake up. It was easily the worst hour of my entire life. It's just . . . I've been trying to keep this overwhelming need to have you separate from our friendship for so long, Eliza. But the lines are all blurred, because our friendship is why I fell for you so hard in the first place. See, I love these." He brushed the back of his hand over my peaked nipples.

I gasped.

"And this." He slid his hand down to my ass. "And I especially love this." He slipped a hand into my pajama pants and lazily glided a finger through my folds.

I sucked in a breath, and he groaned as he dropped his forehead to mine.

"But even if all of that was suddenly gone, I would still be madly in love with you. I wanted to spend forever with you at thirteen. Nothing has or ever will change that. Eliza, I love you. And I am unquestionably serious about spending the rest of my life with you."

They were really good words.

But Till Page was saying them . . . to me.

They were *perfect* words.

It was the truth.

All of it.

"I love you too," she said with tears rolling down her cheeks.

I wanted to wipe them away . . . but . . . my hand was still moving in her pants. It was a serious conundrum.

I pressed a soothing kiss to her mouth and whispered against her lips, "You have to stop crying. I can't put the moves on you if you're bawling."

She laughed, but cried even harder. It was an easy decision at that point.

With two hands, I scooped her off her feet and carried her to the couch. She clung to my neck as I sat down with her on my lap.

"You swear this is real, Till?"

"Well, I'm not exactly an expert on reality."

She laughed into my neck.

"But, Eliza, it's absolutely real to me."

Lifting her head, she stared into my eyes. "I love you."

"I love you too." I gently took her mouth in a slow kiss.

Although it started out slow, Eliza took it deeper as she moved to straddle my lap. Then, dropping her hands from the hold on my neck, I lost her mouth as she murmured, "Show me."

In one fluid movement, she peeled the T-shirt over her head, revealing her lack of a bra, and my cock instantly grew between us. "I could touch you all day long and it wouldn't even be close to showing you how I feel."

She sucked my bottom lip into her mouth, releasing it on a sexy sigh. "Well, I think you should try."

I absolutely agreed with her. She stood from my lap as I dragged her pants down. I wasn't happy until she was completely naked—just the way I imagined her every night before I fell asleep. But even as she stood in front of me, I couldn't picture anything except Derrick's hands on her every curve.

She settled back on my lap, her breasts swaying from the movement.

I dipped a finger between her legs. "Did he touch you here?"

"No."

"Here?" I glided a hand up to squeeze her breast.

"No."

I trailed the tip of my finger up to her neck as she tilted her head to the side, her eyes falling shut. "No," she breathed.

I gently rubbed my thumb over her bottom lip. "Here?"

Her eyes popped open. She didn't respond, but that was answer enough.

"Never again." I kissed her. "No one ever touches these again." I teased my tongue over her bottom lip before sucking it into my mouth. "Yeah?"

"Yeah," she agreed, brushing her nose against mine pleading for more—more that I absolutely planned to give her. "Now, let's see what we can do about that kiss."

I roughly pushed a hand into the back of her hair, causing her to gasp. Then, while her mouth was still open, I took it in a hard, unapologetic kiss. Our tongues tangled as I used her hair to control the pace. She was hurried, but I was steady. There was no rush in eternity.

"Forever." I moaned into her mouth while she rocked against my cock, which was unfortunately still tucked away in my jeans. "Say it." I demanded, lifting my hips to increase the pressure.

"Why aren't you naked?" she groaned, taking my mouth in another hard kiss, as her hand traveled down to the button on my jeans.

"Because I'm erasing where that asshole touched you. Then we're spending the rest of the night rewriting it the way it should've been. I may've been the first, but this time when I make you come I want to know I'll be the last. Now, fucking tell me it's forever."

A slow, sexy smile crossed her lips. "You've always been forever for me."

"No matter how bad I fuck things up, we make this work. Forever."

Her smile grew. "Stop freaking out and start rewriting."

"Eliza . . ."

"Till, shut up." She peppered kisses over my face. "Forever. Forever. Forever. I swear to love you, Till Page. Even if you fuck it up." She leaned back to catch my eyes. "Better?"

I blew out a relieved breath. "Much. Now, just so you know, I want to be the one to tell Bailey to fuck off."

"No way! You'll kill him," she said so seriously that it made me laugh. "You let me handle, Derrick. He's coming over tomorrow night. I'll break it to him kindly then."

"Fuck no you won't! He's not coming over here ever again."

"Are we really fighting over Derrick Bailey while I'm sitting naked on your lap? This seems like a gross misuse of time." She reached down and drew her fingernail over my cock. "Let me tell him tomorrow, and then you can say whatever you want next time you see him at the gym."

I rumbled a groan and pressed my hand between her legs.

"Can we go back to rewriting now?" She circled her hips against my fingers.

"Yeah." I smiled, then began looking around the room. "Where do you want to start? Couch sex has its merits, but I think I'd like to lay you out on that table."

Her eyes heated but she released the sweetest giggle when she answered, "Both."

"Good plan." Standing up off the couch, I slid her down my body until her feet landed on the ground. I began to push my jeans down my thighs, but paused to pull a long strip of condoms from my back pocket.

"Thank God!" she exclaimed, shoving me down on the couch.

I laughed as I fell, but Eliza made quick work of dragging my jeans off my feet as I tore the shirt over my head. She climbed onto my lap while I rolled the condom on between us, and within seconds, she sank down on my cock.

"Fuck." I cursed as she began to ride me.

I wanted to kiss her, but I couldn't drag my eyes from her body. She must have noticed my hungry gaze, because she asked, "You like to watch?" as she slid her hands up over her breasts and into her hair.

"My cock's inside you, Eliza. I could watch this every fucking day for the rest of my life."

"Good. Because you might have to." She quickened her pace.

"That's not exactly a hardship." I leaned forward only long enough to drag my tongue over each of her nipples then reclined against the back of the couch.

Licking my finger, I slid it between us. On every down stroke, I gently tapped her clit, making her go wild on top of me. It was an unbelievably sexy sight.

She reached down and guided my hand to her breast. "No hands. I'm close."

"Come on, baby. Give it to me. This isn't the only time I'm making you come tonight." I stared down as I once again found her clit.

"I mean . . . I don't think I need your hand," she panted and my eyes flashed to hers.

"No hands?" I questioned in shock.

She shook her head as she tightly wrapped her arms around my neck and continued to move over me, searching for her release.

No. Fucking. Hands.

I sat up, shifting to the edge of the couch, and began fucking her from the bottom. I could feel her muscles tense around my cock but I couldn't keep up a pace in that position to make her come.

Jesus, she was so close though. I pushed to my feet with her in my arms.

"Don't stop," she cried. "Please."

"Shhh . . ." I soothed as I leaned her shoulders against the wall. "Hold on, baby." She clung to me as I drilled inside her. With every thrust her muscles contracted, fueling me forward.

"Harder," she pleaded. However, if I fucked her much harder, we were going to be rebuilding a wall in her apartment.

I carried her over to the small dining room table before releasing her legs and pulling out.

"What are you doing?" she objected on a whine.

I didn't say a word as I spun her around in my arms and folded her face down over the table. Poising myself at her entrance, I whispered, "You need deeper. Not harder." Then I slammed myself to the hilt inside her.

She released a strangled cry, but it quickly transformed into a breathy sigh. "Yes," she hissed. My hands gripped her hips as I fucked her from behind, each thrust deeper than the last.

It took several strokes for me to perfect a rhythm. Only the sounds of her moans and clenching of her cunt guided me, but I finally figured her out.

"Oh God, Till!"

I bent down and raked my teeth over her shoulder, and it must have changed my angle because one thrust later—without the use of hands—I claimed Eliza Reynold's final first.

And every. Single. One. Of her lasts.

21

Eliza

"HEY," I SAID, PULLING THE door open.

"Wow. You look beautiful," Derrick lied, leaning in to give me a hug.

I looked like hell. My lips were swollen, and there were bags under my eyes from staying up all night with Till. I smiled at the memory.

"Thanks." I stepped away, allowing him space to come inside.

"You ready to go?"

"Umm . . ." I stalled.

Why the hell was I nervous? I had zero feelings for Derrick, but the butterflies still threatened to overtake me. I was so horrible at confrontation. I would have much rather just avoided Derrick than have this conversation with him, but I sure as hell didn't want Till to do it.

"Can you give me a second?" I retreated to my bedroom.

I needed a little encouragement of the Till Page variety. I looked up at the ceiling and whispered his name. He didn't respond, so I walked over to the wall and gently knocked.

"Hey," I called out, but it wasn't Till's attention I gained.

"You okay?" Derrick asked as he rounded the corner to my room.

"Yeah. Sorry. I, um . . ." Again with the stalling.

"What's going on, Eliza?" He stared at me with genuine concern.

I felt like an ass for making him worry. It wasn't like I was breaking up with him. We had been on one date—two if the Chinese food from the night before counted. I wasn't breaking his heart. I was simply informing him that I would no longer like to see him—in any capacity.

"I'm fine. Sorry. I'm just nervous. Look, some things have changed since last night, and I'm not going to be able to go out with you tonight . . . or, well, ever." I gave him a tense smile and an apologetic shrug.

"Oh," he said, snapping his head back in surprise. "Can you at least tell me what changed? You seemed pretty excited about going out last night."

Clearly, I had been on a different date than Derrick had, because excited was not an adjective I would have used to describe how I'd felt.

"Um . . . it's just . . . Till came over, and we've decided to give a real relationship a try."

I couldn't be certain that he'd heard anything after I'd said Till's name. His eyes had immediately grown dark.

"Page?" he growled. "Did you fuck him?"

I was shocked by his transformation, but not enough to keep my mouth shut. "I'm pretty sure that's none of your damn business."

"You did." He nodded then laughed. "He fuck you on that bed?" He reached down and snatched the blanket off as if the sheets would reveal the proof.

I could have dealt with him acting like a dick, but there was something in his tone that prickled the hair on the back of my neck. Everything suddenly felt wrong, and my eyes flashed to the door for an escape.

"You need to leave."

"So let me get this straight. You're choosing that broke-ass wannabe over . . . *me?*" He pointed to his chest as he took a menacing step forward that forced me to back against the wall.

"Um, no. I just don't think this is going to work out." I inched toward the door.

"Bullshit!" he shouted, leaning close to my face and placing a hand next to my head against the wall. His proximity was intimidating, but it was the absence of emotion in his eyes that sent the red flags flying.

"Backup," I said with a shaky voice.

"Yes. Let's." He laughed. "Let's back up to when I asked you out, and maybe this time, you tell me the goddamn truth about your relationship with Till fucking Page." He bit out his name like it burned on his tongue.

"I didn't have a relationship with Till when you asked me out. We were just friends."

"Liar!" he violently roared, spit flying from his mouth.

I glanced up at the ceiling. Yeah, maybe staying in my bedroom was a better course of action. At least Till could hear if things went sour.

"Please leave." I tried to keep my voice steady, but I failed when a scary smile crept across his face.

He leaned in closer, inhaling deeply as he dragged his nose up my neck. "Where's your boyfriend now?"

"Upstairs. He's waiting on me. Let's not make him come down here." I played innocent, but Derrick knew that it was a threat. And it *absolutely* was.

His body tightened, and he immediately stepped away. I released a relieved breath, but it was entirely premature, because not even a second later, his fist landed hard against my face. My head snapped to the side as I fell over and collapsed against my easel before crashing to the floor.

"You think I'm fucking afraid of him?"

I had but one response. "Till!" I screamed at the top of my lungs, banging my hands against the wall. They were stilled as another fist landed against my cheek. My mind lagged as I tried to remain conscious. I needed help, and I knew he was only one paper-thin wall away.

"Till! Help me!" I shouted again, but a boot under my chin silenced any further cries.

"Till! Wake up. Till!"

I felt Quarry shaking my shoulders, but I could barely make out his words. I opened my eyes and saw his mouth moving, but he sounded a million miles away.

"Get up. Something's wrong with Eliza." His voice began to drift into clarity.

"What?" I jumped to my feet at the very mention of her name.

"She was screaming for help, so Flint took off and went down there. He told me to wake you up."

Without another word, I rushed from my room, and just before I hit the front door, I heard a crash in Eliza's apartment.

"Stay here," I ordered, taking off down the stairs.

When I rounded the corner, I saw Eliza's door wide open and heard a commotion. At a dead sprint, I rushed inside without a single fear of what I would encounter. She was in there. That alone was enough to force me into the pits of hell.

"You Page boys really are fucking stupid! You think you can take me?" Bailey yelled from on top of Flint's chest, raining punches over his face.

Flint's hands were raised defensively, but they did little good.

I dived across the room, catching Derrick off guard and knocking him to the floor. I had been livid when I'd seen him hit Flint, but nothing in my rough life could have prepared me for the way I felt when I lifted my eyes to find Eliza beaten, bloody, and curled into a ball in the corner of the room. Her gaze met mine and the dam broke as tears rushed from her eyes. Her body bucked as a sob tore from her throat. It didn't take long to piece together the situation in front of me.

"I'm okay," she whispered, knowing exactly what I needed to hear.

As soon as the words cleared her lips, my mind checked out completely. Murder and rage quickly filled the empty space it had left behind.

Derrick was just rising to his feet when I threw the hardest punch of my life. It was packed with more than simple determination to win a fight. It was packed with raw and visceral fury.

My knuckles cracked as they landed on his face. I also felt his cheekbone shatter under the blow, and it fueled me forward. Not a word was spoken by anyone in the room as my left hook landed hard on his kidney. He doubled over right in time for my uppercut to snap his head back. His legs were at least smart, because they carried him away from me as they fought to stay underneath him.

I charged after him, nowhere near done yet.

"You fucking piece of shit," I growled, dodging his half-assed attempt at a blow.

"Fuck you. Enjoy my sloppy seconds." He laughed with false confidence before spitting blood onto the floor.

I cracked my neck. I knew he was lying; he'd never had her. But the poor bastard actually thought he had gotten something from her and, in turn, something from me. He might have briefly touched what was mine, but he'd never *had* even a tiny morsel of Eliza Reynolds.

I focused to keep my eyes off her, knowing that one more glance would ensure that Bailey ended the night in a morgue. I needed to get to her, but not until he paid.

"See, clearly, you got confused somewhere." I stepped forward, slamming a fist into his mouth. "That woman you just put your hands on has been mine since she took her first breath of air on this Earth."

I threw a right he surprisingly dodged, but I followed it up with a quick left, knocking him to his ass. Then I lowered myself over him, assuming the same position he'd had on Flint. Grabbing his throat, I cut off his airway. His arms began to wildly seek out contact, but they only ended up sailing through the empty air. His eyes were bulging as he turned red.

"And last night, I finally claimed her once and for all. That date you went on was *never* about you. It was always about *me*. All you got was an angry woman trying to make me hurt. But make no mistake— every single time she looked at you, touched you, or even spoke to you, it was always"—I leaned in as close as I could get—"*me!*"

With that last word, I finished it. Punch after punch, I gave him tenfold anything he could have ever dished out. My vision tunneled as he went limp under me. His head flopped back and forth with every slam. Blood poured from his eyes and mouth, but I was physically unable to stop.

"That's enough, Till. Come on." Flint wrapped his arms around my shoulders pulling me backwards, but I kept going.

I couldn't hit Derrick hard enough to give myself any kind of satisfaction. Not after I'd seen her like that. My arms continued flailing as Flint dragged me to my feet.

"She was always mine!" I roared at Bailey's unconscious body. "Mine!" I landed a kick to his shoulder and a stomp to his stomach before Flint hauled me out of range.

"Fucking stop! You're going to kill him!" he yelled, struggling to get me under control. "Goddammit, Till. Chill out and go take care of Eliza."

At the mention of her name, the blinding rage began to ebb from my system. *Eliza.*

"Eliza?" I called when I didn't see her in the corner anymore. "Doodle?" I yelled as Flint dropped his hands, finally convinced I wasn't after that piece of shit, Bailey, anymore. "Eliza!"

Flint filled in the blank. "She's in her room."

I rushed down the hall to her room. Bile rose in my throat as I took in the mess around me. *Holy shit.* Her easel was broken and all of her art supplies were scattered across the floor. The table next to her bed was tipped over and several frames lay shattered on the ground. *How the fuck did I not hear this?*

My eyes found her small body in the corner by her closet. Her knees were pulled to her chest, her head resting on top of them; her hands were muffling her ears. After walking over, I squatted down in front of her, careful not to touch her even though every fiber of my being was screaming for me to do just that.

"Eliza," I whispered, and I heard her mumble something I couldn't quite make out against her legs. "Huh?" I questioned.

She lifted her head to look at me. I tried really fucking hard not to show any reaction to her injuries, but seeing her in that condition tore away a piece of me I would never be able to reclaim. It gutted me.

There was never a day I could remember where I hadn't wanted to *see* Eliza. I used to wait on bated breath to catch just a single glance of her inky, blue eyes. However, I'd have given anything to be able to erase from my memory the way she looked in that moment. Her eyes were both already starting to swell shut, and a large, purple bruise covered almost one whole side of her face. Blood was pouring from a gash over her left eyebrow, and a split in her bottom lip sent more blood trickling down her chin.

"Did you kill him?"

"Don't know, don't care. Are you okay?" I brushed the hair away from her blood-soaked face.

Her only response was a simple shake of her head before she flew into my arms.

I scooped her off the ground and carried her to the bed. I had to bite my lip when I heard her painfully hiss a curse as I set her down. I battled with the overwhelming urge to finish what I'd started with Derrick, but that would have to wait.

"I'm gonna get you some ice and something to clean up that cut, okay?"

She nodded.

As I began to walk away, I searched her battered body for somewhere to kiss but came up empty. I settled on her hand, pulling it to my mouth and pressing a reassuring kiss to her palm. It might not have done anything for her, but it sure as hell quelled a fire brewing inside me.

She's okay.

I walked back into the room to find Flint leaning over Derrick. He appeared to still be unconscious, but anger once again swept through me.

"I think we need to call an ambulance." Flint said with worry painting his face.

I shook my head and continued to the freezer.

"I'm serious, Till. He doesn't sound good. His breathing is all gargled, and he's not waking up."

"I don't give one fuck if he dies on that floor. He dug his grave when he touched her. If he still has breath in his lungs right now, it's too much."

"You'll get in trouble," he pleaded.

But my mind was made up. I wasn't lifting a single finger to help that piece of shit, not even if it were just to dial 911.

"What. The. Fuck?" boomed from the doorway.

I spun to find Slate's wide eyes resting on Bailey. He hurried inside and knelt beside him.

"Flint, call nine-one-one. Now!" he shouted. "What the hell happened?"

"Not nearly enough." I turned my attention back to packing ice into a bag.

"Um. I . . . uh . . ." Eliza stuttered from the hallway.

"What the fuck!" Slate yelled, but before I could glance over my shoulder to see the reason for his curse, I was pinned against the fridge from behind.

"No!" Eliza and Flint screamed in unison.

"What did you do!" he barked into my ear so loudly that it temporarily deafened me more than I already was.

"Stop!" Eliza cried just as I saw Flint appear beside Slate.

"Slate, no. Derrick did that to Eliza. Till came down and did that to Derrick."

"It's true, I swear," Eliza confirmed.

It must have been enough to convince him of my quasi innocence because I was freed. She quickly moved to my side, wincing as I pulled her close.

"Jesus fucking Christ," Slate breathed, reaching forward to grab Eliza's chin and inspect her face. "Flint," he called out without dragging his eyes off her. "Go upstairs and ask Erica to come down here. Then get on the phone with nine-one-one and tell them we need an ambulance."

"Yes, sir," Flint answered as he headed out the door.

"You all right, hun?" Slate asked with a forced but gentle grin.

"I, um, think so," Eliza squeaked out, moving even closer to me.

"Good."

"What are you doing here?" I asked.

"Q called. Said something was going down and he was worried. Erica and I were just leaving the gym, so we hauled ass over here. I have to be honest. I was not expecting this." He waved his hands around the room.

"Yeah. Neither was I," I scoffed, but it was only to cover the emotions packed into the memories of the moment I'd rushed through that *door*.

"Oh my God!" Erica gasped as she walked into the apartment. Her eyes were glued to Derrick on the floor, but as she lifted her gaze, I saw the exact second in which she saw Eliza. She slapped her hands over her mouth and her eyes jumped to Slate.

He tilted his head to Derrick and walked over, stopping in front of her. "You gonna be okay with this?" He tucked her shoulder-length, blond hair behind her ears.

She stared up at him for a brief second before clearing her throat and nodding.

"Of course you are," he mumbled, kissing her forehead. "I think she's all right, but can you make sure that one isn't dying? The ambulance is on its way."

"Yeah, sure," she answered nervously before lifting her eyes back to Eliza. "Are you okay?"

"I think so." Eliza looked down, embarrassed, and it made me want to kill Derrick all over again.

"You mind if I talk to Till for a minute in the hall?" Slate asked, and her whole body tensed.

"Um . . ." She squeezed me even tighter as her eyes drifted down to Derrick, who was still laid out on the floor. It appeared he was finally starting to come around.

Slate must have caught her pointed glance, because he called over his shoulder, "Johnson."

"What's up?" The scary beast of a man came walking inside.

"I trust that man with my life. He follows Erica everywhere," Slate told Eliza. "She hates it, but it makes me feel better. He won't let anything happen. I swear." He smiled genuinely, but it did nothing to soothe Eliza.

"Can I . . . um, just go up to your apartment and maybe clean up?" she asked, tilting her head back to look up at me.

"Yeah, baby. Of course. Come back down whenever you're ready." I kissed the top of her head, and her shoulders relaxed.

The three of us walked out the door, and Eliza continued past us up the stairs.

Then the sounds of sirens rang through the night.

"All right. You have about sixty seconds before the cops show up. What exactly happened?" Slate leaned around me to look toward the parking lot.

"I walked in. Found Derrick straddling Flint. Knocked him off. Then I saw Eliza. Lost my fucking mind. The end." I pushed a hand through my hair, becoming enraged all over again.

"Shit," he cursed under his breath. "Did he fight back?"

"Yep."

The screaming sirens neared.

"He didn't land anything?"

"Nothing."

"I'm gonna be real honest here, son. I'm not sure the cops are going to feel this was self-defense when he looks like that . . . and you don't have a single mark."

"I know." I shrugged. "Slate, I'm okay with anything the law wants to say about this. I know I did the right thing. No amount of probation in the world could teach that asshole the lesson I just gave him."

"I happen to agree with you." He sucked in a deep breath. "Heads up. Incoming." He nodded his chin toward the breezeway.

I steeled myself for an onslaught of uniforms. Just as I turned my head to look in that direction, a hard fist slammed into my eye and forced me back a step. Before I could even bring my hands up to cover my face, I was popped squarely in the mouth.

"Son of a bitch!" I rocked to the balls of my feet and defensively lifted my hands, readying myself for the next blow.

"Well, look at that! Derrick did fight back." Slate smiled while shaking his hand out.

"Jesus Christ. What the fuck?" I dabbed my mouth to find blood seeping from my lips.

"He looks like fucking hell, but if he'd touched Erica, I wouldn't have stopped until his sorry ass was loaded into a coffin. You did good, Till." He reached forward to squeeze my shoulder, and I instinctively flinched, causing him to laugh. "Go get your woman. The police are going to want to talk to her, too. They'll be here any second." He paused to point to my eye. "Don't ice that shit either. Make it look good."

"Yeah. Thanks," I said sarcastically while dabbing my swelling face.

"Hey, remind me we need to work on your reflexes. I clearly said, 'Incoming'," he joked, walking backwards into the apartment.

I couldn't help but laugh as my shoulders fell. It felt so fucking good to know that he had my back.

"I swear to fucking God," I snarled as I stomped a pattern around Eliza's hospital room. She had just been wheeled out, but my anger and anxiety filled the room in her absence.

"Calm. Down," Slate said from the doorway. "It's no big deal. Derrick's daddy is loaded. It's not as bad as it seems. I'll get it back."

"Fuck you."

"You're welcome. Now, get your shit together and remember who the hell you are talking to."

Eliza didn't have insurance, and she had freaked when the doctor told her that he wanted to run a CAT scan because of the trauma to her face and head. She'd flat-out refused, spouting off some crap about not going into debt by racking up a huge hospital bill she'd eventually have to pay. She'd sworn she was okay, but I'd absolutely not been anything even resembling okay.

So I'd lost it. I'd snapped at her like a fucking asshole. Then I'd shouted at the doctor for reasons that didn't even make sense. In turn, he threatened to call security, which only pissed me off more. It was a clusterfuck in that room until Slate came in and physically pinned me against the wall. While I was trying to get my shit under control, Erica was apparently informing administration that she and Slate would be financially responsible for Eliza's hospital visit. While I was relieved as they wheeled her out of the room, I was sick and fucking tired of feeling like a broke-ass, worthless dick all the time. As it often was, my anger was aimed in the wrong place, and Slate was the only man in the room.

"Get my shit together?" My heart pounded in my chest, and every muscle in my body strained under the mounting stress. "I'd like to see how the hell you'd react if Erica looked like that and there wasn't a fucking thing in the world you could do to help her."

Slate's eyes turned dark as his jaw clenched. "It was different. But I've been there," he stated matter-of-factly. "It was the worst day of my life. I wasn't even the one who got to make the piece of shit pay either. But honestly, Till, sometimes you have to accept that it's not the way things get done or who does them. As long as, in the end, they are *done*. She's getting that CAT scan right now, and you can sleep easy tonight knowing that she's okay. It doesn't matter one bit who signs the check that pays for that kind of peace of mind."

"It matters to me. You have no fucking idea how it feels to be so goddamn helpless all the time. I can't do this anymore. I've only truly had her for less than twenty-four hours and I've already failed to fucking protect her *and* provide for her. My boxing trainer had to pay for her medical bills. It's embarrassing!"

"It's only embarrassing if you let it be." He shrugged and settled into the chair next to the door.

I continued to pace. I couldn't get over the heavy weight of failure compressing my chest. "Why the fuck would she want to settle for someone like me? I failed out of high school. I work sixty-three hours a week for minimum wage so that I can barely pay the bills on a shithole apartment. For fuck's sake, I have two brothers I want to give the world, but last week, she had to buy *us* groceries. Oh, and there is always that fun fact that I'm going deaf. One day, she really will have to take care of me! I can't handle knowing that she has to settle for a future filled with struggles in order to be with me. I love her. I really fucking do. But at what point do I let her go because I know she'd have a better life with someone else?" I finished my rant on a yell.

"Wow. You have really gone off the deep end. She's not some puppy you can find a better home for." He stretched his legs out and crossed them at his ankles.

If possible, it managed to piss me off more. I was in emotional upheaval and he was getting comfortable.

"Just leave me alone. I can't deal with your shit right now."

"You want to go pro?" he asked randomly.

"What I want is for you to leave."

"Is that a no?" He crossed his arms over his chest. "I seem to have an opening now that someone nearly killed my bum."

"What the fuck are you talking about? Nothing has changed. I still don't have the time. Honestly, I think I need to give up boxing altogether. Maybe try to find another job or something."

"I'll bankroll eight hundred a week. Quit your jobs and come work for me in the ring. It comes with health insurance for you and the boys too."

I stared at him, awestruck. That was double what I was bringing home each week.

I'd always heard that you couldn't judge a man's character by the balance in his bank account. Thank fuck for that because character might be the only place I wasn't overdrawn. And right then, Slate's offer sounded a whole lot like pity. No matter how appealing it sounded, I wanted to make it without having to rely on anyone else. I couldn't afford to sacrifice character.

"Why are you doing this right now? What part of that conversation confused you? I don't want your charity."

"It's not charity. I'm gonna make a shit-ton of money off your ass. This isn't a free ride. I'll get all of your winnings until you've paid me back. Then anything you make over that, I get thirty-three percent. Erica's been eyeing this condo on the beach in Florida. I'm hoping you can help me out and buy that for her."

Outstanding. Slate wants to buy a condo on the beach and I just want to keep the electricity on.

"It has to be hard being you." My voice dripped with sarcasm, but it only made Slate smile.

"I guess you won't know until you try. I made every single penny I have from boxing. If you think money will solve all your problems, then put whatever preconceived notions you have about my motives aside and take my offer. But if you decide to refuse, you should know I won't make it again."

"Why now? Less than a month ago, you told me I wasn't ready. Where was your offer to bankroll me then?"

"I'm not going to lie to you. You're not ready. Not if you want to be great! But with enough time, I can get you there. You're raw right now, and despite whatever you think, you're driven by something greater than the almighty dollar or dreams of stardom." He stood up and walked over to me. "To answer your question about why now, I was wrong. You're not hungry for more in life. You're fucking *starving.* I can work with that.

"Did you even listen to yourself while you were talking? Not one single thing you said was because Till Page wanted more money or a nicer car. You were concerned about Eliza and the boys . . . but never Till." He poked my chest right over my heart. "I'm making an investment in you, Till. It's no handout. I believe you're going to set the boxing world on fire, because every time you put on those gloves, you're doing it for *them.* Say yes. Accept the offer. Quit your jobs. Take a week off to take care of her. Then get your ass in my ring."

I had no words. If I spoke, I was going to look like a sniffling little bitch. So I nodded instead.

"Good. I'm going to find Erica and get some coffee. I'll send over the contracts and your first paycheck in the morning." He turned and headed for the door.

I stood in the middle of an empty hospital room where my fantasy and reality had collided. Finally, I had the break I had dreamed of, but it had taken almost losing Eliza to get it. I would forever remember the way I felt in that moment. Cracking my neck and shaking out my arms, I decided I was done letting the world run over me.

Slate had just handed me my one chance to make a better life, and I was going in with gloves blazing. For the first time in my fucking life, I was climbing through the ropes.

22

Eliza

\ONE CONCUSSION, TWO BROKEN RIBS, two black eyes, six stitches, and far too many purple bruises to count. But as I pulled an oversized On The Ropes T-shirt over my head and settled into Till's bed, I was more concerned about him.

"You okay?" I asked as he folded into bed next to me.

His head snapped to mine. "Uhhh, are *you* okay? Why are you asking about me?"

"I don't know. It's been a crazy night."

"It really has." He sighed and pulled me into his side.

I winced from the movement. "And you've been acting weird."

"Huh?" He leaned away to look down at my mouth.

Till had been hard of hearing for years. *Huh* and *what* were probably two of his most used word. Well, those and *fuck*—and maybe *Doodle*. But tonight had been vastly different. Several times, I'd spoken to him at the hospital and he hadn't even acknowledged me. I'd prayed that he had only been lost in his thoughts, distracted by the entire fucked-up day. But I knew in my heart it was more.

So, instead of repeating my vague statement, I blurted, "Where were you tonight?"

It wasn't an accusation, but even as it left my lips, it felt that way.

"Asleep. Shit, Doodle. I'm so fucking sorry."

"Eliza," I corrected just to be positive we were in my reality and not his.

His lip twitched. "It's just habit. Doodle or Eliza—it doesn't change anything."

I nodded, still not convinced.

"I have no fucking idea how I didn't hear that shit in your bedroom. I wish you could have called my name or something. I'm so sorry I didn't get there sooner." His muscles tensed, and I blankly stared at him.

I was struck by the realization that Till had no idea what had really happened in my bedroom. He thought he'd slept through it, and the guilt on his face was staggering. There was no way in hell I was telling him that I'd screamed for him repeatedly or that I'd prayed his name over God's as I'd roused back to consciousness. He didn't need to know that. *Ever.*

"You got there. That's all that mattered." I plastered on a fake smile that hurt my lips.

Only two nights earlier, Till had said, "Bless you," when I'd sneezed. There was no possible way he could have slept through my cries for help. Something was going on, and I couldn't decide which was more worrisome—the fact that his hearing had suddenly gotten a lot worse or that he didn't even truly realize it yet.

To test the theory, I tucked my head low and kissed the muscular curve of his chest. I thought of one single statement that I knew would send Till scrambling. In a voice loud enough that he should have easily been able to make out, even without looking at me, I said, "I don't think we should be together." I lifted my head to catch his eyes with a questioning look. "Is that okay with you?"

His hazel eyes searched my face for the question as my own begged for a reaction to my false statement. All the while, I prayed that I was wrong.

"Yeah. That's fine," he soothed with a smile that splintered my heart.

My chin began to quiver. I didn't care if Till Page went blind, deaf, mute, and dumb—but I knew *he* cared. I rolled over so he wouldn't see me cry the tears he wouldn't understand. With as many black eyes as I had broken ribs, I sobbed for the man whose strong arms held me safely tucked against his chest.

"Shhhh. I've got you. I swear on my life, Eliza. I'll never let anyone hurt you again," he whispered into my hair.

The day had been exhausting, and within minutes, the talking was done and sleep overtook us both. Till held me painfully tight, but I never once moved away. I needed to feel him as much has he needed to hold me.

"Till! Oh my God! Get up! It's seven. You're late for work."

"Mmm," is all he said as he flipped over onto his stomach.

"Get. Up!" I hit his back. "You didn't set the alarm."

"I'm not going to work today."

"Are you fucking nuts? Get up! You don't get paid if you don't go to work." I sat up and my entire body screamed. I felt nauseated, from the pain as my ribs revolted. "Oh, God."

"What the hell are you doing? Get back in bed." Till was suddenly on his feet and shifting my legs back under the covers.

"I was gonna make you some coffee. You have to go to work." I groaned, holding my stomach.

The pain ebbed as I reclined onto my back. As long as I didn't move, nothing hurt. I was about to take up permanent residence in Till's bed. I could think of worse places to live though.

"Just be still. I'll make you some breakfast. You're good with ramen, right?" He smiled a teasing grin.

"You don't have time to make me breakfast, and especially not ramen. You have to go to work!"

"I told you I'm not going to work today. So just relax and let me take care of you." He put his hands on his hips, but his eyes were dancing with excitement.

"You can't miss work. And why are you looking at me like that?"

"'Cause I have a secret," he said proudly.

"Is it that you won the lottery? Because I will repeat: you don't get paid if you don't go to work."

"I'm quitting my jobs."

"Okay, I'm having you committed. Maybe it's too many punches to the head or something, but you have definitely lost your mind."

He barked out a laugh. "Nope. I got a new job." His smile was so wide that I worried his lips wouldn't be able to handle the stress.

"Um, what kind of new job?" I asked suspiciously.

"It pays double what I was making before. The boss is a good guy, although he can be a real asshole sometimes. It's not far from here, so I'll be able to save on gas money. Oh, and you're off duty for taking the boys to the gym in the mornings."

"It pays double?"

"Eight hundred a week." He continued with the weird smile and evasive answers.

"Stop screwing with me. What the hell kind of job is this?"

He seemed to be enjoying my frustration, but he finally spilled it. "Slate's gonna bankroll me so I can go pro."

"What?" I breathed in shock.

Somehow, Till's smile grew impossibly wider.

"Shut up. Are you serious?"

"Yep." The pride on his face as he answered with that one syllable was something I'd never seen him wear, but God, it fit him.

"Holy shit! Till, you're gonna be a professional boxer!" I squealed, and he started laughing. "I want to hug you so bad right now, but I'm too afraid to move."

The tears welled in my eyes, but for the first time in a long while, they were because I was *truly* happy. After years of busting his ass, Till was finally getting something he wanted. And it was huge.

"Get over here and hug me!" I demanded.

"Okay, okay. If you insist." He crawled back into bed and gently wrapped his arms around me.

"You're going to be amazing! I know it."

"God, I hope so. Slate gave me the week off and said he'd send the contracts and my first check over today." He kissed the unmarred corner of my mouth. "Let me take you out to dinner tonight. It will be like our first real date. Oh, hey. You want to get married? My new job has health insurance too."

My heart stopped. I died. Croaked. Kicked the bucket. Bought the farm. All of it.

The amount of times I had dreamed of Till Page asking me to marry him, by all accounts, should have been embarrassing, but never once in my numerous dreams was the proposal ever followed by, "My new job has health insurance."

"Um, did you just ask if I wanted to get married . . . so I could use your health insurance?"

"I asked you out on a date too. Don't forget about that."

"Okay, so I'm going to give you a little warning that will probably benefit you greatly in the future." I painfully rolled to face him. "If you *ever* ask if I want to get married and it's not followed by 'because I love you eternally' or 'I can't breathe without you,' or hell, I will take 'because your body has ruined me for all others'."

He chuckled, and I arched an eyebrow that quickly silenced him.

"I will have the freckle from under my boob permanently removed."

His smile quickly went flat. "You wouldn't!" he hissed.

"Wanna bet?"

He narrowed his eyes, and I narrowed mine right back. The staredown was short-lived because he broke it with a kiss.

A gentle yet still toe-curling kiss.

"Okay. Point taken. However, just so you know, I do love you eternally." He kissed me. "And I can't breathe without you." He kissed me again. "And your body has most definitely ruined me for all others." He squeezed my butt. "And one day, I'll be serious when I ask you to marry me. So start practicing your yes, and let me take you out tonight." He kissed me again, slipping his tongue into my mouth.

"No," I answered when he pulled away.

"No? Well, there's no way I'll ever propose with you throwing *no* around all willy-nilly."

I laughed. "Till, I can't even get out of bed. Much less go out to dinner. I'm sure I look like hell. Let's order celebratory Chinese food and rent a movie. Then save the date for when I can properly sex you up afterwards."

"On the first date?" he mocked in shock.

Just as I was about to give him a detailed explanation of what he could expect after that first date, there was a knock at the door, which was quickly followed by Quarry's agitated voice.

"Till! Wake up! You're late for work."

"Should we mess with them for a little while—tell them I got fired?"

"Oh my God, that's mean!" I slapped his chest, but I couldn't say no to the excitement dancing in his eyes. "Okay, but just for a few minutes."

"I'll get a real job," Flint announced as he paced around the room. "I can quit the gym and start working full time after school."

"Me too," Quarry agreed from his place at the edge of the bed.

"I just don't get why they would fire you. You've never been late before." Flint began chewing on his thumbnail as someone knocked at the front door.

"I'll get it." Till flew off the bed, leaving me with the fallout from his cruel joke.

I felt horrible watching them stress about how to keep the rent paid. "He didn't get fired. He's messing with you," I announced after he walked out of the room.

"That asshole!" Flint gritted out with a mixture of relief and anger.

"Pretty much."

"Son of a bitch!" Quarry shouted, rising to his feet.

Flint pushed a hand against his chest and shoved him back down just as Till rejoined us.

"So listen, Till. I know this is a little unconventional, and I didn't want to tell you, but given the current circumstances, I think I have a solution." Flint said.

"Oh yeah. What's that?" Till bit his lip to fight back a smile as he settled back on the bed, tearing a large, manila envelope open.

"I made, like, two hundred bucks stripping for this bachelorette party last weekend. I lied about my age, but those old women loved that I was young. One even offered me an extra hundred to take it all off. You should have seen her eyes when I did. I could do it, like, once a weekend. My body could pay our rent."

I had to give it to Flint. His face was so serious. I knew he was screwing around, but I'd almost bought into his story.

"Excuse me?" Till dropped the envelope.

Quarry joined the fun. "Hey! I could be your bouncer!"

I thought Till's eyes were about to pop out of his head.

"You did what?" Till took an angry step toward him.

A smile spread on Flint's face as he said, "Your jokes suck."

Till let out a relieved breath. "Your body will pay the rent?" he mocked as he pulled Flint into a headlock. "We'd be homeless in no time if I counted on that."

For a full ten minutes, they wrestled on the floor while Quarry acted as the ref.

God it felt good to have them back.

When Flint finally tapped out, Till climbed back into bed beside me.

"All right, so I didn't get fired. But I did get a new job." He threw his arm around my shoulders and puffed his chest in pride. "Slate's bankrolling my transition to pro."

Flint's eyes jumped to mine for validation that this wasn't another one of Till's jokes. When I gave him a nod, his jaw slacked open.

"Shut up," he breathed.

Quarry did what Quarry always did. He let out a curse. "No. Fucking. Way."

Till didn't even bother to scold him as he responded, "Way."

"Seriously?" Flint asked, still in disbelief.

"You're a professional boxer!" Quarry shouted, jumping up on the bed.

"Oh, God!" I cried out as my body shifted with the bounce.

Flint swiftly plucked him off the bed by the back of his shirt.

"Sorry," Quarry said sheepishly.

Till's hands patted over me as if he were inspecting for new wounds. "You okay?"

"Yeah. I'm fine. Don't worry about it, Q. Go back to the boxing thing," I encouraged even as my ribs throbbed.

"Right." Till stared at me, uneasy, but he dragged his attention back to the boys. "So things are gonna change around here. I'm gonna be busy, but my hours should at least be more predictable. Hopefully, I can swing it so I can work out while you guys are in school. Then I can help you in the afternoons. The other good news is Slate doubled what I was making before. So, Flint, I want you to keep whatever you make at the gym from now on, and, Q, I want to start giving you an allowance for helping out around the house."

"Sweet!" Quarry pumped his fist.

"Oh, and Eliza's moving in."

"What?" I shouted, sitting up and immediately regretting it. "Shit!" I hissed, collapsing back against the pillows.

"See? She's ecstatic about it." Till slid an arm under my shoulders and gently dragged me back into his side.

"When exactly did we decide that I'm moving in?"

"Oh, good idea! She can cook for us all the time now," Quarry announced.

"Yep. And she hates your nasty-ass ramen too, so at least I'd have reinforcements in that department," Flint added.

"Okay, then. It's settled. We'll move her stuff next weekend."

"What the hell just happened? I did *not* agree to move in with you. Last week, you were telling me how we couldn't be together, and now, you want me to move in?"

"Don't give me that look. You told me forever." He smirked.

"Well, what if it doesn't work out? I'll end up homeless!" I snipped back, but waves of warmth were crashing in my chest. I'd fought so hard for so long to get him to take a chance, and there he was, jumping all in.

"What kind of asshole do you think I am, Eliza? I'd never let you be homeless." He looked hurt, and I instantly felt guilty. "I'd at least let you sleep on the couch," he teased.

"How about we just chill and let things play out for a little while. There's no rush, Till. I'm not going anywhere."

"Then why wait? You're the one who pointed out that we're basically married. And after that shit last night, there is not a chance in hell you will ever sleep alone again. I've got the boys, so it makes more sense for you to move in with us."

"Is this about you wanting to live together or you worrying about me? Because if this is about my safety, then I'll pass."

"Why can't it be both? Yeah, I'd kinda like to know you're safe every night. But I also love you and want to spend as much time with you as possible. Why are you even arguing about this? Word on the street is that you're pretty obsessed with me." His lips lifted in my favorite way.

"Obsessed? I'm not the one who has spent the last eight years climbing through windows. If there is a stalker among us, it's most definitely you."

"I don't stalk. I keep tabs." He winked.

While I didn't get his stupid joke in the least, I still laughed with both arms holding my stomach. I looked up, and Flint and Quarry's eyes were still asking the question they were all waiting for the answer to.

"What happens if I say no?" I asked Flint.

"It would be unfortunate. But your belongings have already been scheduled for relocation." He cracked his knuckles. "Welcome home, Eliza." He gave a grand gesture around the room.

"So, what do you say?" Till tilted my head back and stared deep into my eyes.

"I think it's too soon."

"Quarry, you're up!" he called out, never dragging his gaze away from mine.

"Puh, puh, please, Eliza. We're hungry," Quarry exaggerated, full-on batting his long, black lashes.

Till bit his lip to stifle a laugh, but Flint let it fly freely.

I rolled my eyes. "You're moving my stuff regardless of what my answer is, right?"

"Yep."

"Absolutely."

"Hell yeah."

I once again rolled my eyes, but an impossibly wide smile gave me away.

"She's in!" Till declared.

He wasn't wrong.

23

Till

\FOR THOSE FIRST FEW WEEKS after Eliza moved in, I was a nervous wreck pretty much every minute of every day. I waited for her to disappear, proving my theory that she had no business in reality. But each morning as she woke up in my arms, I slowly started to believe that I could possibly have it all.

On the surface, things went right back to the way they always had been between us. Except, instead of sneaking in her bedroom window, I was sneaking into her shower. I couldn't get enough of her. After years of fighting my constant desire to be with her, I couldn't keep my hands off her. She must have felt the same way, because if I was within her reach, she was touching me too. Her body was healing, but she still offered it to me—and I took it every fucking time.

Derrick Bailey was officially removed from our lives. He had been arrested and found guilty of assault. Not even dear old daddy had been able to get him off the hook, and lord knows he tried. Thanks to Slate speaking at his sentencing, his punishment was rather lengthy. It still didn't feel like enough for what he had done to my Eliza, but I breathed easy every night knowing he could never touch her again—not as long as she slept at my side.

After my week off to help Eliza heal, I formally began professional boxing at On The Ropes. Slate wouldn't schedule my first fight until he felt I was ready, and if the way he was training me was any indication, he had been right in holding me back. I was struggling to keep up with the unbelievable regimen he'd created for me. I'd worked hard my entire life, but this was something else completely. By the time I got home from the gym each night, I could barely keep my eyes open. But every day, as I stared up at that painting on the wall, I knew it would be worth it. He couldn't work me hard enough to erase the image I had of someone painting my name into that blank. I was hell-bent on making it happen.

Home of

Till Page

On The Ropes'

First World Champion

With the new paycheck, things loosened up around the Page house. We weren't wealthy by any stretch of the imagination, but for a crew of kids who truly knew what it meant to be *broke,* it sure felt that way. Especially on occasions when we could afford to actually celebrate.

"Happy birthday, Quarry!" Eliza clapped as the waiter brought plates for the cake she'd spent half the day baking.

"Eleven feels pretty good." He rubbed his stomach, sliding down to recline in the booth.

Flint laughed beside him as he polished off his burger.

"I'm serious. I could get used to this life." Q dragged his finger across the side of the cake, scooping off the frosting and shoving it into his mouth.

"So I was thinking. What about Till 'The Terminator' Page?" I asked.

"Lame!" Eliza and Flint vetoed.

"Hey. I kinda like that."

"Thank you, Q!"

We high-fived over the table.

My new boxing nickname had been the hot topic of conversation over the previous few weeks. Slate had put a special clause at the end of my boxing contract stating that, "Till 'The Kill' Page" wasn't cool enough." Yes. He'd actually used that exact sentence in a legally binding document. He'd thought that it was pretty funny, but when I'd asked if he was kidding, he'd answered with a resounding no.

We couldn't decide on anything. It felt like all the good ones had already been used or just didn't fit. Earlier that afternoon, Slate had informed me that my new name was due by the next day or I was fired for breach of contract. He'd said it with a smile, so I doubted that he was serious, but I'd decided to play it safe just in case.

"Vicious Fury?" Flint suggested then popped a fry into his mouth.

"*Fists* of Fury!" Eliza shouted excitedly.

"Been used already, baby." I dropped my napkin on my plate and draped an arm around her shoulders. "The Whirlwind?"

Quarry vetoed that one. "Stupid."

"Okay, what about Till 'The Strong Will' Page," Eliza suggested as she began cutting the cake.

"Oh no." Flint threw his hands over his mouth, feigning fear. "You'll never beat Till Page, he has a . . . a"—his chin quivered dramatically—"strong will!"

We all busted out laughing. Well, everyone except Eliza. She threw a candle.

"Okay . . . how about Till 'The Lights Go Out' Page? Come on! You have to admit that's a good one!" Quarry exclaimed before shoveling chocolate cake into his mouth.

"Oh! I like the play on your name in that one," Eliza replied, passing me a slice.

I rubbed my chin, pretending to consider it. "Well, I love it. My only concern is what if I fight someone who isn't afraid of the dark like Q?"

"I'm not afraid of the dark!"

Even Eliza laughed that time. "The Fatal Kiss." She leaned up and gently pecked my lips.

It caused Quarry to make a gagging sound, Flint to yell, "Veto!"

and me to drop my hand into her lap. Her eyes went wide and her cheeks heated as I snuck it under the edge of her skirt.

"The Hell Greeter! You know, because of you and the whole purgatory thing." Quarry's eyes flashed to Eliza, who was biting her lip as she pried my hand from between her legs.

"I feel like *this* is purgatory," I mumbled. "Come on. Let's get out of here." I slid out of the booth, dragging her with me.

I threw an arm over her shoulders and the four of us walked to Eliza's car. I was *genuinely* happy for quite possibly the first time in my life. I'd just paid for my entire family to have dinner at a decent restaurant, and I hadn't had to save for six months to do it. I had a job I loved, Quarry had a birthday present waiting for him at home, and Eliza was going to end the night calling my name. Life was good.

And it made me *so* fucking paranoid.

"Hey, can you drive home?" Eliza handed me the keys.

"You okay?"

"I have an idea." She rose to her tiptoes and pressed her lips to mine, biting my bottom lip as she pulled away.

"Suddenly, I have ideas too." I looped an arm around her waist and rolled my hips into hers.

"Well, you need to get rid of those ideas," she whispered looking over her shoulder to where the boys were waiting by the car. "I'm on my period."

"Ah, yes. Natures very own cock block." I nodded before releasing a frustrated groan.

She giggled. "Yes, but it also means that I can start my birth control so we can get rid of the condoms." She lifted her eyebrows suggestively.

I sucked in a deep breath. "Oh, woman. Now you are speaking a language I understand." I grabbed both sides of her face and planted a hard closed mouth kiss to her lips.

"Let's go!" Flint yelled, grabbing our attention.

"Next weekend is the lock in at the gym. They will be gone for an entire night. You should rest up while you can." I winked as I walked away.

As we loaded into the car, she pulled a sketchpad out and went to work. I didn't recognize the movements as her pencils glided across the paper. I tried to peek over her shoulder at every red light we hit, but I was never able to catch a single glance. She was acting weird, and my heart raced while waiting for the sky to fall.

"You sure you're okay?" I squeezed her leg.

She glanced up with a warm smile. "I swear. I just wanted to draw something." She lifted my hand from her leg and kissed the palm, reading my nerves like a freaking book.

As soon as we walked through the front door, Eliza sat us all down.

"So," she started, but nothing followed for several seconds. "I'm not sure how you guys are going to feel about this, but I had an idea at the restaurant. I know this is kind of a touchy subject, but I don't really think ignoring it does anyone any good." She flipped the sketchpad over.

I blinked.

Flint gasped.

Quarry cursed.

She had drawn a pistol that appeared to be shooting an intricate sound wave, which eventually fell flat. Inside the spikes of the wave were the words "The Silencer" in block letters.

"Till, I don't mean to sound like a Debbie Downer, but every single day that passes, you fight to keep the silence at bay. I think it's only fair that your opponents should have to face The Silencer."

"Hell yeah!" Quarry flew to his feet.

Flint watched me closely for a reaction, but with one look at the paper, I was rendered speechless.

If I could have taken a step back, I would have realized that the logo she'd whipped up on a twenty-minute car ride home was just good and the nickname she'd picked was just catchy. But I couldn't do that at all. What she'd put on that paper was extraordinary to me.

It gave power to my flaws, purpose to my life sentence, and pride to my future in silence.

It was a symbol depicting who I was, drawn by the very hands that had made me who I was.

I mentally vowed that, from that moment on, I would always be "The Silencer" Till Page.

She nervously chewed on her lip as everyone in the room waited for me to speak. I stood up from the couch and walked over to where she was standing. After grabbing the sketchpad from her hand, I roughly tore off the top page.

"It was just an idea. Don't get mad," she said, starting to apologize.

"Oh, I'm furious," I responded, gripping the back of her neck. "You've been holding out on me. I had no idea you could draw anything but eyes."

She started to laugh, but I kissed her indecently.

I'd forgotten that the boys were in the room until I heard Quarry groan in disgust. I couldn't have given two shits who was watching though.

"I love it," I told her as she pulled away. "I'm giving this to Slate in the morning, and if he doesn't like it, I'm quitting."

"Okay, now, let's not get crazy here," she replied.

"So, that's the one?" Flint asked, snatching the paper from my hand.

I stared into Eliza's dark-blue eyes as I answered, "It is for me."

24

Eliza

Four months later . . .

"QUARRY, GET OUT OF THE car!"

"No." He pouted.

"You look fine!"

"I look like I pissed myself! There might be chicks in there."

"No. It looks like I hit the brakes, causing you to spill pop all over your lap. If the *chicks* ask, just blame it on me. Now, let's go."

Flint chuckled beside me.

"See! He's laughing!" Quarry exclaimed. "I'm not going in like this. Take me back home."

I sucked in a calming breath, but my nerves were shot. That night, "The Silencer" Till Page was set to make his debut in the professional boxing ring, and I was standing in the parking lot of a small, run-down arena on the outskirts of Chicago, arguing with an eleven-year-old drama king.

"It is a three-hour drive back to our apartment!" I looked over to Flint and threw my hands up in frustration.

He shook his head then dragged his royal-blue hoodie off and tossed it at Quarry with a smirk. "Put that on. It's big enough to cover your piss panties."

Quarry fumed as he pulled it on, but he finally got out of the freaking car.

As we entered the venue, it was obvious that the chattering crowd wasn't there because of Till. Every word I heard spoken was about Slate's big return to professional boxing. The venue had printed programs, and Slate's photo was at least three times the size of anyone else's. Till's was on the back.

It was packed with standing-room only, and even though it was the middle of fall in Chicago, it might as well have been a boiler room. Quarry was sweating his ass off inside that hoodie, but he refused to take it off.

"Leo!" Flint shouted from our reserved seats in the front row.

"'Sup, man." He leaned across a metal barricade to shake Flint's hand. "Hey, Eliza."

"I didn't know you guys were coming," I said, returning Leo's friendly hug.

"Are you kidding? We've been waiting a long time for this." He pointed up to the balcony, where Sarah and Erica were waving enthusiastically.

I tried to cover how touched I was that they were all there to support Till. "Thank you," I whispered to Leo as I returned their waves with both hands.

His eyes warmed as he watched me fight back tears. I was a mess. Even more than usual. It was such a huge moment for Till. I was entitled to be emotional.

"Did Liv come?" Quarry asked, jumping to his feet.

"Nah. She's not into the whole boxing thing. Whoa! Q, did you wet your pants?" He started laughing as he looked down at where the hoodie had ridden up.

"No! Eliza made me spill pop. I swear!"

Flint laughed hysterically beside him.

"Right." Leo winked. "Fight's about to start. I'm handling Slate's security tonight, so let me know if you have any problems."

"Thanks," I replied.

He glanced back down at Quarry's pants and chuckled to himself as he walked away.

Just as Leo disappeared around the corner, the arena went crazy. We were all looking around to figure out what we were missing when the crowd started chanting, "Slate." Even through the chaos, I spotted Till the second they started toward the ring. I wasn't even sure the fans in attendance even realized he was there at all.

But I did.

Wearing a red robe with the logo I had drawn sewn across the back, I watched "The Silencer" Till Page crawl through the ropes. Staggering pride forced tears to my eyes. Flint must have seen it, because he tossed an arm around my shoulders and pulled me up against his side. However, judging by their faces, both boys were just as overwhelmed by that moment as I was. Their big brother was a professional boxer, and even if it was only that one fight, he'd made it big time in their eyes.

Four rounds later, Till won his very first fight by unanimous decision.

"How much money did you make?" Quarry asked Till when we made it to the dingy locker room after the fight.

"He didn't make anything," Slate answered. "But I made six hundred bucks." He waggled his eyebrows.

"You didn't make *anything?*"

"Nope. I don't get money until I make more than what Slate pays me every month."

"Well, that blows!" Quarry exclaimed.

Slate began cutting the tape off Till's hands. "All right, so I talked to a few of the promoters before the fight. I got you set up for three more four-round fights. Once every thirty days. Hundred and fifty bucks per round. You good with that?"

"Yeah. Definitely," Till answered quickly.

"After that, we can move up to six-rounders and hopefully get you in the ring with some decent opponents with a larger purse."

"What happened to that possible fight in New York you mentioned the other day?"

"Well, he was willing to take a chance on you as long as I did a fucking meet and greet before the fight. I hung up on him." Slate paused uncomfortably. "Listen, I'm sorry about that bullshit on the way to the ring. This is part of the reason I always hesitated to come back as a trainer. Eventually, the novelty of me being back in the business will wear off and people won't even notice I'm there anymore, but for the next few months, I worry that it might just be the way things go."

"It's okay. I don't mind," Till answered. "Really. It doesn't bother me. You forget that I'm a Slate Andrews fan too. Well, I was . . . until you almost killed me by forcing me around the track in jeans." He gave Slate a one-sided smile I recognized as genuine.

"So, when does Till get to the big money? I refuse to believe that Erica has a bodyguard and you made six hundred bucks a fight," Quarry asked, hopping up onto the table next to Till.

Slate laughed, shaking his head. "I guess that all depends on who he fights. Who he beats. Who he *loses* to. I'm gonna do my job and get him the fights. The rest is up to Till."

"So, he gets paid per round? What about if he knocks someone out?" Flint asked from the corner.

"Promoters want a good show so they can sell tickets. Knockouts are nice, but what keeps people happy is feeling like they got their money's worth. So the opening fights get paid per round. After that, you get paid based on your contract that's negotiated in advance. Win or lose. Decision or TKO, it doesn't matter at that point. The established fighter makes majority of the money, and the opponent makes significantly less."

"Wait . . . what?" Flint stepped closer. "Even if he wins, he still gets paid less money? Shouldn't the loser make significantly less?"

"It doesn't work like that. See, the goal is to become the champ. It's not just the prestige. There are a lot of zeros on the back of that belt that keep people in that ring."

Till tilted his head in confusion. "Why'd you retire when you had the title, then? You must have been making a ton of money as the six-time defending world champion. Why not stick with it until you lost?"

Slate shrugged. "I guess I was just done."

Till barked a laugh, and Slate's eyes turned serious.

"I remember when I won my first pro fight. It was pretty much exactly like things happened for you tonight. I was so pumped up as I walked out of that arena, but then, when I got home, I hit a low. I sat and stared at that envelope full of cash for hours. I was afraid to even touch it. I was convinced that it was all I'd get. For several months, I just let them stack up in a drawer. The promise of money is what drove me in the sport.

"The point is I've been where you are, so I know exactly how ridiculous this statement is going to sound. But I hope that, one day, you will understand that money is only as important as what it gives you. I'm not talking about sports cars or big houses. I'm talking about peace of mind. When I walked away from boxing, I turned down a rematch that would have earned me over sixty million."

"Holy shit!" I heard myself cuss, and it was joined by similar sentiments from everyone in the room.

"For me, money lost its value the day I met Erica. It couldn't buy me time with her. I had more than enough to live comfortably, and that was all I ever really wanted. So I quit. The incentive was no longer worth the sacrifice."

We were all silent for several seconds before the room erupted in chaos.

"You turned down sixty million dollars for a girl!"

"You have got to be kidding!"

"No way! What is wrong with you?"

"Sixty million *dollars* or pesos?"

Slate just laughed.

"You should never tell that story again," Till informed him, making Slate laugh even louder.

"Worst story ever!" Flint declared. "You know what lesson I learned from that story? Till needs to break up with Eliza—stat."

"Hey!" I objected.

"Yeah. I agree." Quarry jumped off the table and faced Till. "If you had sixty million, you could hire her to sleep with you."

Till slapped a hand over his mouth, but his laugh was no less muffled.

My mouth gaped open before I shouted, "I am *not* a hooker!"

"Of course not!" Flint rubbed my shoulder soothingly before he added, "We'd still expect you to cook for us. Hookers don't cook." He winked.

"How the hell do you know what hookers do?" I bit back.

The whole room was rolling with laughter at this point, and I couldn't help but join them.

Till made his way over and wrapped me in his arms. "Okay. Okay. Nobody's getting rid of Eliza. I can make sixty million *and* keep her." He continued to laugh even as he kissed the top of my head.

"Gee. Thanks."

And that was the way we worked. We picked on each other relentlessly and laughed unabashedly. They fought. I refereed. It was perfect, really.

We were a family.

25

Till

One year later . . .

"THE SILENCER IS IN THE house!" I heard called as I walked into the gym.

Quarry laughed as he took off toward the before-school program he had long since grown to love.

I had quickly become a small-time big deal around the gym.

With over seven fights under my belt, I was making my way up the ladder. The fights were getting larger, and I was loving it. By the end of the first year, I had banked over fifteen grand on top of what Slate paid me weekly. I'd dropped it all in a savings account and refused to touch it. I had never felt more stable and secure in my life. Just knowing it was there calmed the anxiety I hadn't even known I was harboring.

Eliza was finishing up her last semester in college and had started looking for accounting positions. She said that she was excited about getting a *real* job, but I knew she was dreading spending her days poring over numbers instead of sketchpads. After a civil case with Derrick Bailey paid off her student loans, I refused to allow her to take out anymore. I was in it forever with Eliza, and the last thing I wanted was to start it out with a load of debt.

God, we fought about money, but not like most couples. It was never because we didn't have enough or one was spending too much. It was always about who got to pay the bills. I was making decent money and hell-bent on taking care of her the way I had always dreamed about. And well, Eliza didn't like feeling like a freeloader being taken care of. I loved those fights. Her nipples would get all hard as I yelled about how much I loved providing for her. Then she would stomp her foot and declare that she wanted to split the bills. Which caused my cock to get hard . . . which caused her eyes to heat as they drifted down to my pants . . . which caused me get so hot that I was *forced* to remove my shirt . . . which caused her to lick her lips . . . which caused me to rush forward and fuck her on the closest horizontal surface I could find. Really, it was a vicious cycle.

"Page, get in here!" Slate yelled from his office.

"What's up?" I asked, settling into the chair across from his desk.

"You and Quarry go to the doctor yesterday?"

"Yeah. I'm good. He's not sure why it comes and goes sometimes. I tested at around seventy percent still."

"And what about Quarry?"

"He's still sitting at eighty percent. No real change."

"That's good fucking news." He stood up, walked to the door, and pushed it shut before drawing the shades that covered his large, glass windows into the gym.

My curiosity grew, because up until that moment, I hadn't known that those shades were even functional.

"All right. Now, there's something else I need to talk to you about." He sat on the corner of the desk. "Clay Page has been calling the gym looking for you. Pretty much every day, we get a collect call from the prison."

"Fuck him," flew from my mouth.

"Right. Well, I've been keeping Quarry off phone duty. I don't want to put him in a position of having to hang up on his own dad if he happened to call."

"I appreciate that."

"Well, just so you know, I'll be contacting the prison to put a halt to that shit. I run a business. I don't need inmates blowing up my phones."

"I couldn't agree with you more." I pushed to my feet, ready to work off some steam.

"Where you going? Sit back down, I'm not done yet."

"Please tell me there's not more," I huffed, flopping back down onto the chair.

"Change of plans on your fight this weekend. Summers got hurt and they can't find anyone to replace him on such short notice. Your fight got dropped from the card."

"Son of a bitch!" I boomed, jumping to my feet. "That was a big fight." I started to pace. "Are we rescheduling?"

"Nope." He smiled in amusement.

"Why the hell not?"

"You're too busy." His smile grew.

"Um, no. No. I'm not. That was twenty-five grand. I'm pretty sure my schedule is wide-ass open."

"I got you a new fight for Saturday night," he announced, and I suddenly understood the smile.

"With who?"

"Oh, you know . . . some guy you've probably never heard of named Larry Lacy."

"Shut the fuck up!" I breathed, taking a giant step toward him. "Former heavyweight champ Larry Lacy?"

"Oh, so you have heard of him." He joked as I started to bounce on my toes. "Well, don't get too excited. It's not a pay-per-view or anything. This tiny, unknown network is actually televising it. Shit. I can't even remember the name." He rubbed his chin.

I knew he was fucking with me . . . hard. He was almost as excited as I was.

"I think it was called . . . ESPN."

I froze. "No. Fucking. Way."

"Eight rounds. Fifty K. Philadelphia. Saturday night."

"I swear to God you better not be fucking with me right now."

He started laughing as he handed me a manila folder. "Lacy's just out of a yearlong stint in rehab and trying to make a comeback. He was supposed to be going against Pryor, but he pulled out yesterday for reasons that were not disclosed to me. And quite honestly, I didn't care enough to ask."

I flipped through the pages of the contract, and sure as shit, everything was there in black ink. My eyes homed in on the four zeros on the second page.

Fifty thousand dollars.

"Holy shit. This is incredible." My heart was banging around in my chest.

"This is a big break for your career. The sheer amount of promoters who will be watching this fight is going to be ridiculous. Everyone is dying to see what Lacy can do now that he's sober, but I want them to leave that arena talking about Till Page."

"Hell yeah," I whispered.

"Now sign that shit and get in the ring. We need to develop a new strategy for Lacy."

As I pushed to my feet, I swear my whole body was numb.

"Thanks, Slate," I called out as I left his office. As I headed down the hallway, I bypassed the main locker room and made my way to one of the dressing rooms in the back. I needed to make a phone call.

"Holy shit. I literally just thought about making twice-baked potatoes for dinner and you called me. That is some kind of serious obsession, Till." Eliza laughed.

"I'm going to be on ESPN," I rushed out, and her laughter stopped. "What?"

My hands were shaking as the shock and exhilaration threatened to overtake me. "Slate got me a fight on ESPN. Fifty thousand dollars." I broke out in manic laughter. "Oh my God, Doodle. This is so fucking huge."

"Wait. When?"

"This weekend!" I yelled as I bounced around the dressing room like a kid on Christmas morning, throwing fist pumps in the most non-badass way possible.

"Shut up!" she screeched into my ear.

I knew Eliza, and I bet she was throwing a few fist pumps of her own.

"Till! That's amazing! Congrats!"

"There is a really good chance my chest is going to explode before I make it home today." I continued to pace around the room.

"Ew. No exploding. So, are you good freaking out or bad freaking out?"

"I honestly don't know. I'm not nervous about the fight, so I guess maybe the good kind? Hell, I don't know. I don't get to good freak out enough to know the difference." I laughed, but it wasn't a joke.

"This sounds like a really good thing, Till. Don't muddle it all up."

I could hear the warmth in her voice, and it calmed me immediately.

"I love you," I said quietly, even though it deserved more emphasis than I could ever give with words alone.

"I love you too. I'm really proud of you. "

I breathed a content sigh. "I have no idea what I would do without you."

She giggled. "You'd probably be emaciated from your all-ramen diet and stuck hanging out of the third-story window."

"Why the third story?"

"'Cause if we ever break up, the boys decided they want to live with me. They told me they liked me better than you." She giggled. "And I lived downstairs for enough of their one a.m. Royal Rumbles to know I'd want my bedroom on the third floor this time."

I grinned as I sank down on the bench. "Wow. This sounds like a big house, moneybags."

"Yeah. My boyfriend was a big-time heavyweight boxer. He bought it for me."

"Jesus. I want to do that," I whispered.

Suddenly, her laughter disappeared. "I don't need that, Till. I was only joking around."

"I know you don't, but I'm going to give it to you anyway."

"I just need you. It doesn't matter where we are."

It was a sweet sentiment that anyone could recognize, but to me, it was everything.

She was everything.

I cleared my throat to cover the intense emotion and then changed the subject. "You're right. This is a good freak out."

"I'm always right." She laughed, and it eased my entire world.

"So I've been told."

"What time are you coming home?"

"Probably late. New fight needs a new plan."

"Okay. I'll see you then." She paused. "I might even be naked when you get here."

I let out a groan. "Mmm . . . I love the way you think. Now, talk dirty to me and tell me you'll be holding a plate of twice-baked pota-toes."

She burst out laughing, and my lips split into a smile. I listened for a while, savoring the sound.

Finally, she got quiet again. "I love you, Till."

"I love you too. I'll see you tonight." After a quick goodbye, she hung up, but I was left staring at my phone for several minutes.

I'd just gotten a fifty-thousand-dollar fight that would be televised for the entire world to see. Yet, somehow . . . it wasn't even the best part of my day.

I sucked in a deep breath.

Yeah. I was definitely going to be late that night. It was time to tap into my savings account . . . and hit the hardware store.

Eliza

Me: The boys are spending the night out.

I sent the message the moment I saw the headlights of Till's truck pull into our parking lot. Then I sprinted to the bedroom and counted to ten.

Me: Twice-baked potatoes. Check.

I sent him a picture of a plate filled with them and then counted to twenty as I settled onto the bed.

Me: Naked. Check.

I snapped a quick selfie of my breasts, making sure that Till's fa-vorite freckle had made it into the picture. Laughing, I pressed send.

Then I screamed at the top of my lungs as I saw his face lit by the glow of his phone outside our window.

"Fuuuck," he groaned, still staring at the phone even as I freaked out on the other side of the glass.

"Shit! What are you doing?" I asked as I pried the window open.

"I'm saving that picture for my home screen." He finally looked up at me.

"Why exactly are you doing it on a ladder?"

"Oh, this? It's nothing. Life was just feeling too real today. I wanted a little fantasy." His gaze raked down my nude body. "And clearly, I've come to the right window."

His eyes were playful, but it still concerned me that he was climbing through a second-story window.

"Till . . ." I started.

"So I have a theory." He leaned on his elbows, popping his head through the opening. "That night when you pushed me out of your door, I had originally come in the window. So what if the life we have been living ever since then is like a fantasy within a fantasy?"

My stomach twisted.

"You have to admit. It's been pretty amazing." He smiled.

Something wasn't right with him. I could feel it, and it scared me to death. I reached out to touch him, but he caught my hand in midair and pressed his lips to my palm.

"See, windows have never let me down before. And this might just be the biggest fantasy of them all. I needed every bit of help I could get tonight." He placed a small, black box on the windowsill. "Marry me, Eliza."

I sucked in a deep breath as tears flooded my eyes. Suddenly, I wasn't sure whose fantasy we were in at all, because Till Page offering me forever had always been mine.

"Till . . ." I stared into his eyes. "Are you serious?"

"Completely. I love you, Doodle. Forever, remember?"

Fully naked, I launched myself at the window. Till was barely able to stay on the ladder as I assaulted his mouth. The ring, which I still hadn't seen, fell to the floor—thankfully on the inside. My tongue rolled in his mouth as my hands threaded into his hair. With one arm secured around my waist, he deepened the kiss as he crawled all the way inside. My feet were lifted off the ground as he walked us to the bed. I dangled in his arms, but I had never in my life felt more grounded.

"Is that a yes?" he asked as he dropped me on the bed and tore the shirt over his head.

"I would have said yes at thirteen." I dragged his mouth back down with the frenzied need to feel him again, but his mouth alone wasn't enough. I remembered his words from all those years ago. "Take me.

Claim me for forever, Till."

With a growl, he stood off the bed and went to the window. Snagging the box off the floor, he said, "Not until you're wearing my ring."

Cracking the box open, he revealed a round diamond solitaire engagement ring. It was small and simple, nothing at all like the man who was proposing to me. It was, however, perfect.

He slid it onto my finger then let out a huge breath of relief.

"It's gorgeous." I rose to my knees, gliding my hands over his chiseled chest.

His eyes watched my ring finger slide over his skin. Mine watched his eyes heat.

"You've always been beautiful . . . but fuck, Eliza. You wearing my ring . . . marrying me . . . It's unbelievable." His eyes glistened with overwhelming emotion, but when I leaned forward to offer him a reassuring kiss, Till Page the man appeared.

His eyes grew dark. With one arm on the back of my neck, he swept my legs out from underneath me with the other. I landed on my back, and Till's mouth went to work biting and nipping my neck. His hands made fast work of removing his pants, and within seconds, he was buried inside me.

"You're gonna marry me," he repeated as he drove inside me.

It wasn't a question, but each time, I still answered, "Yes."

After a while, his hand dived between us, forcing my orgasm before I could even try to fight it off—the orgasm, not his hand. *Never his hand.*

As I came calling his name, Till emptied inside me with his own reverent words.

"My wife."

26

Till

I DIDN'T JUST BEAT LARRY Lacy. I knocked him out in the fifth round.

Slate had been right. There wasn't a person who left that arena who didn't know my name. I was featured on damn near every major sports network, newspaper, and magazine the next day. I might have been a relatively unknown fighter walking into that ring, but I'd walked out as the man of the hour.

I hated that Eliza hadn't been there to see it, but the boys couldn't miss any more school, so she'd stayed at home with them. Before I had even made it out of the ring, I'd been handed a phone with her screaming on the other end. The crowd was going nuts, but she was all I heard. We did a huge press conference the following day before heading home, and for the first time, even as celebrity Slate Andrews sat at my side, the attention was all mine. The fifty-thousand dollar paycheck was nice, although Lacy's was a hell of a lot bigger, but the excitement of that day was intoxicating.

All I could think about, though, was getting home and *really* celebrating.

"Stop!" Eliza batted my hands away.

"No, you stop. I missed you." I teased my way under her shirt and sealed my mouth over hers.

195

"The boys are still awake." She raked her nails over my back.

"Oh hell no. I'm not waiting for them to fall asleep! Quarry had enough Mountain Dew tonight that he may never sleep again. They know we have sex. They'll get over it." I pressed my hardening cock against her core, causing her to throw her head back with a gasp.

"That doesn't mean I want them to be able to tally how many times I come."

"Tally them? How the hell many times are you planning to get off, woman?"

She laughed, and with just the sound, my cock became impossibly harder. I bit her nipple to silence her, but it didn't work, because it turned into a moan that I swear I felt in my balls.

I needed to have her . . . and soon.

"We'll be quiet." I pushed into her panties, finding her clit before she could even object.

"I can't be quiet," she panted, sliding down the bed and out of my reach.

I dropped my head against the pillow. I was debating if it would be wrong for me to give Flint twenty bucks to take Quarry and go sit in my truck for a half hour when her tongue swirled around the head of my dick.

"Fuck," I hissed.

"You be quiet. I'll wake you up in a few hours and take mine. Consider it congratulatory head!"

Her lips formed the most perfect crescent shape as she smiled up at me. It was only outdone by the "O" they made as she sucked my cock to the back of her throat.

I awoke to Eliza's naked ass rubbing against me. After I'd come in her mouth, I'd begged her to let me return the favor, but she'd been hell-bent on waiting until the boys fell asleep. I had no idea how long it had been since we'd fallen asleep, but Flint and Quarry must have passed out, because the house was silent. I couldn't see her face, but she was quiet, the motion of her hips the only proof she wasn't still asleep. Or maybe she was and, even in sleep, her body was craving mine.

I grazed my teeth over her earlobe. "Mmm. Wake up, baby." I felt the vibration in my chest, but nothing came out.

What the fuck?

"Eliza," I called, hoping the outcome would be different, but once again, the silence was piercing.

She immediately rolled over to face me with wide eyes, but I couldn't focus on anything except my inability to speak.

"Eliza!" I shouted as if she could somehow make my voice work again.

I watched her tongue touch her teeth at what I knew to be the "11" at the end of my name, but she couldn't talk either.

It's a nightmare. *It has to be.*

"Doodle, are you okay?" I shouted as loud as I could, hoping to break through whatever unknown force was compressing the sound.

With a painful flinch, she covered my mouth with the palm of her hand. Her lips moved with powerful words, none of which made it to my ears.

I shook her hand off my mouth. "I can't talk!" I yelled, scrambling off the bed. I knocked over damn near everything in my frantic escape, but I didn't still until my ass was against the wall.

Fisting a hand into my hair, I watched the tears fall from her eyes as she mouthed what I decided was the word "stop" over and over again.

She climbed over the bed and snatched a sketchpad off the nightstand, quickly scrawling a message that would effectively end my life as I knew it.

I can hear you. Calm down.

The weight of such simple words was indescribable.

Eliza

His eyes were feral. Every single muscle on his body was taut, and the confusion was only slightly less painful than the utter destruction that crumbled his otherwise strong body the second he read my words.

"It's okay." My voice cracked as I slowly approached the skittish man I recognized as my rock. I wiped my tears away because I knew they would do no good. He didn't need those. He needed *me*.

He blinked rapidly as I soothed him with words he couldn't hear.

"Eliza?" he questioned loudly once more as realization sank in, causing tears to build in his eyes.

"Shh." I placed a finger over my mouth. It trembled wildly even though I desperately tried to keep it still. I didn't want him to see my anxiety, but I broke into sobs when he grabbed the back of my neck and pulled me against his chest.

Somehow, Till was suddenly deaf—and comforting *me*.

"Is everything okay?" Flint called from outside our door.

Stepping away, I dried my eyes and threw a pair of pants in Till's direction. "Get dressed," I told him before remembering that it was worthless. Then I grabbed the sketchpad off the floor.

Get dressed. We're going to the hospital.

"Eliza?" Flint said as he knocked.

"Yeah. Everything's good," I answered, pulling on my own clothes then opening the door.

"I heard Till yelling. Are you okay?" He looked around me to catch a glimpse of his brother, who was nervously fumbling with his shirt. His hands were shaking so violently that he couldn't quite pull it on. "What's wrong?"

Backing him out of the room, I whispered, "Listen, I have to take Till to the hospital. I need you to keep an eye on Q and call Slate for me."

He took a frightened step away. "Why? What's going on?"

"Um . . ." I stalled, trying to figure out what to say, but in the end, there was only one answer. "He can't hear anything. It's gonna be fine though. We just need to get him to a doctor."

"He can't hear *anything?*" Quarry asked in shock as he rounded the corner out of his room.

"Shit," I mumbled to myself.

Telling Flint was one thing. Quarry was something totally different.

"I don't know yet. It doesn't seem like it. Just call Slate. Tell him what's going on." I backed into the room and grabbed Till's hand.

His eyes were all over the place, but as we walked past the boys, he still managed to recognize Quarry's anxiety. He stopped long enough to lick his finger and stick it in Quarry's ear. His halfhearted attempt at teasing did nothing to quell his brother's fears. Quarry's chin quivered as he turned and marched away.

I drove to the hospital with my hand anchored on Till's thigh. Not a force in the world could have torn it away. It wasn't a possessive gesture like I had seen Till do so many times before. No. It was a plain and simple connection of love, and we both needed it.

Hand in hand, we were ushered to the back of the emergency room almost immediately. He sat on a stiff hospital bed with his head hung low. We had no idea what was going on, but I knew Till. I was positive he had entirely too many worst-case scenarios floating through his head. He needed a distraction. Reaching into my purse, I pulled out a notepad and pen.

Crawling into his lap, I kissed every inch of his face that my lips could reach. His chest heaved, but not in the sexual way I was accustomed to. Till was fighting back his own emotions. He didn't need me to witness that.

So I started drawing.

It wasn't much. Just a stick figure climbing through a window. But it seemed to help. I drew a woman on the other side and gave her huge boobs. Till looked up then, a small smile pulling at the side of his mouth. After snatching the pencil from my hand, he added a freckle under her right breast. I laughed, and his eyes snapped to mine. His gaze flashed to my mouth as he swallowed hard. But he eventually lost the battle.

Burying his face in my neck, Till lost it completely. He clung to me as his shoulders shook. I couldn't tell if any tears actually fell from his eyes, but his body was being ravaged. He would never admit it, but I thought he was more scared than upset. I felt helpless, but I held him as tight as possible and whispered encouraging words that would never be heard—those were for me.

A few seconds later, Slate walked into the room, and I threw up a hand to halt him. Till would have been mortified if the only man he considered a father witnessed his breakdown, no matter how understandable it might have been. Glancing down at Till in my arms, Slate nodded understandingly and backed out of the door.

Sucking in a deep breath, I decided the doomsday pity party needed to be over. It wasn't helping anyone. The fact was that, while I hated this for Till, it wasn't the end of the world. No one was dead or dying. Millions of people lived happy lives despite their inability to hear. Till was no different. We would be happy too.

I slid off his lap, and his red-rimmed eyes bounced to mine in question.

"No more," I announced very slowly so he could read my lips. I took my finger and poked into his chest. "You are okay." Then I moved it to my own chest. "I am okay." Then I motioned it between us. "We are okay." I grabbed the notebook and jotted down the words: *Nothing else matters.*

He stared at the pad for a few seconds, but eventually, his shoulders relaxed. A second later, they squared, and a second after that, Till was done with the pity party too. He lifted his head and took a deep breath. He was still pale and nervous as hell, but "The Silencer" Till Page had officially shown up to the fight.

His eyes fearlessly held mine, and I gave him a weak grin.

Lifting his hand, I kissed his palm. "I love you."

He responded with his mouth, but it wasn't in words.

He snaked a hand out, grabbing the back of my neck, and pulled me in for a hard, closemouthed kiss. As soon as he was done, he settled me back onto his lap, but this time, Till's strong arms were protectively holding *me,* not the other way around.

Slate's here, I wrote. *Do you want me to let him in?*

He nodded and allowed me off his lap. When I opened the room door, Slate was standing in the hall, talking on the phone.

"It's okay, Q. He's gonna be fine. I promise," he said, holding the back of his neck and pacing the hallway. "Look, Johnson is gonna be there in a few minutes. Let him in. He's gonna hang with you two until Till gets back. Nah, I know you don't need a babysitter. Just humor me." He shook his head and glanced up at me. "Hey, I gotta go, Eliza just came out. I'll keep you updated." He hung up and slid the phone back into his pocket. "How is he?"

"Better now."

"Can he hear anything?"

I had no answer besides to just shake my head.

"Shiiit," he breathed, raking a hand through his hair.

"He wants you to come in, but we're not grieving anymore, okay? It's fight time."

Slate smiled and squeezed my shoulder before using it to pull me into a side hug. "You're a good woman, Eliza."

"Thanks," I replied, but I embraced the moment of comfort and reassurance his hug provided—feelings that were usually reserved for the man on the other side of the door.

Slate walked into the room first and stopped in front of Till. Then he grabbed the notebook and pencil off the bed and began writing. Till motioned for me to rejoin him. As he kissed the top of my head, I resumed my position on his lap.

For a moment, I thought Slate was writing a novel. Finally, he passed the notebook back and then crossed his thick arms over his chest.

Just so we are on the same page about something, "The Silent Storm" is my nickname. I had it trademarked years ago. I have absolutely no problem suing you for everything you have if you try to steal that shit. No matter how fitting it may be for you now.

Till barked out a laugh as he finished.

Slate watched him warmly before saying, "You'll be fine."

Till nodded, once again refusing to speak.

It wasn't long before the doctor made his way into the room. They swooped Till away for what seemed like a million tests—it at least took

long enough to be a million. Slate stepped into the hall and spent most of the time on his phone while I sat awkwardly, alone, and in silence—just like Till. I cried even though I knew I was supposed to be fighting, but I was just so fucking numb.

Finally, they ushered us into an audiologist's office on the far side of the hospital. The fact that there was an audiologist in his office at three a.m. led me to believe that Slate had been busy calling more than just Quarry while he had been in the hall. Till settled in the chair next to me, taking hold of my hand to rest it on his thigh. I would have preferred to be back on his lap, but this was neither the time nor the place for comfort. This was the place for the truth about the future.

"Okay, Till is currently hearing at less than five percent." He looked at Till and pointed to the screen above his desk, where the words were forming as he spoke them.

"Will it come back?" I inquired hopefully.

"No. I'm fairly certain that it won't be coming back."

Till cleared his throat and cracked his neck as the doctor's prognosis appeared on the screen.

"Given your history, we didn't anticipate your hearing to disappear this suddenly. I've been told that you are a professional boxer, and while trauma can cause hearing loss, it's more likely your genetic condition that's the culprit here. However, like I told you, a cochlear implant is a great solution for your type of hearing loss."

"Wait. What?" I jumped from my chair.

The doctor glanced at Till before looking back at me.

"He's eligible for an implant? He could hear again?"

"Well, that part is up to Till. But yes, he is eligible."

Till shook his head and stood up, wrapping his arms around my shoulders. I wiggled out of his grasp as tears of joy sprang to my eyes.

"Oh my God, you'll be able to hear again!" I laughed, but he watched me blankly. "What?" I asked as my smile faded.

He grabbed a pen and paper off the doctor's desk. *No implant. It costs too much money.*

I snatched the paper from his hand. "You have insurance now," I spoke out loud as I wrote. Then I turned to the doctor and asked, "Insurance will cover the implant, right?"

"Well, yes. Most of it. However, it could still be quite costly. There are programs that can help patients who can't afford the procedure."

"It's not the money," Slate chimed in from behind me. "He knows I'd pay for it."

Till lifted the pen to write again, but I stole the paper before he had the chance.

"Talk," I demanded, and he narrowed his eyes at me. "Why won't you get the implant?"

He just shook his head, so I turned to the doctor.

"What's the catch here?"

"I'll step out for a minute so you all can discuss this alone." He walked from the room, leaving me even more confused and irritated than ever.

I took a deep breath and picked the paper up.

What is going on? What am I missing? You could hear again! This doesn't have to be permanent!!!!!!! I nearly broke the pen as I forcefully added each exclamation point.

Till's eyes flashed to Slate, who was looming behind me. I had no idea what the hell was going on, but I honestly didn't care. There was only one thing that mattered.

You're getting the implant, I scrawled definitively.

Till finally found his voice in the tone of an angry snarl. "No!"

"Why. Not?" I growled right back at him.

"Because he can't box anymore with the implant," Slate said, unleashing the venomous snake of truth into the room, before stalking out and slamming the door.

Oh. My. God.

You would rather fight than hear? I tilted my head, incredulous.

His answer was a shrug that apparently said it all.

The tension was thick as Eliza drove us home from the hospital. I could feel the anger radiating off her, but she didn't once leave my side. She did, however, put the pen and paper back in her purse, effectively end-ing any further conversation. She might not have communicated, but she'd held my hand when the doctor had come back in and scheduled a follow-up appointment for the next day. He'd filled a bag with books and pamphlets, including a schedule for sign language courses at the local community center.

It was so fucking surreal.

When we walked through the door to our apartment, the boys both jumped off the couch. Quarry's mouth was moving a million miles a minute, and just the sight wrenched my chest. Flint quickly elbowed him to make him shut up. They both stared at me, just as unsure of how to react as I was. So I tossed them a forced smile and headed to my room. I could see the concern in Flint's eyes as I passed him, so I reached out and punched him in the shoulder. It was playful and hard, but judging by his face, it wasn't comforting in the least.

Normal. I just needed things to feel normal even if they didn't sound it.

I flipped off the light and fell into bed. My mind was all over the place while trying to figure out how the hell I was going to function with my new existence. I was pissed at myself for not having prepared better for this day. I knew it was coming; I just hadn't expected it to be so soon.

After a half hour, I got bored of being alone and went to find Eliza. She was probably still mad at me, but I could live with that as long as she was at my side.

I found her sitting on the couch, surrounded on both sides. Flint sat on one side with his elbows on his knees and his head cradled in his hands as Eliza scratched his back. Quarry was on the other side tucked under her arm. His body was stiff as if he didn't want the physical sym-pathy, but his head was resting on her shoulder as if he'd never needed anything more. Tears were running from his eyes.

Jesus. *Quarry.* He had gotten so big recently that, sometimes, I for-got that he was still just a twelve-year-old kid who faced my same fate.

When I cleared my throat, they all looked up. Q immediately be-gan drying his eyes and looking away. I casually strolled over to the couch and ruffled his hair. He hated it when I did that, but this time, he didn't squirm. Using both hands, I signaled for them to part the sea and make room for me. Squeezing between Flint and Eliza, I tossed my arms over the back of the couch and roughly dragged them all in for a group hug. Their heads clinked together, and I was sure they all groaned, but I wanted to keep it light. However, those three seconds when my entire life was secure in my arms would be etched into my memory for all of eternity. Tomorrow didn't seem so scary when I was on that couch with them.

We sat uncomfortably squished together for several hours. As far as I knew, no one said anything. We were all lost in our own imagination of what the future would hold. The sun was starting to peek through the window when Eliza nudged me and pointed down to Q, who was asleep on her shoulder. I glanced over to Flint, who was also racked out, his head flopped back and his mouth hanging open. It was time to put the entire day to rest. I scooped Q off her lap then carried him to bed. Flint sleepily stumbled into the room after me, and Eliza leaned against the doorjamb, watching me toss the blankets over them both.

It wasn't picture perfect. Half of Flint's body hung off the twin-sized bed, and Quarry's head was twisted in a way that would cause him to be sore for a week. I was deaf, yet Eliza was still smiling.

It was all wrong.

But right then, it felt exactly right.

After quietly closing the door, I led her down the hall to our bedroom. We collapsed against the cool sheets, exhausted by the evening but miles away from being able to find any rest. I held her close as she doodled my eyes. Then I gave up watching the fluid movement of her hand across the paper and started watching her face.

Her eyes squinted with every curve, and her mouth twitched the moment she started the elongated strokes I knew to be my lashes. She never once glanced up to study my eyes; she knew them from memory.

My attention was drawn away when she lifted the pad into my line of sight.

Talk to me, she had drawn in big bubble letters across the paper.

I shook my head and then slid down to rest on the pillow, facing her.

He's afraid.

I grabbed the pencil from her hand. *Who?*

I started to hand it back, but she grabbed another off the nightstand. *Quarry,* she wrote.

He'll be okay.

Not if you shut down, he won't. She gave me an impatient look.

I couldn't say that she was wrong. Hell, I knew she was right, even though I wanted to pretend she wasn't.

I'll try.

Then talk to me.

"Please," she mouthed. Her chin quivered, and her nostrils flared.

Jesus, she was fighting hard, which was everything I absolutely *wasn't* doing.

I opened my mouth, but not a single sound came out—at least not to my ears.

"Do I sound weird? Like a deaf person?"

She gave me a huge smile that made sounding ridiculous completely worth it. Tears pooled in her eyes as she quickly shook her head and said, "No." In big letters, she wrote, *You still sound like MY Till. But you were always weird, so maybe the answer should be yes.*

I watched as her mouth opened and her chest shook with laughter. It damn near killed me to know that I was missing the sound that should have accompanied it.

You need to talk to them tomorrow. Show them that it's still you.

"Okay."

But maybe quieter. You're yelling.

"Shit. Sorry," I replied, trying to speak softly even though I had no idea how to gauge my volume.

Better. She smiled. *Now talk to me about why you won't get the implant.*

I guess there was no beating around the bush.

"Doodle, I don't know. I have to fight. I don't have anything outside of that ring."

That's not true at all and you know it. You have me and the boys.

"That's exactly it! I *have* you and the boys. And I finally found something I can make enough money at to provide for all of you. I'm not giving that up. I can't! I just *can't!*" I was sure I was yelling, but I couldn't stop.

Two days ago, I'd made fifty grand in fifteen minutes That was more than I'd made in two years working my ass off. I couldn't go back to the struggle just to keep food on the table—not even to hear again.

I'm not asking you to give it up, Till. I just want to understand your reasons. I didn't even know the implant was a possibility until today. You never talk to me about this stuff.

"I only found out a few years ago—back when I'd *never* have been able to come up with the money for it. But honestly, I don't want to think about it, Eliza. Not with you."

Fantasy?

"It's kinda my thing." I smiled sheepishly.

Her mouth began to move, and I just blinked at her. I watched her bite out the word, "Shit," before going back to the paper.

How about you just make us your thing?

"I can do that. But I can't get that implant," I announced again.

She bit her lip and rolled away.

"Look at me." I flipped her back over, and the expected tears were already present.

"Did you know that Slate thinks he can get me a fight in a few months for double what I made the other night? That's a hundred thousand dollars, Doodle. Think about it. If I win that one, who knows! We could be millionaires by the end of the year."

She wasn't impressed and rolled her eyes

"I'm serious. It could happen."

She forcefully scribbled on the paper, *It's just money!*

"No, it's not!" I roared, jumping off the bed. "It's a life. It's security. It's being able to provide for you. It's being able to send Flint to college and pay to get Quarry to the best doctors so he never has to experience *this shit.* It's buying you a home and a car, maybe a whole fucking studio where you can sit and draw for the rest of your life. Fuck accounting! You hate it." The more I spoke, the angrier I became. I wasn't mad at her. I just fucking hated reality. "It's more than money! It's being able to make babies with you and not having to bust my ass at a job I hate when all I truly want to be doing is sitting on that fucking couch"—I pointed to the living room—"with *our family.*

"Do you have any idea how it feels for a man to not be able to provide for his *family?* It's crippling! Don't make me feel guilty for making this choice. Damn it, I'm doing it for all of us. If it means you guys are taken care of, I will sit in silence for the rest of my fucking life."

By the time I finished, tears were streaming from her eyes. She didn't want me to suffer—I understood that. This was my life though. Suffering was a guarantee. Security was not.

"Okay."

I read her lips as she rose to her knees and wrapped her arms around my waist. Then I held her, smoothing her hair until I was able to calm down.

I cupped both sides of her face and studied her eyes. "Okay? That was too easy."

Her response was nothing more than a shrug.

As we crawled back in bed, I took her mouth in a gentle kiss. It didn't grow any deeper, but it was there for comfort, nothing else.

Eliza pulled away first and grabbed her notebook.

I have two conditions.

I rolled my eyes, but she ignored me.

Swear to me, that the minute your boxing career is over, you will get the implant.

"You know Slate didn't retire until he was thirty-three," I teased.

I don't care if you are three hundred. Promise. Me.

"I can't box at three hundred!" I laughed, and she narrowed her eyes. "Okay. Fine. I promise. Just give me ten years."

"Ten. Years?" She gave me a sad-puppy-dog face that made me laugh harder. God, it *felt* good.

"Maybe more." I grazed her jaw with my teeth before looking back at her paper. "And number two?"

The Page family is officially enrolling in sign language classes. All of us.

"The Page family, huh?" My smile grew painfully wide. "You're a Page now?"

Well, not legally. You know I'm still married to Justin Timberlake.

I laughed then snatched the pad from her hands. "Then send my apologies to Justin, because I'm about to fuck his wife."

The sparkle of humor vanished from her eyes, but longing and desire appeared just as quickly.

"Are you sure?" She over-enunciated so I could read her lips.

"Uhh . . ." I quirked my eyebrow in confusion. I was always sure when it came to her. "Please don't tell me deaf people can't have sex," I joked and pulled her shirt over her head. "I just want things to feel normal, Eliza. And the normal I want to feel tonight is you coming against my cock while I empty inside you."

A shy smile crept onto her mouth, but her hands boldly slid over my cock, which was thickening in my jeans.

I couldn't get my clothes off fast enough.

It started out slow, with me kneeling beside her, watching my fingers as I glided them in and out. She lazily stroked my shaft and watched me, watching her.

I licked over her breasts; she raked her nails over my back.

I was into it. Completely. But as I guided myself inside her, her head fell back in pleasure and it was as if someone had kicked me in the stomach. There wasn't a single noise to accompany it.

With every thrust, I watched her quietly fall apart underneath me. I willed my eyes to somehow magically transmit the sound I saw coming out of her mouth to my ears, but no matter how hard I tried, she still came on a silent cry.

I struggled to find my own release, fucking her harder than ever before. I was on a mad mission for over an hour, drilling into her in every possible position I could think of. I was in no way gentle, and by the end, it had to have become painful for her. But she never once tried to stop me as she took every ounce of the anger that was aimed at my own body.

I was covered in sweat as I began to tire, still no closer to finding my orgasm than I was when we started. I was ready to give up, when she flipped us over and began to ride me. Then Eliza Reynolds proved once again that she was magic. She made me better. I was still deaf, but she showed me that there were other ways to hear her.

She lifted my hand to cup her throat and moaned as she slid down on my cock. I heard it. Maybe not with my ears, but the vibrations of her throat gave me just enough sensation to make me believe I had. My eyes got wide as she did it over and over again. Then a small smile tilted my lips, and hers filled with absolute love.

It was by far the worst sex we had ever had, but within seconds, I was coming harder than I ever would again.

Soon after we finished, Eliza fell asleep. She was never a snorer,

with the exception of her final conscious sigh, there was no sound asso-
ciated with her sleeping. So I lay awake for hours watching her. It truly
felt normal and made it easy for me to forget the panic that continued
to build in my chest.

I was okay.

She was okay.

We were okay.

Nothing else matters.

27

Eliza

TILL'S FRUSTRATION WITH HIS INABILITY to communicate was overwhelming for all of us. The simplest of tasks had become impossible, and the slightest trigger would send him off the deep end. My easygoing fiancé was gone. Hell, even the nervous, stressed-out boy had disappeared. In his place was a pissed-off man with a grudge against the world.

We enrolled in sign language classes and started integrating it into our every conversation. Flint and Quarry picked it up rather quickly, but Till was a little slower on the uptake. He took it upon himself to learn every possible curse word, but that was the extent of his thirst for knowledge. He hated spending two hours every night in class, and he skipped any time he could find a plausible excuse. It was a hard balance, because we could learn all of the signs we wanted, but if Till didn't understand, they were worthless.

Our relationship took a hit as well. He still held me every chance he got, but it was oddly reminiscent of our younger years. It was affection, but never sexual. I missed him even when he was sitting directly in front of me. We still had sex when I initiated it, but it was rough and it took forever for him to come. It just wasn't the same. Boxing seemed to be the only thing he cared about, and even that was a challenge for him.

We didn't announce to the public that Till had suddenly lost his hearing. He had made his way onto the professional boxing scene after his win over Lacy, but it wasn't like the press was beating down our door for an official statement or anything. I thought Till liked it that way too. He hated advertising his shortcomings—and that was exactly how he viewed it.

Slate spent months developing a system that would enable Till to know when the round was over. Most of the time, the ref would dive in and divide the fighters, but if Till was still swinging after that bell, he would risk losing a precious point. Back home in the quiet gym, Till could faintly make out the bell, but in a crowded arena, it was swallowed by cheering fans. Ten seconds before the end of the fight, Slate would pound three times on the mat, and Till would count it down in his head before he quit swinging. It was simple, but it took some getting used to. He eventually perfected it—probably a little too well.

"You son of a bitch!" Slate screamed as Leo James tried to drag him away from the other boxing trainer.

Tears fell from my eyes as Till lay on the mat forging his way back to consciousness.

"I will ruin you!" Slate threatened wildly as the crowd snapped pictures of "The Silent Storm" losing his shit.

It was all I could do not to join him.

"The Silencer" had just suffered his first defeat. TKO in the sixth round. There was not a single doubt in my head that the judges' cards had him up by several points. He was dominating the fight in every aspect—except for hearing the bell.

I saw the other trainer watching Slate each round. He'd see Slate pound the mat and his eyes would fly back to Till to watch for a reaction. He knew something was going on; he just couldn't figure out what.

In the sixth round, with thirty seconds left, that opposing trainer pounded three times on his side of the ring. Slate started shouting immediately, but it was too late. I sat in the front row, holding my breath as I nervously counted to ten. When I got to nine, I watched Till throw one last punch knocking his opponent back a step. As the ref got close, Till dropped his hands and started to turn away. Because he was completely unprotected, a glove landed on his chin and sent him to the ground.

Celebration erupted across the ring, and well . . . that's when Slate erupted as well.

"Calm the fuck down!" Leo barked as Slate continued to scream profanities at the other corner.

Flint hopped the railing and rushed to the ring, where they were trying to get a stool under Till. I was breathless as I watched him slowly come around. Flint was signing a million miles a minute, but Till's face spoke the real words—and they were tragic.

"Come on." Leo appeared beside me as I watched a much more subdue Slate helping Till from the ring.

"Is he okay?" I asked as I pulled on Quarry's shirt to drag his attention from his brothers.

"Yeah. His pride's the only thing that took any kind of real damage."

"That was so fucked up," Quarry said as Leo ushered us back to the dressing rooms.

"It really was," he replied.

When we got to the door, I could hear Slate yelling, and I steeled myself for a similar reaction from Till, but the second I walked through the door, he smiled and I burst into tears.

"Oh, Jesus. She's crying," he teased as he walked over and pulled me into his arms. "I'm fine," he reassured me, but they were angry tears. There was no soothing them.

I leaned away and signed as I spoke, "*That was so messed up.*"

"Yeah. It was. I'm good though."

"*Are you sure? You're entirely too calm right now.*"

"I think he's pissed enough for both of us."

We both looked over at Slate, who was marching around the room with his phone glued to his ear. He was barking at someone about the boxing commission and integrity. It was so unlike anything I had ever seen from Slate that I couldn't help but laugh.

"*So, what now?*" Quarry asked as he signed.

"Now, we go get some food," Till replied.

"*No, I mean, how bad is it that you lost?*"

"Well, it sucks. But the check still cashes the same." He winked. "Yo, Slate. Let's get some food. We're gonna need to figure out a new bell plan."

Slate waved him off as he continued to rant on the phone.

I watched as Till walked away seemingly unfazed. It was eerie and worrisome.

Till

Oh, God, I silently whispered to myself as I sank down the wall to the cool bathroom floor.

I replayed that ten-count in my head at least a million times. Over and over, I tried to figure out how to make the outcome change.

Quarry's words scrolled through my mind. *"What now?"*

I had no fucking idea.

It wasn't career ending to lose a fight, but maybe going deaf was. And that little revelation shook me to the core. I had no plan B. I loved boxing, but it was always about the paycheck. Watching that savings account grow meant more to me than any belt I could wrap around my waist. The pursuit of greatness and the dreams of being a legend were great, but Eliza and the boys didn't rely on me for those things. Their futures rested on my shoulders. The same shoulders that had been flat out on the mat because I couldn't even hear a fucking bell.

It was a hard pill to swallow, but the effects were what really did the worst damage.

Being hungry for more was one thing, but I was so sick of groveling for the scraps life tossed at my feet. And just when I'd thought I had found my one chance to escape the dungeons of reality, my own fucking body had sabotaged me.

I needed to get out of there. I pushed to my feet and tugged on some clothes, not even bothering with the shower.

I couldn't let them see how much losing had shredded me. My whole body ached with disappointment; I didn't need theirs as well. Flint would just try to fix it, Quarry would worry, and Eliza would have to save my ass once again. I was so sick of being a burden on all of them. I was barely a man anymore. I couldn't even fuck my own woman without having a goddamn nervous breakdown.

I just needed to leave. But as I caught sight of myself in the mirror, I realized that running would do me absolutely no good. There were no more windows.

"Fuck!" I yelled as I slammed my fist into my reflection. It shattered against my hand, and I wished like hell that I could do the same to life's vendetta against me.

As predicted, Eliza came rushing in, ready to care for the broken patient who masqueraded as her fiancé.

"*Are you okay?*" she asked then lifted my hand to inspect my bloodied knuckles.

I snatched it out of her grasp. "Don't fucking baby me," I growled. "I can't handle it tonight. Just leave me alone."

"*Let's just talk about it.*"

"No. I don't want an intervention tonight." I snatched a towel off the ground and wrapped it around my knuckles. "I'm all maxed out on feeling like a bitch tonight without you making it worse."

"*Making it worse?*" She tilted her head in confusion.

"Yes, worse. Just let me hang on to my own balls for the evening. I'll be sure to return them first thing in the morning."

"*Wow. I didn't know that helping you was the same as taking your balls. But you know what? Now that you mention it, maybe you're right. I'll be happy to stop trying to talk you down when you go into one of your full-blown tailspins. Would that stop you from being a broody asshole all the time?*" She threw her hands out to the sides in frustration.

"A broody asshole, huh?"

"*Yep. You're always either pissed off, angry, or moping.*" She flicked her fingers at me as she finished the sign.

"I just got knocked out because I can't hear. I think I've got a right to feel that way."

"*So is that*"—she pointed to the broken mirror—"*about the fight? Or were you in here wallowing in bitterness and pity?*"

I fucking hated that she knew me so well.

"I have the right to be bitter!" I roared.

"*No. You. Don't!*" She punctuated every single silent syllable. "*You may not have chosen to lose your hearing, but you chose to be deaf.*"

"Excuse me?"

She narrowed her eyes, but it wasn't in the playful way that usually instigated one of our staring matches. It was actually a little fright-
ening. Her hands started moving rapidly, but her lips didn't accompany
it. My sign language was usually only good enough to give me context
clues on what their lips were saying. Without them both, though, I was
worthless.

"I have no idea what you're trying to sign."

"*That's because you refuse to learn!*" she screamed as she signed.
Her face turned red from the exertion, but it hit my ears. It was probably only a single note of her voice, but I *heard* it.

It was both painful and invigorating.

I sucked in a breath, and a real, honest-to-God smile formed on my
mouth for the first time in months.

"*And now you're smiling. Fantastic.*" She threw her hands up in
the air and headed for the door.

"I miss your voice. I miss listening to you talk while I figure things
out. Hell, I even miss Justin Timberlake right now, because that terrible
CD was like the Eliza Reynolds soundtrack. I'd give anything to hear
it right now."

She turned around to face me with tears sparkling in her eyes.
"*Well, you know what? I just miss you.*"

"Doodle, I . . ."

"*This is temporary, Till. And it sucks really fucking bad, but this
was a decision you made. I understand why you chose this life, and I
support you completely. But I can't live with this miserable man you've
become for the next ten years. Give me back my man. I'll even take the
boy if that's all you have to give. But damn it, I'm struggling too and I
really need Till right now.*" Her chin quivered and it broke me.

"*I'll do better.*" I signed awkwardly, walking toward her. "I'll do
better, I swear." I looped my arms around her waist and pulled her
against my chest. I didn't know if she spoke any more, but her words
played in my head.

She needed me, and I had been too wrapped up in my own shit
to realize she was struggling too. It was time to man the fuck up. I
couldn't do it for myself, but I damn sure could do it for Eliza.

28

Eliza

"HOLY SHIT!" TILL JUMPED OFF the couch and was quickly followed by Flint and Quarry.

"Three . . . Four . . ." Flint counted, creeping closer to the TV.

"It's over! It's over!" Quarry screamed at the top of his lungs.

"Oh my God." I covered my mouth.

"You knocked out the heavyweight champion of the world!" Flint signed excitedly then shoved Till's chest. He laughed wildly as he fell down onto the cushions.

"I can't believe that fucker actually won."

"Won? I can't believe someone gave his ass a title shot," Flint replied.

"Are you kidding me? He's The Brick Wall! He's *never* been knocked out! What choice did they have?" I said sarcastically.

Rick "The Brick Wall" Matthews had just won the title belt. He was the same Brick Wall Till had knocked on his ass during his first and only amateur fight. The same Brick Wall who had quickly been making his way up the ladder. His arrogance about having never been knocked out and his ability to back it up made him a fan favorite and enabled him to skip a few of the rungs Till was still navigating.

"I cannot believe he has the fucking title now," Till signed as he spoke.

My stomach twisted as I waited for the fallout from watching someone so obviously lap him, but it never came.

Over the course of four months, my Till had come back. He had thrown himself into learning sign language, and even our sex life had returned to somewhat normal. Without words in the dark, Till was forced to read my body language—now that was something he excelled at. Things would never go back to the way they were before Till lost his hearing, but we were all busy forging a new path with the life we had been handed. Sometimes it sucked, but, as a family, we never focused on that for too long.

"Hey Flint, you still meeting up with Tiffany?" Till asked when I flipped off the television.

"*Nah. Her curfew's eleven. By the time I got over there, I'd just have to turn around and come home.*"

"Quickie?" Till waggled his eyebrows teasingly.

"*Till!*" I smacked his chest.

"Don't Till me. When we were his age, I'd already had you!" He laughed.

"*Oh sweet Jesus.*" I closed my eyes, shaking my head.

"*He's a man, Eliza.*" Quarry interjected. "*Men have quickies.*"

"*I'm gonna puke.*" I stood up and walked to the kitchen, but Quarry continued.

"*Sex is a natural part of life. It's nothing to be embarrassed about.*"

I curled my lip in disgust and pleaded with Till. "*Make him stop talking about sex.*"

"No way. I happen to agree with Q. Besides, you didn't seem to be embarrassed in the shower this morning."

My eyes bulged as I glared at him. Flint shook his head, but they all burst out laughing.

You're so getting cut off for that, I signed behind the boys' backs.

Liar, he replied with only his hands. Then he stood up from his seat on the couch and dug his wallet out of his back pocket. "Besides, who said I was talking about Flint having a quickie? I was talking to you." He handed Flint a twenty, but his eyes were glued to mine. "I'm starving. Go grab some pizza, and go to that good place down by the gym. It's worth the drive."

"*Oh shit! Are you two going to do it?*" Quarry asked, looking back and forth between us until Flint slapped him on the back of the head.

"Let's go." He grabbed the truck keys off table, and they both headed out the door.

As soon as it clicked behind them, Till was on me. His mouth crushed into mine while he lifted me onto the kitchen counter. I wasn't going to fight him. We so rarely got time alone that I didn't even care that he'd just announced to the boys that we were planning to have sex. More embarrassing things had happened.

He moved his mouth to my neck as my hands slid under his shirt and up to his hard abs.

"So I was thinking. Since I won the fight last night, I'm off for a few days." I wasn't looking at him, and I wasn't about to remove my hands to reply, so I hummed my acknowledgement. He continued to kiss my neck. "I know things have been crazy over the last few months, but you've been wearing that engagement ring for entirely too long. What do you say we get married tomorrow?"

I jerked my head away to catch his eye. "*Tomorrow?*"

"Yeah. I was thinking we could hit the courthouse, make it official, then do a big dinner with the boys and Slate and Erica, maybe some of the guys from the gym. Then we could get a hotel room for a couple of nights. Spend some time having way more than quickies." He bit my bottom lip.

"*Tomorrow?*" I asked again in shock.

"Tomorrow."

"*But we don't have rings,*" I signed my petty excuse.

He grabbed my hand and pulled it to his mouth, kissing my palm. "*We'll get some.*"

"Umm . . . " I stalled, but I wasn't quite sure why. There wasn't really anything to think about. I'd been married to Till since the first moment I'd laid eyes on him. He hadn't known it for a long time, but I always had. There was really only one answer. "*Okay, but hotels are expensive. Let's just see if the boys can spend a few nights at Slate's.*"

"Stop being a cheapo. We have more than enough in savings to cover something like this. We're getting married. I want a couple of nights at a nice hotel where we can order up room service and a nice bottle of champagne. Maybe get a little tipsy and spend the rest of the night finding new ways to make each other come. You'll need the extra day for recovery."

"*All right, baller. Then I want a new dress too.*"

"Jesus Christ, Eliza! I'm not made of money." He winked.

I melted.

"Baby, you can have anything you want if you just promise to marry me tomorrow. I'm not waiting anymore."

Okay, I signed, unable to speak around the lump of emotion lodged in my throat. *I'm so glad you're back.*

"Good. Now, get naked. I'm gonna fuck you one last time as my fiancée."

I laughed as he peeled my shirt over my head. Then I quieted as he sucked my nipple into his mouth. A few minutes later, I moaned as he made good on his promise and fucked me on our kitchen counter.

Till

In an ill-fitting rented tux and a pair of black Converse shoes, I watched Eliza Reynolds become Eliza Page.

My little courthouse scenario had been quickly nixed when I'd called Slate to invite him to dinner the following day. Erica had gotten her claws in Eliza, and within three hours, they had planned for the entire wedding to take place in the gazebo of Erica's garden. I had no idea how they'd pulled it together, but by six p.m. that evening, Eliza had walked down a makeshift aisle covered with rose petals. She was wearing a short, strapless, white dress that hugged her body in ways that spoke to my soul—or, at the very least, my cock. Her long hair cascaded over one shoulder, and a sheer veil floated in the breeze behind her.

I was a man. I didn't cry—at least, not right then. No, I saved that exhibition of manliness for when I actually had to talk and choke over every other word for everyone to hear. I was reasonably sure I'd never live it down. I was also reasonably sure I didn't give a single fuck.

I was marrying Eliza.

Erica had found a nice officiate who had been instructed to do the traditional wedding vows. But as I stood there looking into those dark-blue eyes that represented the rest of my life, I knew I needed to say something of my own. The problem was figuring out *what* to say at the moment when every single dream I'd ever had was suddenly realized.

"Excuse me for just a second. Can I say something?" I sucked in a shaky breath. "Eliza, I have absolutely no idea what I did to make you fall in love with me. But I can honestly say that, no matter what happens from this point on, it will always be my greatest accomplishment in this life. You're incredible, and the fact that someone like you fell for a poor kid in dirty jeans who was too scared to walk through doors proves it." My voice hitched, and I felt the moisture fall from my traitorous eyes. "When I told you that this"—I pointed to my ears—"was my future, you never batted an eye. And when reality became more than I could handle, you declared war on the inevitable for me. You always say that you love me, but you have given me so much more. And because of that, I will spend a lifetime fighting to give you the world."

Tears fell from her eyes as she responded with only her hands. *I already have it.* Then she launched herself into my arms, kissing me way before she was supposed to.

Her hands shook as we exchanged wedding bands. As soon as she settled mine on my ring finger, she broke the unwritten wedding rules yet again by kissing me once more.

We were pronounced husband and wife, and Flint immediately stole my wife in a congratulatory bear hug. Quarry was more excited about dinner, so he gave me a high five and headed inside, where Erica had turned her dining room into an elegant wedding reception.

She and Slate had insisted on paying for dinner as our wedding gift, and I'd begrudgingly agreed when I'd found out she wanted to do something at home. I had been thinking chicken on the grill, but she'd had other ideas. By all accounts, she had gone overboard. It was less than ten people, but she had three private chefs and a cupcake tower that was roughly as tall as Eliza. When my jaw dropped after seeing what she had put together, Slate pulled me aside, slapped a beer in my hand, and told me to keep my mouth shut. He had never steered me wrong before, so I did just that.

At the end of the evening, Johnson drove Eliza and me to our hotel. It was a nice place, and I smiled proudly as Eliza oohed and ahhed over every thing. Then I made sure she oohed and ahhed under me when I took her against the wall for the first time as my wife.

Hours later, as we lay in bed naked, we removed our rings and read what the other had inscribed inside.

Hers: *My wildest fantasy.*

Mine: *This is reality.*

That day had been such a surreal combination of the two that I'm still not sure who was right.

29

Eliza

FOR THREE FULL MONTHS AFTER the wedding, our lives became blissfully boring. I found an accounting job I hated, Flint graduated high school, Quarry was starting to draw national attention in the amateur boxing circuit, and Till . . . Well, he smiled more often than not. And with another win under his belt, his career was looking even more promising—each fight bringing in more money than the last. There was money in the bank, food on the table, and plans to move out of our crappy apartment as soon as we could find a house to rent. For the first time in as long as I could remember, life was easy.

That was until one Friday night when Quarry came down with the stomach flu. It quickly ravaged its way through Flint and Till. I served as a nurse to all three of them until I got sick too. As the guys got better, the roles were reversed. While I thought it was really sweet to watch them all coddle me, I showed no signs of improvement after a full week. It honestly appeared that I was getting worse. Then Till really began to worry and finally dragged me to the doctor.

"*Are you freaking out?*"

"No."

"*Yes, you are.*"

Till's lips twisted in a one-sided smile. "No, I'm not."

"*You're totally freaking out.*"

He sat down on the edge of the examination table and squeezed my hand. "Doodle, are *you* freaking out?"

I sucked in a deep breath before the floodgates failed me. "*Yes!*" I cried as I dropped my head against his chest.

I felt his shoulders shake before I heard his quiet chuckle.

I sat up back up, sniffling. "*Why are you laughing?*"

"Because after everything we've been through, you decide to freak out about being pregnant? I'm happy and my little Miss Fix It is panicking. I'm sorry, but that's funny."

"*You're happy?*" My voice squeaked at the end.

"Um . . . why wouldn't I be happy? My wife is pregnant, and I'm finally at a point in my life where I think we could afford to start a family. It might not be ideal timing, but who cares? It's not the *wrong* time either. We'll make it work. It's what we do."

"*You know, I'm really not fond of this sensible Till.*"

He barked out a laugh. "You're okay. I'm okay." He reached down and placed his hand over my stomach. "We're okay." Kissing the top of my head, he said, "Nothing else matters."

The familiar words soothed my nerves.

There was a knock on the door, and I nudged him off the table. The doctor and nurse came in pushing a large cart that nearly filled the crowded room. Till scooted back against the wall to allow them more room, and I felt the loss of his comfort even though he was only a few feet away.

"Okay, Mrs. Page. Since you don't know how far along you are, we are going to do a quick ultrasound to see if we can get a fetal measurement and estimate a due date."

I nodded with my eyes glued to Till. I was so nervous, and apparently, it read on my face. He quirked a smile and signed, *I've heard pregnant women are horny all the time. This could really work in my favor.*

My faced heated, and I prayed that no one in the room understood sign language. Till was entirely too far away, and as the doctor lubed up my stomach, I motioned for him to join me. With a smirk, he squeezed his muscular body around the doctor and took my hand, kissing my palm.

From our vantage point, we couldn't see the screen, but the doctor squinted and leaned in closer with every twitch of his wrist.

"When did you say your last period was?" he asked.

"About two weeks ago."

"And you were on birth control, right?" he asked, still staring at the screen.

"Yeah. The pill."

"That was definitely just breakthrough bleeding, then. It appears that you're around eight weeks." He reached forward and turned a tiny knob.

A beautiful whooshing sound filled the room. A hand flew to my mouth as my eyes began to swim.

Till gripped my hand and nervously asked, "What?"

The heartbeat, I signed unable to say the words then made a flashing sign by opening and closing my fist to the rhythm of the sound.

Till's face formed a fake smile that proved he knew exactly what he was missing and he fucking hated it.

Thankfully, the doctor must have seen our exchange. "Here." He turned the monitor to face us. "You can see it on the screen." He placed his finger below a tiny blinking light.

Nothing about that black-and-white image was even remotely recognizable as a baby, but its little heart still beat steadily. It made sense. It was Till's baby; the heart had always been his most defining feature.

Till gasped as he pulled my hand to his mouth and kissed it repeatedly. He silently stared at that screen until the doctor turned it away, and even then, he moved toward my feet in order to keep it in his line of sight.

"Can you tell if it's a girl?" he asked.

The doctor snickered before turning to face him and shaking his head no.

"No, it's not a girl, or no, you can't tell?"

"It's way too soon to tell," he replied.

Till's eyes flashed to mine for the translation.

At the answer, he released a loud breath and raked a hand through his hair. "Okay. I'm gonna need it to be a girl, and if you could sway that for me, I'd really appreciate it."

The doctor laughed as he handed Till a few grainy pictures that would serve absolutely no purpose other than wasting hours of our time as we tried to make out the nonexistent shape of our baby. Maybe that made them the most precious pictures of all though.

"Go ahead and get dressed. Everything looks great, and we can discuss details and future appointments in my office." The doctor walked out of the room, leaving us both still shocked and emotional in his wake.

I waved a hand to catch Till's attention, but when he looked up, his eyes had lost their playfulness.

"*Are you okay?*" I asked.

He swallowed hard before painting on a painful-looking smile. "Way better than okay," he responded unconvincingly.

"*Till . . .*"

"Come on. I want to hear what he has to say about my daughter." He turned away from me, halting any further conversation.

I became instantly worried that Till had joined me on the freak-out train. I threw my clothes on as he stood with his back toward me, but I could see his eyes focused on the pictures in his hand. As I got close, I reached out and traced a hand down his shoulder. He caught my arm and spun, wrapping it around his neck.

"We're gonna have a baby," he choked out with that a one-sided grin of Till the boy. I was transported in time to the moment I'd fallen in love with him.

"I want to buy a house with a big yard. I want to put a huge swing set out back and get one of those stupid tea sets."

I pushed my hands in front of the paper and signed, *I kinda want a boy.*

His eyes snapped to mine.

"*One with your hazel eyes and that crooked grin.*"

"No way. She needs to be smart like you."

"*No way. He needs to have your heart,*" I countered.

"We're having a baby," he repeated, but it wasn't said with happiness or even fear. It was said with pride and victory. "When I first lost my hearing, I stayed awake one night freaking out about the fact that our kids might have to deal with this one day." He pointed to his ears. "But, Eliza, who cares? Look how perfect she is." He held the picture up.

"Till, listen to me. He—"

He narrowed his eyes.

"—won't ever have to experience this. Quarry either. They can get the implant. You've shouldered this for everyone. You wanted to give us all a better life. And you've done it. We aren't millionaires, but we've made it. The only question now is: When does Till get the better life?"

30

Till

"HAVE YOU SEEN THIS?" SLATE asked as soon I walked into his office.

"Seen what?" I replied.

He turned his laptop around to face me, and I immediately recognized the still preview. It was the setup of amateur night at On The Ropes. He pressed play and I watched myself rise from the corner stool. My eyes were glaring across the ring.

I leaned in close to the computer and could barely make out Eliza seated with Derrick Bailey at her side. His arm was around the back of her chair, and even though I knew it had been well over two years since that night, the same rage bubbled in my stomach. Both on the screen and in the present, I watched Eliza until Rick "The Brick Wall" Matthews rush toward me.

I saw my attention only leave her long enough to step forward and throw two punches—which dropped Matthews to the mat. I didn't even stay to celebrate my win. I simply stormed back to the corner and started pulling off my gloves. I could still feel my desperation to get her away from him. *Justified desperation.*

The video suddenly cut off, and I looked up at Slate as I arrogantly dusted off my shoulder. He let out a silent laugh.

"I woke to a million phone calls and emails this morning. This

thing has been viewed over a million times in twenty-four hours."

"Nice!" I smiled and pressed play again.

"*People are going nuts trying to find out more about the only man to ever drop The Brick Wall.*"

I lifted my eyebrows in shock. "Really?"

"*His balls are aching.*"

"I can't blame him." I watched as he once again crumbled while I walked away unfazed.

"*He has built an empire on the fact that no one can knock him out.*"

I rolled my eyes and pressed play again. Each time, only watching her.

Slate shoved a hand in front of the screen. "*Apparently, he's catching a lot of shit over this little video. It was played on a loop on ESPN last night while he was on a phone interview.*"

My eyes grew wide. "Seriously?"

He wants a rematch.

Time froze.

Dollar signs flashed.

My smile grew.

"*I told him to go fuck himself.*"

I jumped to my feet. "Why?" I yelled. "Call him back!"

"*No title on the line and they want to pay you shit. You made more at your last fight.*"

I rolled my bottom lip between my fingers. "Can we negotiate pay? How big of a fight are we talking? Vegas?"

"*Potentially. His image is hurting. They are going to want to make this huge. Listen to me. They are trying to use you like a bum to save his reputation, and if you lose, that is exactly what you will become.*"

But what Slate couldn't possibly know was that, in the span of twenty-four hours, my priorities had dramatically shifted.

"Eliza's pregnant," I blurted.

Slate's jaw dropped open as his mouth formed a shocked "O."

"We went to the doctor yesterday, and I. . . ." I paused because it was the first time I was going to admit my decision. I hadn't even told Eliza yet. Up until that moment, saying it out loud had seemed too final. "They did this little ultrasound, and I couldn't hear her heartbeat. I realized that I wouldn't be able to hear her cry, or laugh, or talk." I stopped to give myself time to let it really sink in. "All I can think about is what if she sounds like Eliza. Slate, I can't miss that. You told me a while back that money is only as good as what it can give you. Well, it's official. The incentive is no longer worth the sacrifice." I sucked in a deep breath and finally threw in the towel. "I want the implant."

"*Okay,*" he said as if it were nothing.

And maybe it wasn't. Maybe it was the logical choice I had been fighting all along.

"I've got some money in the bank, but it won't last. I need this fight, Slate. My career is over, win or lose. Bum or champ, I don't give a damn."

"*So, that's it? You just want the cash?*"

I shook my head. "No. I *need* it. I have no clue what the fuck I'm going to do after this. I don't have an education or any great skill besides manual labor. I need this opportunity to set me up for a while. See what you can negotiate for pay. I'll fight a dancing bear at this point as long as they put my name on a fat check."

"*What if we take a different approach?*"

"Does your different approach allow me to hear my daughter when she's born?"

"*No. But it will give you a long-term solution.*"

"Just spit it out," I bit out as I began to lose my patience.

"*We refuse to step in that ring unless he puts the title on the line.*"

"He'll never agree to that. He has too much to lose."

"*Then we force his hand.*"

I tilted my head in confusion and motioned for him to continue.

"*If he's already catching enough heat from this video to offer a rematch, let's add some fuel to that fire. Let's hit the media. We do a press release to tell the entire world how easy it truly is to crumble the invincible wall. Make it known that he won't give you a shot at his belt because he's scared of The Silencer. We'll set you up some interviews and let the world get to know Till Page. We can make the public beg for this fight.*"

"I can do that," I answered as I mulled over the possible scenarios.

"*But this is going to take time.*"

"Time is the one thing I don't have."

"*When's Eliza due?*"

"Seven months."

"*I need you to commit to one more year.*"

"A year?"

"*It's two fights. We're going to shame this asshole into offering up that title, and you're taking it from him. Then you're defending it. **Then** you're getting the implant.*"

"Let's assume I beat him. How much could I make in the next fight as the defending champion?"

"*Millions.*"

The sound of his word never made it to my ears, but I heard it all the same. It was the crystal-clear ringing of a lifetime of security.

"Set it up," I breathed.

Slate clapped his hands together and jumped to his feet while I sat dazed counting dollars in my head. *Millions of dollars.*

I sat with sweaty palms for hours as Slate made numerous phone calls between agents, attorneys, managers, and even trainers. In the end, going to the media wasn't even necessary. When Slate told them that we would be willing to make concessions on pay in exchange for a title shot, they pounced. Considering the instantaneous hype of the fight, it would reel in at least thirty million, and with less than three hundred thousand dollars written into my contract, it would all go to Matthews.

It was well worth the gamble though. They had no plans to pay me anything substantial for that fight, but with the title on the line, the dollar signs were infinite.

31

Eliza

Four months later . . .

"HOLY. SHIT." QUARRY SPUN WITH his arms stretched wide in the middle of our Las Vegas suite. Then he lost his balance and almost plowed me over.

"Hey, dumbass." Flint caught him by the back of his shirt at the last second. "Watch where the hell you're going!"

"My bad." Quarry patted my stomach then excitedly went back to dancing around the room.

"Christ. What did you pack, Eliza?" Till huffed then set down my three huge suitcases. "And what the hell is that?" He pointed to the small, pink bag with a pink B monogrammed on the side.

"It's Blakely's bag—" I replied, and he captured my hands before I had a chance to completely finish signing my explanation.

"Our unborn daughter, Blakely?" He bit his lip to stifle a laugh.

"You can't be too safe, Till. What if I suddenly go into labor while we are here? What would she wear home from the hospital?"

"Well . . . we're only gonna be here for seven days. If you went into labor, she would be three months early. We'd have way bigger issues than what she would wear home from the hospital." He winked and dipped me back for a wet kiss.

"Hey, I quit my job to be here. Don't you dare get all snippy about

what I packed."

His lips twitched. "You hated that job."

"No. I didn't hate it."

His smile grew to full-blown.

"I loathed it! Thank you." I pressed an exaggerated, humor-filled kiss to his mouth.

He laughed against my lips. "I love you."

"I was nervous about the flight, okay? It made me feel better to have a little bag for her just in case."

He teasingly pretended to bite at my hands as I signed.

"Stop!" I hit his chest.

"Um, I said I love you." He kissed my forehead.

"Oh, right. I briefly forgot how needy you are," I teased. *"I love you too."*

Till began tickling me, and when I looked up, I caught Flint watching us. He smiled and quickly looked away. I made a note to talk to him later. He'd really been acting off recently, even more withdrawn than usual.

There was a knock at the door, and Quarry darted over to answer it.

"Dude, you are huge!"

Slate laughed as he walked in with Leo, Johnson, and a new guy I didn't recognize. But Quarry was right. He *was* huge.

"Okay. Listen up!" Slate's lip twitched, and Till shook his head at his attempted joke. *"Leo's running security for all of us this weekend. I know you've seen the hype, but this isn't going to be like it is at home. You guys are celebrities here. You will be recognized."*

Till moved behind me and folded his arms around to rest on my stomach.

"Do not leave this room without security. Period. This is Alex Pearson. He's been with Leo for about a year, but this is his first trip with us. Please don't scare him off. I'm talking to you, Q."

We all laughed, except for Quarry, who smiled mischievously.

"I will repeat. Do not leave this room without one of them." He passed us all a card. *"Program all of their numbers into your phones. Leo will be with me and Till most of the time, but Alex and Johnson are all yours if you want to go out exploring or whatever. Erica will be here*

this weekend, along with Sarah and Liv."

"Liv!" Quarry shouted before slapping a hand over his mouth.

Leo's lip twitched, but he glared down at Q. "I'm watching you, boy."

Quarry bit his lip, but his smile showed past it.

"Okay. Now that we have that out of the way, Till, get dressed. Let's go check out the gym."

Slate walked out, leaving Leo, Alex, and Johnson to chat with Flint. Quarry went back to flittering around the suite.

"You want to go out to dinner tonight?" Till asked me.

I pointedly looked down at my stomach. *"Like I'm gonna say no."*

He smiled then pressed a soft kiss to my lips.

"Eliza, look! There's a kitchen! You can cook for us here too!" Quarry shouted from over the bar dividing the rooms.

I rolled my eyes, but my smile snuck out, giving me away.

32

Quarry

One Week Later . . .

"QUINN."

"No."

"Queen."

"God no."

"Quillan."

"Uhhhh . . . I'm pretty sure you made that one up, so I'm going to stick with my original answer. No," Eliza said, shooting me down for the hundredth time.

"Come on!"

"While I appreciate your efforts, we already picked a name."

"Blakely is stupid though. Everyone will end up calling her Blake for short. Q is a badass nickname."

"It's also *your* nickname. Trust me. I don't need to yell 'Q' any more than I already do. I can't handle two of you." She laughed as she scraped the mushrooms she had been slicing into a pan on the stove.

"Oh, whatever. What are you cooking anyway?"

"Hell if I know. Mushrooms just sounded really good."

"Plain mushrooms?" I curled my lip as I settled on the barstool across from her.

"Yep!"

"You're disgusting." I laughed just as someone knocked on the door. "Oh! I bet that's our The Silencer T-shirts for the fight."

"God, I hope! They were supposed to be here yesterday."

I yanked the front door open, and a well-dressed man I didn't recognize stood on the other side. His hands were shoved in his pockets of his jacket, and a bright, white smile covered his face.

"Can I help you?"

"I'm looking for Till. Is he around?"

"Nope."

"Perfect," he purred as he slowly pulled his hands out of his pockets, revealing a massive, green tattoo with the head of a dragon shooting red flames down his fingers—the same fingers that were poised on the trigger of a gun. "Quarry, I presume?" He used the tip of his gun to push me inside.

As the door clicked behind us, I heard Eliza from the kitchen.

"Who was it?" she asked just as we rounded the corner.

I didn't even have a chance to react before his arm quickly looped around my neck to rest the gun at my temple. Her eyes popped wide and her hands flew to her mouth.

"Oh my God."

I was in absolute shock. I didn't know this guy, but I was terrified—and not for myself.

"It's okay." I tried to soothe her as my heart slammed around in my chest.

"Who the fuck are you?!" the piece shit spoke to her, and it enraged me.

"Um, who are *you?*" Her shoulders moved as if she were searching the counter, but the bar blocked our view of her body.

"Get your fucking hands up!" he barked.

It caused her chin to quiver and rage to radiate through me.

"Eliza," she answered slowly, lifting her hands in surrender.

"Okay. *Now, Eliza.* Who the hell are you and where the fuck is Till Page?" He turned the gun on her.

Even through my blinding fury, I knew that she did not need to answer that question.

"She's my babysitter. Till's at the gym." I quickly covered, praying to fuck he thought thirteen-year-olds still needed babysitters.

"Okay. Well, Eliza, this could actually work out. I need you to deliver a message to our good pal Till. Call him and let him know that Frankie Dragon stopped by to close out some unfinished business. It's imperative that he gets this message. Do you understand?" His tone wasn't harsh, but it was downright menacing.

She quickly nodded. "Yeah. Absolutely. I'll tell him."

"Great. Now, for insurance that this message is delivered in a time-ly manner, I'm taking Quarry with me." There was a smile in his voice, but Eliza's face slid to ghostly white.

"No! I'll deliver the message. I swear. Just leave him here."

"Yeah. That's not going to happen." He laughed. "I think Till's going to need a little extra incentive for what I need. We all know how much he loves our little Quarry here," he said condescendingly.

A rush of relief hit me as the gun was turned away from her and aimed back against my temple.

"Please don't do this. Just leave him. I'm positive Till will do any-thing you want. You don't need Quarry."

"Yeah. Sorry. I like my plan better."

I felt him shrug as he began to drag me backwards toward the door. I wasn't struggling. I was all too willing to go with him if it got him out of that suite and away from *her.*

"Stop! Wait! Please. I'm Till's wife. Take me instead!"

"No!" I screamed over her words, but it was too late.

She ran from behind the counter, revealing her pregnant stomach and causing Frankie to gasp.

"Just take me. Leave Quarry alone," she cried.

"What the fuck are you doing?" I yelled, but Frankie leveled the gun back on her.

"His *wife?*" he asked before cackling.

"Please. Just let him go."

"This just got so much better."

My entire body went stiff, and Eliza's eyes grew impossibly wid-er as he roughly shoved me, sending me scrambling forward. Just as quickly, he grabbed Eliza and dragged her to the door.

"No!" I jumped to my feet. He had no fucking business even talking to her, but I'd kill him before I let him hurt her. "Get your fuck-ing hands off her! You're not taking her anywhere!" I rushed forward.

I heard Eliza screaming with every step, but adrenaline fueled me. She was ours. I wouldn't let him have her.

"Oh for fuck's sake." He spun Eliza to the side just as I got close, sending her crashing to the ground.

I landed a blow to his side, but his hand folded around my throat and the cold, metal butt of his gun landed hard against my face. Pain exploded as someone dimmed the lights.

I felt my body crash onto the floor, but I struggled to keep my eyes open. I was vaguely aware of Eliza screaming my name as she fought against his arms.

"No," I slurred, but my body had betrayed me.

Seconds later, the darkness consumed me completely.

Till

My phone vibrated in my pocket as Slate and I watched Rick's last fight for at least the hundredth time. I had long since memorized his every nuance in the ring, but I still watched every single second as if it were going to change.

"Hey, pause it."

A text from an unknown number lit my screen.

Unknown: I believe I have something that belongs to you.

I read the text a few times, trying to let it process, but before I could respond, a picture I would never be able to unsee came through. A vision that, with one glance, was branded into my soul.

It was Eliza. Her mouth was taped and her eyes were pouring tears. She was sitting on the floor of a hotel suite that looked exactly like ours. I could barely make out the round of her stomach as my eyes followed her arm up to a doorknob she was tied to.

Entire dimensions folded upon themselves in that moment.

In less than three seconds, I'd plotted the death of whoever had put her there. That picture could have been the joke I prayed it was, but someone would absolutely pay for the way my chest was caving in as I stared at my phone.

Me: Who the fuck is this?

I blinked at the phone, desperate for an answer, but my mind finally kicked into gear. There was carpet behind her—carpet I recognized.

I sprinted from the conference room with one destination on my mind.

My legs moved faster than I'd thought possible as I raced to the elevator. The seconds I was forced to wait for it to arrive were the longest of my life. It was only the last rational brain cell I had that forced me to stand there, knowing that it would take longer for me to run up the stairs to the thirty-seventh floor. Just as the doors opened, Slate caught up and stepped in front of me.

His mouth and hands moved angrily, but I couldn't focus enough to figure out what he was saying. Shoving him out of the way, I frantically pressed the button to our floor and he barely made it inside before the elevator started moving. I was losing my mind trying to speed it up when my phone again buzzed in my hand.

Unknown: Your old friend Frankie Dragon of course.

It was followed by another picture of Eliza with her eyes closed and a booted foot pressed against her stomach.

The world turned in slow motion, but my wrath grew rapidly.

Me: I have no idea what you want, but your life is over.

Him: Mine? Or Hers?

The text was followed by a photo of a gun tilted to Eliza's temple. My hand gripped the phone painfully tight.

Slate snapped in front of me to get my attention. *"What the fuck is going on?"*

"They took Eliza!" I shouted as the eternal elevator ride ended.

When the doors started to open, I squeezed between them, sprinting to our suite. My shoulder slammed into the door as I twisted the handle, but the door remained in place. I patted my pockets down, suddenly realizing I didn't even have my keycard to open it. I was in absolute hell. She was in there, with a gun to her head, and I was stuck on the other side of a fucking *door.*

I pounded as hard as I possibly could. "Open the goddamn door!" But if someone responded, I'd never know.

Slate appeared at my side with his phone to his ear, and something on the other side of the door immediately piqued his interest. He leaned in close and pressed his ear against the wood. I watched his mouth form a word that sank my heart even further.

"Quarry!" He began to shake the handle to open the door.

As I backed up, ready to bulldoze through that fucking door, I caught sight of Flint and Leo jogging down the hall. Flint quickly pulled a key from his pocket and swung the door open. He tried to enter first, but I snagged the back of his shirt to prevent him from rushing inside. I had no idea what was waiting on the other side of that door, but I was going to find out first. I swung him back in to the hall and then stormed in with Leo directly behind me.

We found Quarry lying on the floor with blood pouring from his nose. He was struggling to sit up, and his mouth was moving a million miles a minute.

"What's he saying?" I yelled as I helped him sit up, but my eyes scanned the room, desperate to find her.

I rose to my feet, ready to haul ass down the hall to the bedroom, but Leo stopped me. With his gun drawn, he motioned for us to leave. He must have lost his goddamn mind though, because I wasn't going anywhere without her.

Quarry waved to get my attention. *"She's not here. He took her. I tried . . ."* His hands dropped to his sides and his head hung.

Leo made fast work of clearing the suite and verifying that Quarry was right.

I focused back on my phone. When my fingers started flying over my keyboard, Leo, Slate, and Flint sidled up beside me to read over my shoulder.

Me: Where the fuck is she?
Him: Phew, that took you long enough.
Me: I swear on my life, I will kill you. Give her back to me.
Him: No cops. Tell your daddy Slate to stand the fuck down.

Slate's head snapped back as he lowered the phone from his ear.

And my phone immediately buzzed once again.

Him: Better.

Leo started looking around the room.

Him: Tell Mr. James that he should probably be more worried about his own family than where my camera is located. His daughter seemed frightened when I killed her worthless bodyguard.

Suddenly, with wide eyes and pale faces, Slate and Leo flew from the room.

Me: I swear to god, I will kill you.

Him: Yeah. Yeah. Yeah. I've heard it all before. So now that we are alone, I have a favor to ask in exchange for your precious wife's return.

Flint tugged on the edge of my shirt. *We have to go. Don't talk. Just sign. Leo told me to get you two to the conference room.*

Me: What do you want?

Him: I need you to throw the fight. I've got 200k that I don't exactly have riding on you losing in the third round. TKO.

Me: Done. Now let her go.

Flint continued to tug on my arm as he led me from the room.

Him: As soon as the final bell rings, she's all yours.

Me: And what happens to her if something happens before then? I can't guarantee that I'll make it to the third round.

Alex rounded the corner as soon as we cleared the doorway. He ushered the three of us to the elevator, while I stared holes in my phone.

Him: Oh, I have a feeling you'll do just fine.

Him: Tell me, Till. How good is her mouth?

It was followed by a picture of Eliza leaning against the leg of his slacks. Her eyes were squinted shut, and his hand was wrapped firmly around her throat, the tips of his fingers digging into her flesh.

Me: Don't you fucking touch her.

Him: We'll be in touch. You should go get

ready. You have a fight to lose.
Me: I'll pay you more than what you'll make
on the fight. Just fucking give her to me.

But as we made our way to the conference room, my text went unanswered.

Eliza

"I really didn't think this would be so much fun!" He laughed manically as he ripped the tape off my mouth. "Shhh. Keep your fucking mouth shut or I'll go back for the boy." He winked.

I'd sat helplessly, watching the camera feed on Frankie's laptop as every single message he sent landed on Till's face. The pictures were the worst.

"Who the hell is that?" A man I vaguely recognized asked as he strolled into the room.

"*That* is the insurance policy that allows you to live another day."

"What the hell are you talking about? I thought Till throwing the fight was the insurance policy. I just need to talk to him for a few minutes. I couldn't get him alone earlier—"

"Well, you know what? I got really fucking tired of waiting for your lazy ass to make a fucking move. The fight is tonight. I was starting to believe that you weren't going to follow through with this at all." He tilted his head to the side accusingly. "This is both of our asses."

"I told you I'd handle it. I'll get you your money. Then I'm done."

"Well, pardon the fuck out of me for not trusting a lying piece of shit who just got out of prison. You should be kissing my fucking feet right now. You're welcome, by the way." He shook his head in annoyance. "Clay, meet your daughter-in-law." He clapped his hands. "Congratulations! You're going to be a grandpa!" He mocked enthusiasm before rolling his eyes.

My stomach knotted, and bile rose to my throat. *Clay fucking Page.*

"Whoa. Wait just a fucking minute. You never said anything about involving his family."

"Well, originally, I was only planning to involve *your* family. But I figured she would be a little more enticing than your youngest spawn."

"You went after Quarry?" Clay yelled as he took a huge step forward.

Frankie moved to the kitchen and poured a glass of amber liquor. "You know, I have to give it to you. For such a pussy, you managed to raise some fearless kids."

"He didn't raise them," I interjected into their conversation as I glared at Clay. "Till did. *I did.* He had nothing to do with those boys. Don't you dare give him any credit for who they have become," I growled. I shouldn't have said anything, but Clay Page was somehow involved in this bullshit and it enraged me that he could do this to his own fucking son . . . again.

He put his hands on his hips and leveled me with a glare. "Bullshit. Those are my kids. I raised them all until I got locked up."

"You are so full of shit. You've thrown Till to the wolves twice now. Flint's a fucking nervous mess, and when I was dragged out of that hotel room, Quarry was unconscious in a pool of blood. Is that your idea of raising them?" I pushed to my feet, my arm still connected to the door. "You know what?" I turned my attention to Frankie. "You never needed me for insurance. Till would have been happy to throw the fight if you just promised to put a bullet in that asshole's head." I nodded toward Clay. My chest heaved as I finished.

Frankie burst into laughter, spraying liquor from his mouth. "That bitch is tied to a door and still talking shit to you, Page. I like the spunk."

Clay held my eyes as his tongue slid over his teeth. Then he cracked his neck but didn't respond.

"Oh, look! The dip-shit bodyguard is back." Frankie leaned over the computer that showed a grainy feed of my hotel room.

I tried to lean around him to see the screen, but his back blocked my view.

Clay waved to catch my attention. I sucked in a breath as his hands brokenly signed, *They're still my kids. Sit down. Shut up.*

Till

"Why was no one watching them?" I yelled at Slate.

"*They were inside the room. Leo was on the door, but he took Flint down to grab some food. They can't be everywhere.*"

"Bullshit!" I boomed. "What the fuck about Alex?"

"*He's pulling nights!*" Slate explained for at least the tenth time. "*Not a single one of us could have anticipated something like this happening. All that matters now is that we get her back. So calm the fuck down and let's figure this shit out.*"

Every muscle in my body twitched, but calming down wasn't a possibility—not when she was missing. I intertwined my fingers and rested them on the top of my head.

"Found it." Leo rushed into the room and slammed a tiny, black camera the size of a pencil eraser down onto the table. "It's cheap. Low end that you can grab almost anywhere. This guy's no fucking professional."

As soon as we had gotten to the conference room, we'd found that, while Frankie obviously did know that Johnson was assigned to Sarah and Erica, nothing had actually happened to them. They were all safe and unharmed in the restaurant downstairs when Leo got in contact with him.

We all congregated in the conference room with Alex and Johnson standing guard at the door.

"He's no pro. He's a small-time, cracked-out bookie. I met him once when I was eighteen. This has something to do with my dad. I don't know if he's in on it or what, but you find Clay Page. He'll have some fucking answers."

"He was released last week and already skipped parole. It'll take me longer to locate him than it will Eliza," Leo answered as Flint furiously signed for me.

"*This is out of control. We need to call the cops,*" Slate announced.

"No!" I yelled. "No cops."

Leo stepped in front of me and began talking, but I was forced to watch Flint fill in the words. "Till, there is no guarantee that he will even release her after you lose. We need some backup here."

"No, we don't. Just find her."

"I'm working on getting access to the hotel surveillance cameras. It's a casino. There isn't an inch of this hotel we can't see. But I'm hitting walls at every turn. I need a badge. I'll explain the situation and get minimal officers, no uniforms."

"What if he finds out? He'll kill her . . . He'll kill them!" I roared before I felt my throat close and I was forced to depend on my hands. *I can't risk it.*

"I'm sorry, but I think you're wrong about this. I'm calling it in."

As Flint finished signing Leo's words, I exploded and rushed across the room. "No! That's not your fucking choice!" I batted the phone out of his hand, sending it flying across the room.

Slate wrapped his arms around my shoulders from behind, and Flint stepped in front of me.

"That's my wife. My daughter. Goddammit, I get to decide how this goes down."

"Till, you're making decisions with your heart based on fear right now. I'm trying to think logically."

My eyes flashed from Flint back to Leo. "Fuck, your logic. I am not taking a gamble on calling in the cops when my entire life is on the line. And if you even try to tell me you wouldn't play it safe if it were Sarah and Liv, then you're a goddamn liar." I stopped fighting and pinched the bridge of my nose, barely clinging to the edge of sanity.

Slate released me and shoved me toward a chair in the corner. He tried to force me into it, but there was no possible way I could have relaxed. I wanted blood.

Slate signed for my benefit as he explained the situation to Leo. "*If we call in the cops, the Boxing Association will cancel the fight if there is any suspicion that Till might throw it. This guy has made it more than clear he has money riding on this fight. But there has to be more to it. Till offered to pay him off, but he hasn't gotten a response. Sounds like someone has a vested interest in the actual winner of the fight.*"

"You think Matthews has something to do with this?" My murderous rage became palpable.

"*I don't know. Maybe. More than likely a big-time, dirty bookie is using a small-time, dirty bookie to make an ass-load of money. I bet this Dragon guy doesn't even know how much money is actually on the line."*

"Someone, please just fucking find her. Jesus Christ, I don't give a shit about this fight anymore. I just need someone to find her!" I pushed a hand into my hair. The anger was quickly subsiding as my anxiety took up root.

Flint moved to where we were all talking. *"What if we do call the cops—"*

My eyes grew wide, but he held up a hand to silence me.

"—but don't tell them about throwing the fight. Just tell them that someone took Eliza. That way, if at fight time, they don't have anything on Eliza, Till can still throw the fight. We have two outs instead of one."

Slate turned to look at me. *"Now that's an idea."*

My eyes jumped to Leo.

He shrugged. "I'm okay with that."

I toyed with my bottom lip as my mind ran over every possible scenario, but I came up empty. Losing her wasn't an option. "No uniforms. No cop cars. Nothing."

"I can do that," Leo announced, walking forward and holding my gaze. "I'll find her. I promise."

I sucked in a deep breath as I read his lips. He could promise all day, but nothing would make me relax until she was in my arms again.

Flint

"Find her!" Till screamed at the top of his lungs. His words slurred from the force.

"We're trying," Leo explained, slapping the laptop closed.

Till had insisted on watching the video Leo had acquired of Eliza being dragged from the hotel. After over an hour of trying to talk him out of it, Leo had finally given in when Till went off and started demolishing the entire conference room.

We'd all huddled around the computer and watched as Eliza walked willingly from the room with Frankie. Everything was fine until he tried to push her out of the hotel through a back exit. She planted her feet and tried to snatch her arm out of his grip, but it only caused him to slingshot her out the door. She stumbled and landed facedown. She immediately got back on her feet, but watching her fall on her pregnant belly had been more than enough to send us all into a fit of rage.

"Try fucking harder!" Till seethed.

"Look, we know she's in the building. Or at least she was when those images were sent to you. We're going through footage of every single entrance to see when and where they came back in. It just takes time," Leo said as I translated. "You get in that ring and do what you have to do. I'll do what I have to do out here."

The entire thing was so surreal. I couldn't wrap my mind around any of it. Leo had made good on his word, and everything was very low-key. So much so that it almost felt like nothing was being done at all. Two plain clothed detectives milled around, but when I found one sitting around eating a sandwich, I'd lost my shit too. It took Leo and Slate to keep me from shoving that goddamn sandwich down his throat.

We'd all spent the day in upheaval. Sarah and Erica buzzed around the room, trying to coddle us, but they were a nervous wreck right alongside the rest of us. Till was a fuming mess, understandably. He paced a lot and ranted at anyone who would listen. Quarry had been transformed into a depressed, weeping child. He sat alone in the corner, refusing to talk to anyone. It seemed my brothers had figured out their coping mechanisms, but I flipped back and forth between anger and hopelessness.

God. Eliza. She must have been so scared. It twisted my gut and sent flames through my blood. I had never experienced that level of fear before and was clueless about how to channel it.

But then again, I'd never felt for anyone the way I did for Eliza Reynolds Page.

I'd been in love with her since the day she'd first walked through Till's front door. I had barely even been a teenager, but when she'd smiled at me, I had known I'd never be the same. And I wasn't. There wasn't a girl in the world who would ever make me feel the sense of belonging I felt when I touched her. She was beautiful, and funny, and so good to all of us. It was so fucking wrong for me to want her the way I did, but even the guilt couldn't stop me.

I always knew she was in love with Till. I couldn't even be mad about it because it was obvious how much he loved her too. At least, if they were together, I had a way to keep her in my life. But right then, with her missing and having absolutely no control over where she was or what was happening, it was excruciating.

A sudden knock at the door grabbed all of our attention.

"Ten minutes!" was shouted from outside the door.

Slate stepped in front of Till. "*You need to calm to fuck down or you're going to get your ass knocked out in the first round. What good is that going to do her? You have ten minutes to get your head in the fight.*"

Till might have nodded, but I knew for certain that he wouldn't be into the fight while Eliza was missing. I didn't know how he was going to do it. I could barely breathe, yet he had to fight.

"Let's go, Flint," Alex called from the door. "Time to get you seated."

Slate had made the decision that Erica, Sarah, and Liv would watch the fight from their hotel room with Johnson standing guard. I'd insisted on watching ringside. I *needed* to be there. Quarry had been given the option, but he'd only shrugged and followed the women as they'd left.

Alex had been assigned as my bodyguard for the fight, and while I absolutely loathed the idea that they assumed I couldn't protect myself, I hadn't argued. I knew that my bitching would have only stressed Till out more. He had enough going on without having to worry about me too.

I walked to the door and stopped to sign to Till, *You got this.*

"Yeah. I got it." He forced a tight smile then turned away to shrug into the robe Slate was holding open.

I walked toward the arena with Alex barely a step behind me. "Can you not make me look like a pussy with a babysitter?" I smiled tightly.

"Sorry, man. It's my job."

"Can I have a little breathing room at least?"

He chuckled but dropped back a few feet.

We navigated through numerous winding hallways, the crowd getting thicker the closer we got to the arena until it eventually bottle-necked at an intersection.

"Sorry," a man said as he slammed into my chest.

I only glanced at him long enough to notice a baseball cap pulled low over his eyes. "No problem." I smiled—until I felt something being shoved into my hand. I looked down at a room key as the man quickly walked away. Written in black marker was the number 3716.

Confused, I watched the man weave through the tight crowd. Just before he rounded the corner away from the arena, he turned to face me. Similar blue eyes lifted to mine.

"Dad?" I whispered to myself.

He gave me a tight smile then raised his hands and signed, *I didn't know he was going to take her. Tell Till I'm sorry.*

I gasped then glanced back down at the card in my hand.

Eliza.

Eliza

"You ready for the big fight?" Frankie asked me as he settled on the couch with a drink in his hand.

"Are you really going to let me go if he loses?"

"I don't know. He'll be pretty useless to me after he gets knocked out." He kicked his feet up on the coffee table and crossed his legs at the ankle. "Plus, the last thing I need is you popping that baby out on me. I don't like kids as it is. I can't imagine how much I would hate one with Page blood." He stirred his drink with his finger and then flipped the TV on.

I watched from the floor as Till's picture and stats flashed on the screen. My chest ached to get out of there and back to his side, but it pained me that he was losing his one shot at greatness. I should have been sitting ringside, giddy with excitement and hope. He should have been walking to that ring with his head held high and his determination firmly intact. We'd all lost though.

"It's about fucking time you got back. Did you bring me—What the fuck!" Frankie shouted, jumping to his feet as Flint came storming through the door. His blue eyes were dark and barbaric.

Frankie rushed to the table where his gun was, but Flint was faster. Grabbing his throat, he slammed Frankie to the ground. Their tangled bodies knocked over the table, sending the gun tumbling across the carpeted floor. Flint didn't say a single word as he landed punch after punch with his right hand. Each blow landed harder than the one before, but he never released his hold on Frankie's throat. Flint's knuckles turned white as Frankie's face turned red.

I scooted away as far as the door I was tied to would allow as Flint unleashed a savagery I had never witnessed before. I wanted to stop him. That brutal look didn't belong on my Flint's face, but I didn't exactly belong tied to a door either. Frankie lay immobile underneath him, and with the threat gone, I really just wanted to get the hell out of there.

"Flint!" I yelled, and his head snapped to mine.

"Shit. Eliza." He crawled over and patted down my stomach and sides, searching for injury. "Are you okay?"

"Um . . . I want to go home." I tried to choke back the sob, but it was a losing battle.

Flint grabbed both sides of my face and tipped it down to kiss my forehead. "Then let's get out of here." He rose to his knees in front of me and went to work untying the knot at my wrist.

Hope began to swell in my chest. We were so close to getting out of there. Everything was falling into place the way it was supposed to be. The cruel universe had given it a good shot, but the Page family had won in the final round. Till was in the ring, the roar of the crowd on the TV told me that much, and now that I was safe, he could actually have a fair fight.

My entire body buzzed with the idea that for the first time ever we really could have it all.

Maybe.

"Don't fucking move!" was barked from the doorway.

Flint's hands froze as he turned to look over his shoulder. I caught sight of Alex in the doorway, his gun aimed at Frankie. Flint immediately slid in front of me and pushed me over backwards. It wasn't until

I felt the first shot that I realized how wrong I truly was.

I heard the second shot as I lay on the ground with Flint on top of me. Blood sprayed from Frankie's head as he too collapsed on the floor.

Maybe having it all was never meant for us.

Till

As the bell rang to end the second round, I sat on the stool, exhausted. After the day's events, I was in no condition to be fighting at all. However, I was fighting for her—there wasn't a boxer in the world who could have taken me down. But I would fall anyway.

I opened my mouth to spit out my mouthpiece when one of the water boys stepped in front of me. As my trainer, Slate should have been the one to do it, so my senses immediately went on alert. I looked over my shoulder to find him just outside of the ring, secretively whispering with Leo. It was a sold-out arena in Vegas. No one should have been whispering in that chaos.

Leo pointed to the side, and Slate's eyes drifted for only a second before he rushed to the ring. His face was pale, but his expression was murderous.

"What's wrong?" I stood up, but he roughly pushed me back down. "Is she okay?"

He squatted in front of me. "*One round. Then I'm calling the fight. You knock this motherfucker out right now or it's over.*"

"I'm supposed to fall," I stated as panic built in my stomach. I pushed to my feet. "What the fuck is going on? Where is she?"

He looked down to Leo and swallowed hard. Leo responded with a nod, and Slate slowly lifted his arm and pointed to the far side of the arena. I swung my head to follow his direction.

My breath failed me as the weight of the world fell away.

Eliza.

She was wrapped in a blanket and surrounded by two uniformed officers, but she was more beautiful than I had ever seen her before.

The second our eyes met, she burst into tears, and it was all I could do to keep my knees from buckling.

"Oh, God." I breathed. I lifted my hands to sign before remembering my gloves.

"I'm okay," she mouthed with a steady stream of tears dripping from her chin.

I nodded and swallowed the lump in my throat. I wouldn't believe it until I held her. I'd started to climb through the ropes when Slate grabbed my arm.

"*No. Finish this.*"

I looked back at Eliza and smiled weakly.

"Why only one round if she's okay?" I asked Slate without tearing my eyes off Eliza. I bounced on my toes and shook out my arms, trying to get myself back into the fight but finding it impossible.

Slate didn't have a chance to respond before Eliza gave me the answer.

From under the blanket, she lifted a shaky hand to wipe away her tears, but her fingers left a streak of blood across her cheek.

My eyes went wide. "Eliza!" I called out, but there was no way she could hear me over the crowd.

I love you. I'm okay, she signed as one of the officers started to guide her away.

"Eliza!" I yelled as I traced the ropes down the side of the ring to follow her. I was vaguely aware of the ref pushing me back to my corner, but all I could see was the blood painting her face.

Slate moved in front of me as she disappeared around the corner. "*One round.*"

"Why is she bleeding? What the fuck is going on?" I shoved his chest.

"*She's fine. Get your ass in that corner. Three minutes. Then you are out of here.*"

I studied his eyes. "Swear to me she's okay? Swear it!" I barked, backing into my corner.

"*She'll be fine. Now, hurry this the fuck up. You have one round to secure your entire future. There are millions on the other side of that bell. Claim them.*" He pointed across the ring as he folded out. "*Silence him.*"

That I could do.

With a deep breath, I called up every bit of strength I had left. I drew from Eliza and the images of the life we were going to have together. The future I could provide not just Blakely, but also Flint and Quarry. I could win this for them.

The fight had been somewhat one-sided until that point—and not my side. It was obvious that Matthews wasn't the same fighter I'd easily knocked out all those years ago. Unfortunately for him, I wasn't the same Till Page either.

Sixty seconds later, with the same combination I'd knocked him out with the first time, I made my own dreams come true. Rick Matthews stumbled back against the ropes before collapsing to the mat. The combination wasn't anything special or unique to boxing, but it was conceived from a desperate need for me to get to Eliza's side. And for that alone, it was unstoppable. I counted around my mouthpiece as the ref issued a ten-count, but I could have told you at three that the fight was over.

When the ref waved his hands to call the fight, the crowd went nuts. The vibrations from the cheering fans were unforgettable, but it was the sight of thousands of fans twisting their open hands in sign language applause that choked me up. I lifted a glove in appreciation to the fans on all four sides of the ring, but that was my only celebration.

"Let's go!" I barked at Slate as he started pulling my gloves off. For a man who had just won his very first championship belt, my corner was entirely too subdued.

"*Wait,*" he signed back. "*Let them lift your glove and we're out of here, okay? There's a car waiting out back.*"

"A car? Where is she?" I asked as the opposing trainer came over to offer a handshake and the customary congratulations. But I wasn't having it. I stepped around him and got into Slate's face. "Where the fuck is she?" I growled.

His hands lifted to respond, but he dropped them and mouthed, "I'm sorry."

"Sorry? What the fuck is going on?" My stomach dropped.

I searched his face for answers, but he had them all stoically hidden away. Fuck having my glove lifted in the air. If there was a car out back headed for Eliza, I was getting in it.

I shoved him out of the way and climbed out of the ring, not even bothering with the steps as I jumped off the skirting and made my way through the crowd. People were slapping my back as I rushed from the ring, and it wasn't until I slammed the back door open that I realized Leo and Slate had followed me.

Slate yanked the door open to a blacked-out Escalade, and I crawled inside. No sooner than the door was shut, I yelled, "Start fucking talking. Now!"

"*Eliza's fine. So is the baby.*"

I blew out a relieved breath, but he continued.

"*She's at the hospital with Flint.*"

My head snapped back in surprise. "Flint?"

"*I'm afraid so, son. He's the one who found her. Frankie put up a fight, and Flint was shot in the scuffle.*"

"Flint?" I barely squeezed out as my chest took the painful blow of his words. "Is he okay?"

"*He was shot in the back, but according to Johnson, he was talking as the paramedics wheeled him out.*"

"In the back?" I whispered.

Leo said something and my eyes flashed to Slate for the translation. With a quick swipe of his hands, pride—and guilt—consumed me.

"*He was protecting Eliza.*"

33

Eliza

"TILL!" I CRIED AS SOON AS he shoved the door to my hospital room open.

His hands were still taped from the fight and he was only wearing his trunks and an On The Ropes T-shirt, but it was the anger in his eyes that looked the most out of place. His whole face softened as soon as he saw me.

He rushed to the bed and wrapped me in his strong arms. I had been mildly holding it together up until that moment, but I lost it as I buried my face in Till's neck.

"Jesus fucking Christ, Eliza."

As he lifted me off the bed, the wires dangling from my stomach all snapped off. I clung to him anyway.

He gently sat me back down. "What is all this?" He pointed to the monitors attached to my stomach. "Is the baby okay?"

"*She's fine. When I was talking to the police, I started having contractions.*"

His eyes widened.

"*It was just stress,*" I quickly clarified. "*I haven't had any more since they hooked me up to the monitors.*"

"Thank God," he exhaled, resting his hand on the curve of my stomach.

"How's Flint? Did they tell you anything?"

He swallowed hard, and instead of speaking, he only signed back. *He's in surgery.*

I nodded sadly, and he lifted my hand to kiss the palm. I sat there for several minutes just staring into space. I was in Till's arms, but my body remained stiff.

"Eliza, the police and Alex filled me in on what went down at the hotel, but do you want to talk about it?"

I shook my head and nervously toyed with his fingers. I fought really fucking hard to hide what was really going through my head. It was wrong, and I felt extremely guilty for even thinking it. However, that didn't stop me from feeling it. And as tears leaked from my eyes, I knew I wouldn't be able to keep it hidden from Till.

"It's just . . . I'm so fucking mad at him right now." I paused to collect myself but failed. *"He's so goddamn stupid. Why the hell didn't he go to the police instead of storming in and trying to take care of it himself?"* My chest ached as the memories filled my mind. *"He shouldn't have been there at all. It's so messed up, but I want him to get out of surgery so I can . . . kick him or something."*

Till coughed a laugh that was dripping with emotions. "I'm pissed too. But he took a bullet for my wife and daughter. I'm gonna have to figure out a way to get over it."

I couldn't let it go though. I would have done anything for those boys, and apparently, he felt the same.

"I met your dad," I said as I tried my damnedest to stop envisioning Flint when he rushed through that hotel door.

"I heard." Till snapped.

"How the hell does he know sign language?"

"I have no fucking idea. But if I ever find that motherfucker, he won't be alive long enough for me to ask." He looked down and kissed my forehead.

We quietly sat there for a few minutes, lost in our own thoughts, but mine were just a never-ending replay of the day. My anxiety climbed with the vision of a gun being smashed into Quarry's face, then Flint—

Till interrupted my spiral downward. "You're shaking. Talk to me."

I couldn't stop the words as they flew from my mouth. *"It was ter-*

rible, Till. I'll never be able to forget the way Flint's body jumped when the bullet hit him. Even as he fell on top of me, he was thinking enough to catch himself with an arm so he didn't land on my stomach. He has to be okay. We can't lose him."

Till was chewing on his bottom lip, and I knew for certain he didn't need to hear any of it, but I also knew for certain that it would engulf me if I didn't talk to someone so I selfishly kept going.

"*Oh, God. I really thought he was dead. Then he woke up when the paramedics got there, but he just kept repeating my name.*" I dropped my chin to my chest and tried to rid myself of the memories that would haunt me forever.

"Shhh. I've got you. He's okay. We're all okay," Till choked out before pulling me into a hug.

I couldn't see him, but it was okay. Talking wasn't helping the ache in my chest that was threatening to devour me.

He eventually wedged his massive body onto the bed beside me and let me cry into his chest until I fell asleep. I loved Till Page, but not even his arms brought me comfort that night.

Till

"I'm sorry," the surgeon said, pulling off his hat. "I don't have any answers."

Slate translated beside the doctor. Eliza was sobbing in the bed, and I blindly reached down to hold her hand.

"You . . ." I paused as my legs started to shake. "You're a doctor. How can you not know?" I swallowed hard.

"Spinal injuries are difficult to predict. It's case by case, really. We're going to do everything we can, but there is a good chance that he may never walk again."

I choked on a shocked breath. Quarry bolted from the room, Erica hot on his heels.

"We'll just have to wait and see. Give him some time to recover and let his body heal."

I watched Slate's hands, but when I made it to his eyes, they mirrored the devastation in my own.

"No. That's not a good enough answer. Fix him." It was worthless. I knew there was nothing the doctor could do, but that didn't prevent me from taking an angry step forward and demanding again, "Fucking fix him."

Slate stepped in front of me, but I didn't explode like I was sure he was expecting me to. I was exhausted. So instead, I backed up and sat down on the edge of Eliza's bed. She wrapped her arms around my neck from the side, and I looked up to Slate.

"I'm so sick of fighting."

He reached forward and squeezed my shoulder. "*I can't blame you. But let's just hope Flint doesn't feel the same way. This isn't your fight anymore.*"

I kissed the top of Eliza's head and rested a hand on her stomach. It was going to kill me, but Slate was right. I would have to watch this one from outside the ring.

It was Flint's turn to fight.

Epilogue

Eliza

BLAKELY PAGE WAS BORN THREE months after that horrible day in Vegas. She was the bright light during a dark time for all of us. With a head full of Till's straight, black hair and my deep-blue eyes, she was beautiful—there was no disputing that. She had a tiny freckle-sized birthmark on the top of her hand that Till quickly fell in love with. He was such a great dad. He always had been though.

"The Silencer" Till Page lost his title belt after a rematch with Rick Matthews only a few months later. However, as the defending champion, the contract read a little differently that night. With a guaranteed eight figures in his pocket, "The Poor Kid Fighting For A Better Life" Till Page smiled with genuine excitement as The Brick Wall's glove was lifted into the air. It didn't matter one bit that he'd lost his final fight as a professional boxer. Till was the absolute winner as he walked out of that ring.

The day Till received his cochlear implant was extremely bittersweet. There wasn't a dry eye in the room as he heard Blakely cry for the very first time. Unfortunately, not everyone was there to witness it firsthand.

Flint and Quarry never truly came back from Vegas. Sure, they both returned home with us when Flint was well enough to travel, but my boys weren't on that flight.

They lived under our roof, but after that the smiles were never as wide nor were the laughs as loud. The apartment became entirely too quiet. I understood why Flint had changed so drastically, but even my sweet, foul-mouthed Quarry withdrew. We tried too hard to make everything go back to how it used to be, but ultimately, we were forced to let go and make the best of the present.

The first thing Till did after he lost his title was write two enormous checks. Slate was more than happy to sell him fifty percent ownership of On The Ropes. Even though the funds were transferred electronically, Slate made a huge production about Till coming up to the gym late one night to deliver the check personally. It was all a ploy though. When Till walked through the door, Slate surprised him with his name painted in the coveted blank on the wall. Till was, in fact, On The Ropes' first world champion, and he had been on every possible news and sports network you could imagine, but nothing validated his success more than seeing his name on that wall.

The second check Till wrote was to the old construction company where he used to work. We spent over a week sketching our dream house. As soon as we were finished, Till rushed it down to the architecture firm to have formal plans drawn up. It wasn't anything huge, but it was a mansion for us. I was banned from visiting the build site. I knew he was hiding something, but Till gave me a classic one-sided grin every time I brought it up, so I let it slide. Finally, the day we were presented with our keys, he let me in on his little secret.

"Close your eyes, Doodle!"

"I'm carrying a baby, Till!"

"Well, then, give me my baby." He pulled Blakely from my arms.

She went more than willingly and squealed as he tickled her stomach.

The entire house was empty since we hadn't moved in yet, but when we entered the large master suite, there were pale-pink curtains drawn over one of the windows.

"I didn't take you for a pink kind of guy."

"You know, when we bought this land, I wasn't completely sold on it. But one look at the view outside of that window and I decided that I never wanted to live anywhere else. Seriously, check it out." He tilted his head.

I narrowed my eyes at him as I moved toward the window. He held my stare, but a massive smile threatened to split his face.

After one last look over my shoulder, I pushed the curtains back.

I gasped as my hand flew to my mouth and tears made my vision swim.

The other side of that window wasn't outside at all. It led into a small room laid out exactly like our old abandoned apartment. There were cushions against the wall for a couch, our filing cabinet pantry, and the easel he had built for me years earlier. Till had made a few additions of his own too. There was a table covered by sketchpads, and various art supplies and paints lined a shelf. A picture from our wedding hung on one wall while black-and-white photos of Blakely, Flint, and Quarry covered the other.

"Till," I whispered, unable to drag my eyes away.

With Blakely in one arm, he wrapped the other around my waist. I swayed back to lean against his chest.

"I know how you feel about doors, so I had them add one in the closet."

I turned to look up into those hazel eyes and said, "I think I'd rather use the window."

He smiled and placed a gentle kiss on my lips.

"This is amazing. I . . . I can't even tell you how much I love it."

Using his thumb, he wiped the tears from my cheeks then shrugged. "What can I say? I'm good at fantasy."

I sucked in a shaky breath as I watched Till Page, my *husband,* hold *our* daughter inside our *home* with pictures of my *family* covering the walls. I couldn't have asked for more.

"You're pretty good at reality too."

The End

The fight's not over.

Coming Summer 2015

Flint Page is
Fighting Shadows

Acknowledgements

I hate writing acknowledgements. Seriously, the second I type *The End,* I curl my lip and shake my fists, knowing I have to do this part. It's not because I don't have a million people to thank for each and every book, but rather because there are a million people to thank for *each and every book.* I would be absolutely nowhere without the endless support of the indie book community. This includes the readers, bloggers, and authors.

I'm probably going to forget someone. I always do. But that is *not* because I don't appreciate the endless amount of support that I receive. It's because I'm writing this with a glass of wine in my hand. Cheers . . . and please forgive me.

These ladies keep my on track and harass me on Facebook when they know I should be writing: Bianca J and Bianca S. I usually just say Bianca and Bianca, but every single person who has ever read my books say, "Is that a typo or do you have two betas named Bianca?" Nope. I have two! And they are invaluable to me.

Then I have my picky betas. These chicks keep me in check on my details: Tracey and Alexis. I know the word 'picky' doesn't sound like a positive thing, but trust me it is the most precious of all traits in a good beta. I love these ladies.

Let's not forget my sweet beta: Lakrysa. This woman always points out such amazing positives about my books that it fuels my words.

Then . . . oh, lawd . . . my dirty betas: Amie and Miranda. These ladies just joined the team for Fighting Silence and I have never had more fun. They pretend to be innocent, but honestly they are just amazing. I couldn't love them harder. Don't worry they will be sticking around. I've promised some spankings.

Oh, we can't forget the crazy beta: Natasha. This chick. . . . THIS. CHICK. She bulldozed her way onto my beta team a few books ago. I've never turned back. I love her so much. She makes me laugh and gives me shit for drinking boxed wine. *sip*. We even snuggled at WBW. Be jealous.

Last but not least on the team, we have the real life betas: Ashley and Autumn. I don't even have words to describe to you how much these ladies ground me on a daily basis. We may fight and roll our eyes, but every day ends with a text and the mornings start bright and early the same way. I love them hardcore.

Let's talk formatting for a moment. I've said it a million times before and I'll say it again, Stacey Blake is amazing. I can't even begin to tell you how much I LOVE this part of the process. You know why? Because working with Stacey is a DREAM! She is prompt, on time, and always available when I start to go crazy because I found a typo the night before release. HAHA!

Oh, and my editors. Lord do these ladies know how to polish a potato. (I hate the word turd. SHIT! I said it anyway.) Mickey and Claire. You ladies are top shelf.

The final proofreaders: Gina and Danielle. These are the ladies who make sure I don't screw up the edits. (Which I usually do!) I can't even begin to tell you how much they improved this book. Isn't that right, Danielle? It was almost the Flinter fiasco of 2015.

I need you all to strap on your imagination cap for a minute. Now, in reality, I'm holding my glass in the air. Pretend you are here with me because I need to tell you about some amazing ladies.

M. "Mo" Mabie is one of the most incredibly talented ladies I have ever met. I don't mean only because she writes amazing books though. Mo excels at being an amazing friend too. Her heart is always in the right place, and her mouth can move at exceptional speeds at one a.m. while plotting books via Facebook messenger. I can honestly say that Till Page wouldn't be who he is today without her. Better yet . . . I wouldn't be the author I am today without her. Okay okay, I'm getting sappy. Yes, we MIGHT have a lady love affair going, but I'll always be the top! *Flirty wink* DS for life! <3

Erin Noelle is another on of those magical people who make this author thing the best job ever. This time last year I would have fan-girled her . . . Oh wait, I totally did that. Now, I can honestly call her a friend. She still thinks I'm weird, and I still stare at her boobs like a creeper, but I'm okay with that. Hopefully she is too!

Chelle Bliss. This freaking woman. I know there is a (hopefully) humorous exchange in this book that goes like this . . .
"If you have a problem, I solve it—"
"That's actually Vanilla Ice."
Well, guess what? Chelle Bliss is officially Vanilla Ice. No matter how big or how small my question, Chelle is always there with an answer. And if she doesn't have the answer, she will call you a dirty name and tell you to Google it. HAHA! I love her so much!

Alissa S: What in the world would I do without her? She is a fantastic PA who keeps my butt in line and holds down the fort when I spend weeks locked away in the cave. I'm insanely lucky to have her and also be able to call her a friend.

About the Author

Born and raised in Savannah, Georgia, Aly Martinez is a stay-at-home mom to four crazy kids under the age of five, including a set of twins. Currently living in South Carolina, she passes what little free time she has reading anything and everything she can get her hands on, preferably with a glass of wine at her side.

After some encouragement from her friends, Aly decided to add "Author" to her ever-growing list of job titles. So grab a glass of Chardonnay, or a bottle if you're hanging out with Aly, and join her aboard the crazy train she calls life.

Facebook: https://www.facebook.com/AuthorAlyMartinez
Twitter: https://twitter.com/AlyMartinezAuth
Goodreads: https://www.goodreads.com/AlyMartinez

Made in the USA
Lexington, KY
16 February 2017